For Jenifer, Adara, and Arthur, who are funnier than DuckBob,
and even more precious than cookies

And to Bob, whose insight is as invaluable as his friendship

Too Small for Tall

Aaron Rosenberg

CRAZY 8 PRESS

"What we do," Tall starts, "it's dangerous. Really dangerous. We're facing aliens all the time that're bigger than we are, stronger than we are, faster than we are, smarter than we are, and a lot of 'em have way better tech than we do—and much bigger guns. We're putting ourselves at risk every day, in order to protect the American people and their way of life."

I'm now picturing aliens that look just like Tall, only bigger and stronger and faster and with oversized brains and carrying huge guns. "What do they do, most of these aliens?" I ask after gulping a few times because my throat's gone dry all of a sudden. "Are they all trying to take over the world? Man, I'm glad I moved away!"

Tall looks down at his hands, which're now clasped in front of him. "Take pictures, mostly," he admits after a second. "And try to steal stuff for souvenirs. We get a lot of tourists."

Chapter One
If I wanted one of those, I'd order it

Tall is trying to kill me.

No, he really is.

Oh, sure, he calls it something else:

"Exercise."

Yeah, right.

I call it "Tall shouting and screaming at me like my step-dad used to, and making me run around and do jumping jacks and a lot of other hideous and evil things designed to kill me by making my heart burst out of my chest and dance the watusi around the room."

When I tell him that, he just laughs at me.

And then yells at me to get off my fat butt and do some pushups.

Have you ever tried to do pushups when your bill sticks out past your elbow? It ain't fun. I can manage the full extension part, but dropping back down I get stuck halfway. And trying to lever yourself up when your arms are already partially extended? Not so much.

Once he realized the pushups weren't going to work, Tall switched to sit-ups.

Uh huh.

Most people, they've got maybe half their weight above the waistline. Me? Two-thirds. And half of that is my head. Hey, duckbills aren't light! So here I am, lying on my back on the floor, Tall standing over me yelling, and he wants me to lift around a hundred and sixty pounds using just my stomach muscles? Even if they got out and pushed that's not going to happen!

"Don't you want to get in shape?" he demands. "Don't you want to look good and feel good?" That expression that flits across his granite features is supposed to be sly, I think, but when you've got the same face as Mt. Rushmore (he's got Lincoln's jaw and brow but Washington's nose) it's tough to manage the subtle stuff. "Don't you want to look good for Mary?"

Okay, that's low. "Mary likes me just fine the way I am," I reply from the floor. Y'know, it's surprisingly comfortable down here. I guess that's because instead of carpet it's actually like grass or little fuzzy caterpillars or something, so laying on it you feel like you're getting a massage from a thousand fingers all at once. Small, soft, squishy fingers.

Right, getting up now. Ick.

"Look, I'm trying to help you," he says, and the funny thing is, I know he means it. We didn't start out as friends—hell, I'm pretty sure Tall started out thinking of me as something between a juvenile delinquent, a lab rat, and a loaded gun—but during our trip across the galaxy, well, we kinda bonded.

What can I say? I'm a people person.

"I'm just not built like you," I tell him, limping over to the couch and plopping down on it. "You're, like, modeled after a Greek god or something. I take after Mr. Potato Head. Or Donald Duck." All of which is more or less true. Tall's a MiB, a Man in Black, and I guess they've got even tougher entry requirements than the FBI or any of those agencies people actually know about, both mentally and physically. You've gotta be in good shape to chase after little green men, or something. But I met a few other MiBs and Tall could probably take 'em all on in arm-wrestling, using only his pinkie, and still win. While distracted. And feverish. He's not only tall, he's got the broad shoulders, the thick upper arms, but then the narrow waist and the long legs—he's like an Olympic athlete, if they had an event for skulking and brooding and shooting things.

Me? Even without the whole duck-head thing going on, I was never like that. I'm a decent height, but I was always a little on the doughy side. Having all this happen to me hasn't really changed that any. If anything, I'm more sedentary now—I figure I lied, cheated, snuck, stole, conned, fought, and fled my way across the galaxy, battled a race of invaders from another dimension, restored the Matrix, and saved our entire reality. That's gotta be enough exercise for anyone. I deserve to take it easy after all that.

Still, I can see this is killing him. "I appreciate your concern," I promise him, and I really do. It's nice to know he cares, if in a gruff and borderline homicidal fashion. "But don't worry about it. I'm comfortable with who I am and how I look." I am, too. That's why I didn't have the Grays change me back after the whole invasion thing, despite their offer. Who wants to go back to being just another pudgy guy with a weak chin and pug nose and watery blue eyes and a receding hairline? I'm resplendent in my feathers, my coloration is striking—once literally, when I found out that the people from Rasmussen Nine-Five-One actually experience physical pain from bright colors, and accidentally knocked out an amiable pair of floating noodles who'd come to see if I wanted a magazine subscription—and I've never met anyone else who looks even remotely like me, at least away from a duck pond. I'll take that over "pudgy and boring" any day.

Besides which, Mary does like my looks. And my feathers. Hey, once you've slept on down, you never go back!

And then there's the job. As the Matrix's Guardian and "sentient operator"—read here, "living component"—my staying plugged into it via the Mad Scientist wired headband Ned whipped up keeps it running, which in turn keeps the universe balanced and safely sealed from outside intrusion. But I couldn't do that if I got changed back to the old me—it's the fact that the Grays had altered me that made me suitable to be the human plug-in in the first place. Give that up and I've got to go back to Earth and find another boring, normal job, probably another cubicle somewhere. I think that'd kill me.

"Yeah, yeah." Tall drops onto the couch beside me. "Fine, we'll call it quits for today, but this isn't over. In the meantime, when you run out of breath climbing the stairs, or drop a jar of pickles because they're too heavy for you to manage, don't come crying to me." He gives me one last chance. "Come on, just a little more today. Three months and you'll have a six-pack and killer guns, I guarantee it."

"Dude, if I want a six-pack I'll just order one, and I hate guns. Besides, who would see it under all these feathers? But thanks."

"What about swimming?" he suggests. "You're good at swimming, right?"

"Yeah." And it's true. Hell, with these webbed feet and the feathers, I could probably outrace Michael Phelps—hell, I could probably get to the end, double back, stop to do a quick water ballet routine, and still beat him. Though that might come across as gloating, I'm not sure. There's just one problem. "You see a pool around here anywhere?"

"Oh. Right." He actually looks abashed, which is pretty funny on him—it's like a dragon after a major browbeating. But the thing is, he's knows I'm right. Being Guardian of the Matrix is a cool gig, and looks great on a resume, but it's very much on-location—as in, I'm actually wired into the damn thing at all times. And even with the tether our tech-buddy Ned rigged up, I still can't leave the Matrix building. Which is odd and sparkly and pink—and doesn't have a pool.

"Don't worry about it." I scoop up the remote. "Now, you wanna watch the game, or what?"

"Who's playing again?" He eyes the remote warily—after that one time, he tends to steer clear of the tech around here. Hey, I warned him to stroke it before trying to push any of its buttons. It's sensitive. And it gives off one hell of a shock.

"The Yarmoths versus the Ma-bin-yo."

"Right. And what're those, exactly?" It does get hard to

keep track sometimes.

"The Yarmoth are those little guys that look like they're made of marshmallows and toothpicks but can melt anything with a touch," I remind him. "The Ma-bin-yo are the ones that look like emo Goths drawn by a six-year-old with sticky fingers, purple crayons, and a lot of glitter."

Tall shakes his head. "I don't know how you can keep all those straight." He glares at me for a second. "Especially when you can't remember which temperature to use for laundry."

What? You've never gotten confused and washed reds—and maybe a few whites—on hot before? So his shirt shrank a little. And turned sort of a tie-dyed pink. It was a whole new look for him. That was the last time Tall brought his laundry over—now he does it at home or something, though I suspect he has his mom do it for him. If he has a mom. It's possible he was born from a granite quarry, a chisel, and an overly ambitious sculptor.

"Different kinds of knowledge," is all I tell him. "I've got a vast capacity for useless trivia." Which is true. It's why I'm so good at Trivial Pursuit. That and whenever I'm not sure about an answer I go with either "Whistler's mother," "the Himalayas," "butterflies," or "The War of 1812." You'd be surprised how far you can get with just those four.

We turn on the game and settle in to watch for a bit. There're over a thousand different televised sports in the galaxy, it turns out, and I can get all of them here. One of the advantages of being "the guardian of the Matrix"—I'm at the very Core of the galaxy, smack dab in the middle of everything, so I've got phenomenal reception. There's always a game on somewhere.

And, oddly enough, most of them look an awful lot like football. Oh, the uniforms change, and the fields, and the balls, and the use of additional weaponry, but underneath, they all boil down to the same thing—Team A is trying to get past Team B to score points, and then Team B tries the same thing with Team A. As long as you don't try to remember all the smaller rules and especially all the penalties, you're fine.

But Tall's not really into it today. Usually he gets psyched— he picks a team, more or less at random, and roots for them, and he gets pretty vocal about it, cursing out the other team and threatening their lives and waving his pistol about and the whole bit. Kinda reminds me of the sports bar I went to back in college, only without the cigarette smoke. Today, though, he's just staring at the screen, and even when a dozen of the Yarmoths surround this one poor Ma-bin-yo and swarm all over him, melting holes through his torso until he looks like he's made of Silly String, Tall doesn't react.

"You okay there, amigo?" I ask gently—gently because he is armed, and I've seen him punch reflexively. That poor old lady just picked the wrong time to ask directions, is all.

He sighs, and starts to nod, then turns it into a shrug, which then becomes a shake of the head. Yeah, he's off his game. Either that or he's developed palsy overnight. "I don't know," he admits. "It's just—work's been getting me down lately."

"Work?" I click off the game—this is way more interesting. Tall's usually real close-mouthed about his job, which I get—without being all spooky and secretive the MiBs are just undertakers with sunglasses and guns. Which could be cool, actually, but not the same thing. So if he wants to tell me something about being a MiB, I'm all ear canals. "Do tell," I urge. "Lay your troubles at my feet, my friend, and I'll happily squash them flat." I wave one pontoon-sized webbed foot at him. "Free of charge."

He sighs, and for a second I think damn, he's gonna clam up again like always. But then he starts talking. And once he starts, it's like he's never going to stop.

Chapter Two
The end of the world—in triplicate

"The first few weeks I was back," Tall began, "everything was fine. It was all 'Agent Thomas, good job,' and 'Agent Thomas, nice to have you back,' and "Agent Thomas, damn fine work.'"

"That's swell for this Thomas dude," I cut in, "but what's that got to do with you?"

He glares at me again—Tall's really good at glaring. Especially at me. He's got lots of practice. I can almost feel a bruise right between my eyes when he does it, like he's added a little lead shot to his stare somehow. Must be a MiB thing. Either that, or he's wearing contacts.

"I'm Agent Thomas, you numbskull," he hisses—yes, he's actually an expert at hissing intelligibly between his teeth. You read about people hissing things all the time in cheesy novels, but really? If you actually try it, most of the time all you can manage is "sssssssss" or maybe "sssssssssssaaaaaayyyyyyy" or ever once in a great while "sssssssssssaaaaaaasssssssssssssssssssaaaf-raaaaasssssssssss." Me? Forget about it, I can't hiss at all. When I try it's just a spatterfest, spit flying everywhere. But Tall, he can actually make full words, complete sentences, the whole bit, all without moving his jaw or parting his teeth. I think he's cheating—maybe he's got a speaker built into a molar or something.

But I admit, I forgot his actual name is Roger Henry David Thomas. Apparently his parents couldn't decide between a bunch of first names, so they gave him all of them at once. I just call him Tall, sometimes to his face. He says it's not the worst nickname he's ever had, not by a long shot.

"Anyway," he continues, "eventually things calmed back down, people sort of forgot what we'd done, and everything went back to normal. Which was fine by me. I don't particularly like getting that much attention." Which shows just one of the many differences between Tall and me—I love attention. The good kind, anyway. I've had plenty of unwanted attention, from bill collectors to bird fanciers to nosy bosses to those people who just won't look away or pretend to be asleep on the subway. Give me somebody who tells me how awesome I am and how I've saved the universe, I'll happily take second and third helpings of that and come back for more, and diet of humble pie be damned!

"So what happened?" I prompt Tall when he doesn't pick up the story again after a few seconds. "Things were good and back to normal—normal for a shadowy, semi-official, quasi-government agency, anyway, I'm guessing, which probably leaves a lot of room for interpretation—and now you're moping around being a Gloomy Gus. What gives?"

He grumbles something in response, but he must be chewing on marbles again because I can't quite make it out. "What? You hate your work? That was fast—you used to love that job!

Especially the cheap suits and the sharp ties!" I'm not kidding about the ties, either—one time we were playing Varsuvian Ping Pong, which is just like regular Earth Ping Pong except the ball moves on its own and you've gotta browbeat it into standing still and letting you hit it with the paddle—and Tall'd just come from work so he was still in full MiB getup and he shucked his tie and coat and I picked them up off the couch so I could sit afterward and I got a paper cut from the damn tie! Right on my thumb, too—stung like a mother!

He's shaking his head, though. "Paperwork," he corrects. "I said 'paperwork.'"

"Oh, well that makes more sense. Only, no, not really." Yeah, I tend to think out loud. I like it better than thinking and then speaking. Saves time.

"New orders from the top," Tall explains with a deep sigh, the kind you usually only make when you've just found out someone shot your truck and totaled your wife and ran off with your dog, or some iteration thereof. "Changed our operating procedures. Now we've got to fill out all this extra paperwork every time we do anything—in triplicate."

"Oh, I hate those," I agree. "Those carbons always leave ink all over my fingertips, and do you have any idea how hard it is to get that stuff off feathers? It stains, man! I've had to bleach my fingers before!"

"We don't use carbons," he told me. "And we can't photocopy them, either, or just print out three copies. We have to fill out each form three times, from scratch." I must be making a face because Tall cracks just the barest hint of a smile. "There are times," he says slowly, "when the Men in Black are a little . . . old-fashioned."

"I'll say!" I can't imagine having to do a whole heap of reports on who knows what—and then having to do them all over again. And then a third time! "Well, yeah, no wonder you're in a bad mood, then! Sorry, dude."

He slaps me on the back, and suddenly I know how those Varsuvian Ping Pong balls feel! "Don't worry about it," he says then. "It's not a big deal."

But he won't look me in the eye, and he's shuffling his feet a little bit. I'm a pretty good judge of when somebody's telling the truth—hey, I've got brothers and sisters! "Talk to me, man," I urge him. "You need to let it out, whatever it is."

He hesitates again, then nods. "There is something else," he says slowly, like he's gotta drag the words up from the vault himself. "Something that just started recently." I lean in—this is the good stuff! "It seems," he whispers, "that they've decided, that we should—" he looks around "—start admitting"—the suspense is killing me, or at least mildly spraining the one arm where it's still tender from playing the Horseshoe Nebula version of Guitar Hero, which involves playing this thing that looks a lot like a guitar but also intercepting small poisonous throwing stars at the same time—"girls."

I stare at him. I can't help it. And after a minute or two, when it's clear he's not going to elaborate, I practically squawk at him: "That's it? That's what's got your panties in a twist, that they might let women join the MiB?"

"You don't understand." He looked a little shell-shocked,

maybe from the recent meetings and paperwork and whatever but also presumably because he's flown, what, two or three times to the Core and back. I wonder sometimes if that's dangerous— not just to him, but the universe in general. I don't even know what it'd do if he somehow met himself while traveling, but I feel like that's possible because of the time change and relative speeds and all that other good stuff. And while it might be nice to gab with somebody who understood all your in-jokes, and to get a little advance warning about what's going down next Tuesday or whatever, I'm pretty sure it'd still wind up being a bad thing for the universe in general.

He's right, though, and I tell him so: "You're right. I don't understand. So explain it to me." And I lean back into the couch. I have the feeling this is going to take a while.

Chapter Three
WiB just sounds wrong

"What we do," Tall starts, "it's dangerous. Really dangerous. We're facing aliens all the time that're bigger than we are, stronger than we are, faster than we are, smarter than we are, and a lot of 'em have way better tech than we do—and much bigger guns. We're putting ourselves at risk every day, in order to protect the American people and their way of life."

I'm now picturing aliens that look just like Tall, only bigger and stronger and faster and with oversized brains and carrying huge guns. "What do they do, most of these aliens?" I ask after gulping a few times because my throat's gone dry all of a sudden. "Are they all trying to take over the world? Man, I'm glad I moved away!"

Tall looks down at his hands, which're now clasped in front of him. "Take pictures, mostly," he admits after a second. "And try to steal stuff for souvenirs. We get a lot of tourists."

I suppose that makes sense—Earth's a pretty hip place, for a backwater, or so I've gathered over the three months I've been out here. "What's this got to do with letting women join?" I ask. "Or are you trying to tell me that it's too dangerous for 'the fairer sex'? Because if so, I dare you to repeat that in front of Mary."

Mary's ridiculously hot—I often have to pinch her to make sure I'm not dreaming, which she says isn't how you're supposed to do it but she seems to like it so what the hell—and incredibly smart, but she's also tough as nails and Tall visibly quails at the idea of pissing her off.

"No, women can handle it," he says quickly, shrinking back into the couch a little, which is always a bad idea because it decides he wants to get past and flows out of his way, turning itself into two corner chairs with me on one, the other on Tall's far side, and him flat on his butt on the floor. Yeah, it's Trasgamine modular furniture, responds to your movement and some vocal commands. I'm trying to figure out how to turn it into a pup tent but I keep getting a doggie bed instead. I did get a Papasan once, though, so I have hope.

"So, what then?"

He picks himself up, glares at the couch, and claims one of the actual wooden chairs over near the side table instead. "Look, it's a dangerous job, okay?" he tries again.

"Yeah, yeah, you already said that."

"Right, and we're putting our lives on the line."

"Uh huh. And if there were women MiBs—would they be WiBs? Because that just sounds wrong—then you'd worry about them getting hurt and that'd get you all distracted and probably killed by these oh-so-dangerous alien tourists." I shake my head, accidentally knocking over a nearby lamp. "That's really 1950s of you, man."

"That's not what I'm saying!" he claims. "The problem isn't them getting hurt, or us worrying about them getting hurt, or anything like that!"

"Oh, so you wouldn't care if they got hurt, just because they're women? Wow, that's really low."

"That's not what I'm saying, either!" He's got that look again, the one where his face goes red and his eyes bulge and his jaw juts out and it looks like he's gonna breathe fire any second. I'm really good at getting him to make that face. Or almost anybody, actually.

"Okay, so talk sense, buddy. What, exactly, is the deal?"

"The deal," he says slowly, spacing out each word, "is that men in my line of work don't have a lot of time for . . . socializing."

I scratch at my bill. "Um, okay, so you need to get out more?"

"We don't have much opportunity to mingle . . . with members of the opposite sex." He's slowing down still more, dragging each word along until it's stretched like taffy—and that image brings back bad memories.

I'm still confused, though. "So, what, you guys wanna hold a coed dance?"

There's that grinding sound again, which I hear a lot around Tall. Poor guy's gonna need new teeth before he's forty, at this rate. "We don't see many women." He's switched tacks and now he's practically hurling each word at me like a dagger. I saw a game show like that once, but this one guy basically cheated and used compound words—it was like those old French cannon that fired two cannonballs linked by a chain. It wasn't pretty. He did get full points for taking down a dozen targets at once with "multi-inter-bi-dimensional," though. "Not women who can hold their own. So when we do, it can be . . . distracting."

And finally I get it: "So you're saying having WiBs would be a problem because all the MiBs would fall all over them?"

I must have gotten it right, because he actually nods. "There was a female MiB once," he explains softly, but at least he's working his jaw again, so it's a lot easier to understand him—and less hazardous to my health. "Her name was Mercer or Messer or Miezer, something like that—most of the records have been expunged. She was only with the organization for a month, back in the early seventies."

"What happened?" I wish I had some popcorn—this is better than the game by far!

"She indirectly caused the death of twelve other agents," Tall tells me. "They were all so busy trying to impress her they did stupid things to get her attention, and it got them killed. Damn near got the planet taken over or blown up or strip-mined or mind-controlled several times, too." He shakes his head. "The higher-ups finally had to let her go—it was just too dangerous to everyone else."

"Huh." I think about that. "I didn't even realize you could fire a MiB. How does that work, exactly? Do you get a letter of reference for your next job? 'Such and such was an exemplary member of something we can't tell you about, and during the course of his employment for a period we can't reveal, he took care of several responsibilities we can't divulge'?"

The smile he manages looks a bit sad, and maybe a tad guilty as well. "When a MiB leaves, his memory is erased all the way back to when he first joined. He's given false memories to fill in that period, and a cover story to explain away any gaps and discrepancies, and then he's set up with a new life somewhere."

"So somewhere, the former Agent Mercer-Messer-Miezer may still be out there, never realizing she was once the world's only Woman in Black?"

"Precisely. But after her they decided not to let in any more women, just to avoid another situation like that."

Something else occurs to me. "Was she hot?"

Tall gets a dreamy look on his face, which is a little creepy, if you ask me. "Yeah, she was," he almost whispers. "I ran across a picture, once, where she was in the background—apparently whoever did the cleanup hadn't noticed and pulled the image. But she was tall and busty, with long blond hair she kept up in a tight bun. Very hot, very capable, and very distracting." I'm getting this horrible mental image of the other MiBs getting mowed down not just because they're trying to show off in front of her but because they're busy covering their crotches, and I wish I had some of that mental bleach I saw advertised the other day: "Scrub bad memories away!"

Then I have an idea: "So just hire ugly women." He stares at me like I've gone crazy, but I really think I'm onto something here. "No, seriously. Just don't allow any of them to be attractive at all, and you're safe, right? Nobody'll lust after them, nobody'll get distracted by them, nobody'll die because of them, you're all set!" I try to pat myself on the back but I'm not a big fan of touchy-feely (except with Mary) and keep twisting away, so in the end I have to settle for a supportive hand on the shoulder instead. I don't think I'm getting the recognition I deserve.

Tall doesn't seem as impressed by my revelation—good

thing he's not in charge of back pats! "This isn't a beauty contest!" he snaps, then adds, "or an anti-beauty contest, or whatever! MiBs are very carefully selected—we're the best of the best! And if they decide to let a woman in, she'll be the best of the best, too!"

"And you're betting that means she'll be another Amazon, dangerously hot in a black tie and shades." I don't know whether to laugh at his naiveté, cry at his stupidity, or applaud his optimism. I'd do all three at once but that'd just get messy and it'd look and sound like a drenched seal with a head cold. "Tall, man, you do know how the process actually works, right? At my old job I was stuck in the cube right next to HR—trust me, genuine ability has nothing to do with it. It's all about who you know, how you look, what you can do for them, and whether you're willing to take a little less money than advertised, and a cut in benefits, while doing as much or more work. Don't worry about the Amazons—you're a lot more likely to get some mousy little chick who's real good at typing and filing but sucks at everything else, or one of those super-friendly types who makes a mess of everything but who's so nice no one wants to tell her." I tried that last strategy myself at one point, but I must've been doing it wrong, because it backfired—everybody liked me and wanted to be my friend, but that just made them feel they could be honest with me about my own shortcomings, and owed it to me to be as blunt as possible when telling me what I did wrong. I tried not to have any friends after that.

Tall laughs, which is at least an improvement over the moping and the glaring. "Maybe you're right," he tells me, which might just be a first, or at least a second. "I'm probably blowing this all out of proportion." He turns toward the TV and switches it back on, intent now upon the game. "Aw, man, the Yarmoths just scored again!" he complains. "Come on, Ma-bin-yo, let's lick their little fluffy asses!" Okay, that might have been "kick," but either works, right? Regardless, he's back to shouting curses and death threats at the screen like it's done something to personally insult him, his mother, and his puppy.

Good to see he's feeling better about his life.

Chapter Four
One Choco-Mint is never enough

"Look what I got!" I practically shout the next time Tall shows up, two weeks later. I'm sitting out in the Matrix Chamber, as I like to call the football field-sized room that houses the thing, and I've got my feet in my latest acquisition.

He stops short just the other side of it, and stares. I bet he took courses on staring in college—he's real good at them. You can actually catalog Tall's stares. I'm up to nineteen so far. This is good ol' number three, "what the hell is that, exactly, and should I be drawing my gun?" Which is a lot nicer than number one, "are you a complete flippin' moron?" or number two, "remind me why I don't just shoot you and incinerate the body?" Sometimes I practice those two myself, just me and the mirror. I figure they'll be useful if I ever have kids and they try to bring home their dates.

Finally he says, "Is that what I think it is?"

"I don't know," I tell him. "What do you think it is?" Hey, I'm not a mind reader!

"It looks like a kiddie pool," he tells me. "But shaped like the Milky Way."

"Man, you're good!" I admire it again, splashing my feet

about and almost drenching his feet. He must've had time to go home and change this time, because instead of his usual MiB suit Tall's wearing worn blue jeans, a Texas A&M jersey-style T-shirt, and cowboy boots. I should've known.

"Why do you have a kiddie pool in the Matrix Chamber?" See, I've got everybody calling it that! Now if I could just train them to refer to the bathroom as "the shrine to the porcelain god" I'd be all set!

"Because a real pool wouldn't fit," I answer. "Duh!"

He's just staring at me again, and it's starting to shade from three to one—you can tell by the way his left eye is twitching. So I stand up, still in the kiddie pool. "Look." I walk around the central part and then out along one of the spiral arms, then turn—carefully, because my feet're a lot bigger than most adults, let alone kids or small elephants, and I don't have a lot of extra room here—and make my way back to the center. "See, it's exercise! And the water creates resistance, which means it's more of a workout than walking the same distance on dry ground!"

I'm all pleased with myself, but Tall looks like he's trying not to cry, or sneeze, or spit out curse words like they were sunflower seed shells. "You only walked about ten feet," he points out.

"So? At least it's something!" I stop and face him, hands on my hips. "Look, you were the one who suggested swimming, remember? Well, it turns out full-sized pools aren't exactly cheap, even out here—plus there's the delivery fee to consider." Somehow, the Matrix isn't in anybody else's galactic zip code, which makes it really easy for mail to reach me but really hard on delivery charges. "I couldn't afford one. But then I saw this baby on the Interstellar Shopping Network—they've got everything on there!—so I ordered one. I thought you'd be impressed!"

He's shaking his head like this's all a bad dream, or at least like he's hoping that's the case. "I am glad to see you're taking exercising seriously," he says finally, though I can tell that was hard to get out from the way he's breathing like he just did the power walk instead of me. "And yes, walking through water adds some resistance." He glances down at the pool again, and at my feet in it. The water's lapping against my ankles. Feels nice. "But it's best if the water comes up to at least your waist," he continues slowly. "Not your ankles. Plus"—he sighs—"if you were willing to walk all the way around this chamber a few times a day? That'd be a whole lot better for you in the long run."

"But look!" I cut through the middle toward another arm, race through that and back, cut through again, go to one back on this side, and do that a few more times. "Didja see? I drew a star! It's exercise—and art, all at the same time!"

This time I get hit with number five, which I've labeled "I can't decide whether to laugh, cry, or just starting shooting."

To change the subject, I ask, "Hey, what's that?" Usually when I do this I just point somewhere at random, in order to distract people. But this time I mean it, and I'm gesturing at the bag Tall's holding in one hand.

"Oh, this?" A smug little smile takes up residence on his face, and sits there sneering at me. "This was supposed to be a reward if you agreed to do ten minutes of exercise."

"I've been exercising," I argue. "I've been in this pool for at least an hour!" I splash some water at him for emphasis.

"I didn't see that," he tells me—typical hall monitor mentality—" so it doesn't count. Show me you can exercise for ten minutes and I'll give you what's in the bag."

I eyeball him, the bag, then him again. "How do I even know I want it? Maybe it's a bunch of smelly old socks or something. Maybe it's leftovers from your lunch." Though those I would want, probably. Hey, it takes a lot of fuel to protect the galaxy!

"It isn't." And the way he says it, I can tell it's true. Tall's not one for lying, anyway. He's too straight-arrow for that. Unless he's on the job and feels it's best for everyone, in which case he'll lie his butt off and do it with a completely straight face.

"Oh, fine. If curiosity could kill the cat, I suppose it can at least make me exercise for ten minutes." I start walking again. "I've never really understood that phrase, anyway," I say as I pace along another arm. "How did curiosity kill the cat? Was that the name of a really big dog? Or a runaway freight train? Or did the cat just get so curious about something that it wouldn't leave and forgot to eat and wasted away? Or was the curiosity itself toxic somehow? Can a mental state be lethal like that? I mean, I know people say they're bored to death—can you really die from boredom? Wouldn't death just be even more boring because now you can't even complain about being bored and it's a lot harder to hide other people's keys just for the fun of watching them freak out and go running around looking for them? What?"

Tall's just standing there, staring at me again. This is number four, "How could anyone talk so much and make so little sense?" Well, whatever, my mind thinks these things and so my mouth says them. Filters are for the weak.

Besides, it helps to pass the time, and by the time I've exhausted this idea of dangerous emotional states and emotion assassins and rogue killer emotions and so on, I'm exhausted too. But Tall's watch beeps—yes, he's old-fashioned enough to still wear a watch, even though his phone has a clock on it and that and his watch always have the same time—and he looks as relieved as I feel when he says, "Okay, ten minutes. Shut up, dry your feet off, and come over here." And he stomps over to the couch I've set up along one wall of this room.

I follow him, taking a second to shake the water off my feet and ankles—as a part-duck I'm actually really good at shedding water; too bad I can't seem to shed the pounds as easily—and then plop down. "Okay, what's in the bag?" I'm all out of breath, but I'm proud of myself, too. Ten whole minutes of exercise! Underwater! Go, me!

Tall gives me a big, proud-of-himself grin, reaches into the bag, and pulls out—a box of cookies.

But not just any cookies.

"Are those ChocoMints?" I grab at the box, and he actually laughs at the glee I know is showing but I don't care. "They are! Where the hell did you find ChocoMints?"

"My niece is a CampGirl," he says, shrugging. "They just got their cookies in."

CampGirl is this big, big organization all over the U.S. that's just for girls but it's for any girl at all, and they do things like nature hikes and clothing drives and all sorts of arts and crafts.

It's really sweet, actually, and I've had at least one niece who was in a troop—at least, until she got kicked out. Turns out if you light someone's house on fire you don't get the Firestarter badge, even if you did a really good job gathering the kindling and creating the spark. Especially if it's the local troop leader's house. No, I don't know where my nieces and nephews get it from.

I pause in trying to tear open the box. "Wait, they just got their cookies now? Isn't it like May or something? I thought the cookies came in March." I know they used to. When I was a kid my friends and I would mug CampGirls for their cookies, then hole up somewhere and gorge ourselves.

And when I say "young" of course I mean college. Hey, nobody got hurt. Victimless crime. Or something.

"It's actually spread out," Tall's telling me. "Because that way they can ship to a few troops at a time." He shrugs. "My niece's down in Austen with my sister and her husband, and they get their cookies in May." He leans forward, plucks the box from my hand, and tears off the top, then tips it to slide out two waxed-paper-wrapped cylinders. One of them he sets aside, and the other he hands to me.

"Yes!" I rip open the paper and shovel three or four cookies into my mouth at once. I love ChocoMints! They're so thin and crispy and chocolaty and minty! I'm happily chomping and chewing when I realize Tall hasn't taken any. "You want some?" I manage to mumble, holding out the open sleeve.

But he shakes his head. "Naw, those are yours."

"You're not gonna have any CampGirl cookies?" Now I

guess I'm the one staring at him like he's nuts.

But he just grins. "I've got a dozen boxes at home," he confides. "Most're going in the freezer—they hold up really well in there. But I'll keep a few boxes out to eat."

"Yeah, that makes sense." Moderation always makes sense to me. Unless it's money. Or sex. Or friends. Or hot chocolate with brandy and butterscotch syrup and whipped cream—man, I could drink that all day long! For right now, though, I'm thrilled to be gobbling down ChocoMints. It was smart that he only gave me the one sleeve, because when I finish it I half-consider trying to get the other sleeve from him and downing that as well. But that would be bad—then I wouldn't have any cookies left! So instead I just toss the empty sleeve in the trash, lean back, and belch. "Thanks."

"Not a problem." He tucks the remaining sleeve back into its box and hands it over to me. "Save these for later."

"Right. Thanks." I'm gonna hold onto them until Mary gets back, and then we can enjoy them together. Assuming I can control myself for that long. "Hey, how's it going at work? Any better? Any sign of the WiBs?"

"No better," he admitted, "but no worse, either. They're still debating the whole WiB issue, so I've got a little time. We're getting some kind of security upgrade soon, too, but they swear it won't interfere with our daily operations." Which usually means, of course, that it'll shut the entire office down for days, and play havoc with everything for weeks beyond that.

"Cool." I look around, watch the Matrix for a second, manage to pull my eyes away after a bit—the way it rotates and bits of it turn and flash and so on, it's pretty hypnotic, especially if you can also hear the music it makes, which of course I can—and then look at Tall. "So, you wanna dip your feet in the pool?"

He looks down at it, shrugs, then sighs. It's like MiB semaphore—if I had the dictionary I could translate that and all the other gestures and get a full language. "Sure, why not?"

I shift over to make room, not that that's really an issue—there're whole arms still available. I'm considering starting a water fight, though. Or challenging him to a rousing game of Marco Polo, though admittedly the trick there would be not toppling out of the pool while searching. But I'm determined to show him that this is not only a cool conversation piece, it's also a good investment and a wise purchase.

Besides, after inhaling a whole sleeve of ChocoMint cookies, I'm gonna need a little more exercise.

Chapter Five
My ingredient list is in code

"**Enriched flour, yeah,** okay, sure," I'm muttering to myself the next time Tall shows up, trying to make out the little tiny print on the box. "Lots of stuff in the flour itself, guess that's why they call it 'enriched.' Always figured that meant it was wealthy somehow, like flour that'd hit the lottery or made a killing in the stock market and now retired to relax and sit back and make cookies—literally—but what do I know? Let's see—"

He sits down next to me. "What are you doing?" He's not glaring at me for once, and I glance over to make sure this isn't some stranger wearing a Tall-suit. Hey, the things I've seen, you never know. But no, it looks like him all right. Though how I'd know if it was somebody in a Tall-suit, I haven't a clue. Ask to see the label? Tell him I've decided to put the Matrix through a car wash to give it a good rinse, and listen for the sound of his teeth grinding? Say something about that one WiB and watch for drool?

Well, whatever—I'm just gonna assume it's Tall for now and leave it at that. Assumptions are handy things, I've found, especially if you're secure in them. One time I just assumed I still had a job and kept coming in to work day after day, even though my boss had yelled at me one time to "get the hell out and never come back!" But I played it off like he was just kidding around, and Monday morning there I was like nothing had happened. I managed to pull that off for two weeks before he finally decided to call security. Turns out, assumptions? Not so helpful against big, beefy guys with low IQs and stun guns. Worked out okay, though—after they threw me out I called HR and told them to send all my back pay, overtime, vacation pay, and 401k made out to cash instead, and quoted a number at them. I got the check a few days later. Which was pretty good, considering I only really had the job for four days.

But yeah, he asked me a question, and one of the things you're supposed to do for your friends is actually answer stuff like that. Hey, I'm learning! "I'm reading the ingredients on the ChocoMints," I tell him. "The second sleeve lasted a little longer—I actually ate a few of them one at a time!—and something about 'em tastes a little funny. Not bad, but I'm just wondering if they changed something in the mix." I did hold out long enough for Mary to have a few when she got back from her latest assignment and before she headed out on this one—the Grays do keep her hopping!—but she said she didn't notice anything unusual.

"I'm sure they're fine," Tall says. "Mine were delightful."

Did he just say delightful? "Did you just say 'delightful'?" I ask him. "What're you, moonlighting for greeting cards now? Applying to join a tea club?" He just shrugs.

Fine, whatever. Back to my reading. "Sugar, duh. Vegetable oil, okay. Cocoa, obviously. Caramel color, right. 'Contains two percent or less of cocoa processed with alkali'—does that mean they're made with batteries? Or maybe from batteries? Explains why I'm always so wired after I eat 'em—'invert sugar'—is that where you take sugar and hold it upside down? Or turn it inside out? Or is that sugar that doesn't like to talk much and sits off in a corner by itself reading most of the time?—'whey, leavening'—so no eating this on Passover, I guess, which sucks—'cornstarch, salt, soy lecithin, natural and artificial flavor, oil of peppermint.'" I toss the box at Tall's head. "Huh."

Now, normally when I do something like that—throw something at Tall, not read off a list of ingredients—he bats it aside like a large, angry, suit-wearing cat. And then he throws it back at me, but harder. While glaring. This time, though, it just hits him in the face and falls in his lap. He barely even blinks from the impact.

"Yo, dude, you okay?" I take a closer look at him. He isn't wearing his sunglasses, though he's got the rest of his MiB uniform on, and his eyes look a little glassy. "Are you high or something?"

"Of course not," he says, focusing on me finally, but there's none of the usual bite in his tone. "I'm fine."

"Really? Because you're not acting fine. You're acting stoned." To test this theory, I lean in a little closer. "You want something to eat?"

That gets an immediate reaction—he sits up straighter, like somebody just zapped him, and snaps his head forward so he's just staring off straight in front of him. "Yes, I would like some-thing to eat, thank you. Do you have any cookies?"

"Cookies?" I think about that. "Yeah, maybe. Hang on a

sec." I hop up and head into the kitchen, and the big alcove I've made into a pantry. So I've been redecorating a little, sue me—you try living inside a giant, sparkly pink skull and not wanting to put up some drywall and some paneling and maybe some French doors. I needed somewhere to prepare my food, anyway, and you can only order out so many times a week—when they start knowing your order by heart, and being surprised when you change it, but then suggesting that you might want to try one of the healthier options because they're worried about the amount of trans-fat you're ingesting every day, yeah, you should start to worry. So I rigged up a little kitchen in one of the wacky alcoves this place has—apparently whatever kind of creature this was, its brain was not just lobed like ours but actually segmented and split off like kids being sent to opposite corners of the room. I've got a grill, a microwave, a slow cooker, a fryer, a popcorn maker, and an espresso machine. Really all I need. Plus a cute little dorm-sized fridge and a sink. Those're all arrayed against one wall, and I curtained off the area opposite it and put in some metal shelving to hold all my cans and packets and boxes and whatnot. Instant pantry!

Anyway, I go in there now and start rooting around. Sure enough, I've still got half a box of Nonniung Critter-cakes. Those were just a little weird for me—they're shaped like lizards, those cute little ones that scamper around on walkways and in gardens, and they actually try to get away when you take them out of the box, so you've got to gulp them down immediately. And they're filled with some kind of jelly, plus the cakes themselves are spongy but have like a glaze or something that gives them almost a hardened-gel crust, like some gummy candies. It all makes sense, and it's clever, and they taste good, but I just shudder every time I eat one.

I bring the box back out with me and hand it to Tall. "Here you go, man. Knock yourself out." Just the thought of him eating them is enough to make me shudder again.

I'm a little surprised when he accepts the box—I told him about these things after the first time I tried them and he thought they sounded disgusting—but I'm even more surprised when he tries smashing it into his forehead. What the hell?

"Aim for the mouth, dude," I tell him. "Or, if you don't want 'em, fine, give 'em back."

He doesn't do either. Instead he bashes the box against his temple again.

"Okay, this is officially going from 'just plain weird' to 'getting kind of creepy,'" I say. "Tall, man, snap out of it!"

He stops hitting himself with the box and looks over at me, and I can almost see the clarity coming back into his gaze. It's like a film washing away.

"What?" he mutters. He glances at the now-crumpled box in his hand, then thrusts it at me. "Get these away from me! You know I think they're gross."

"I know. But you said you wanted cookies." I take the box back. Hey, if I'm really desperate for sweets I might try one again. Maybe. Or if I ever get a cat he can have them to bat around a bit.

"I did, didn't I?" He rubs a hand over his face, then does it again. "I remember saying that, but I can't imagine why."

"Got me. You've definitely been acting weird since you got here." That gets him to glare at me again, which feels like coming home after a long trip, but it's only Number Seven, "I feel like you know more about something than I do, and it's making me crazy." "Hey," I defend myself, "All I know is, you show up, you act like a robot, you ask for cookies, you hit yourself in the head with the cookie box, and now you're being you again." That Tall-suit theory is starting to look better and better.

He stands up, stretches, and does some of those arm-popping things you see athletes and bullies do occasionally. "I am a bit foggy," he admits while he's flailing about. "Odd. I may need to get that checked out."

"Yeah, well, you're acting normal—for you—now," I point out. "And I think the Madrigoran spikeball semi-finals are on." I flick the TV on.

"Nice." Tall sits again, leaning back and stretching his arms across the couch back to either side. It's a good way to make sure the couch stays together. "Too bad about the ChaosFiends getting knocked out last round."

"Yeah, yeah, rub it in." The ChaosFiends are my team. They had a good season, but lost the quarterfinal on a technicality. Technically, the other team scored more points. I still think they should have contested it.

We settle in to watch, and I go grab some Omegan fire-beer after a bit. I even try another Nooniung Critter-cake. Turns out if you shake the box enough beforehand, they're stunned and can't try to get away. Still a little squicky, though.

Chapter Six
There's a WiB in the house!

"Well, they went and did it," Tall grumbles as he stomps in. I'm just chilling in front of my computer—literally, because its screen is formed from giant holographic ice crystals. Gives you a wickedly good picture, fantastic resolution, but you need to don a parka if you're gonna do more than quickly check your email. I've been playing a new game I found online and I can't really feel my fingers anymore, even with the feathers, so I use Tall showing up as an excuse to log out and turn the whole system off. Probably for the best anyway—a few times I've wound up in a War Games sort of situation, where it turned out I wasn't so much playing a game as actually dictating lives and a few times even meteorological events on some distant planet. Turns out proximity to the Matrix has done some pretty weird things to my computer. Like, when it first arrived and I set it up, it wasn't actually supposed to respond to voice commands. Or raised eyebrows. Of course, it also didn't open my email beforehand and decide what I should and shouldn't read, which is getting to be a real problem—three times now I've had to explain that Sue Louise is just my cousin and that's the way she writes to everybody and no, I'm not cheating on Mary.

"Did what?" I ask. He's brought a six-pack with him and tosses me one, and I catch it without a problem. Hey, I may not always be graceful but I never drop my beer, not unless I'm standing on or near something really expensive and easily stained. Or my date's wearing white.

"Hired a woman." He drops onto the couch, which tries protesting until he slams one hand down on it, and it shuts up and goes still. And sulks. But quietly. "She starts tomorrow."

"Huh. Interesting. You okay?" He doesn't look okay, but he doesn't look completely pissed off or anxious, either.

"Yeah, I'm all right." He pops open his beer and I do the same with mine, then take a long swig. It's regular old-fashioned Earth beer, none of the weird stuff we usually drink these days, and it's kind of nice to guzzle something that doesn't turn my skin transparent or make flames shoot from my eyes or let me hear colors (green is incredibly raunchy, it turns out. Who knew?) or make me irresistible to dandelions (that played havoc with my hay fever, let me tell you!) or any of those other things. Kind of nice, but kind of dull, too.

"Have you met her yet?" Tall shakes his head. "Huh. Have you even seen her?" Another head shake. "So, what, they're keeping her under wraps so nobody'll panic?"

"Something like that," he agrees. "I know her name—Violet Melody Jones—and that she's twenty-nine, she used to be CIA, and she's borderline diabetic. That's about it."

"That's it?" I laugh, then take another sip of beer—trust me, it's better than doing it the other way around. "You already know her name—her full name—her age, her last job, and her medical condition. That's not enough? Though, yeah, what about her blood type?"

"AB negative," he answers immediately, then flushes and looks away. I don't think I've ever seen Tall embarrassed before. Wow.

"Okay, so maybe I peeked at her medical record," he admits after a second. "So what? I like to keep informed."

"That's informed, all right," I tell him. "Go to the head of the stalker class!" Tall actually doesn't have a comeback for that, and we sit and drink our beers quietly for a bit. Then he spots something off to the side of my computer, which also makes a great freezer.

"Hey, what've you got there? Are those . . . CampGirl cookies?"

"Hm? Oh, yeah." I pick up the box of ChocoMints and toss them to him—he catches it with one hand. Show off.

"I thought you ate all yours?" He's staring down at the box like it's made of diamonds and rubies, or like it's gonna tell him the answers to all life's little questions. Which it doesn't—I asked.

"Yeah, I did, so I ordered more." I grin at him. "Thanks for letting me know about that rolling sales period thing. Did you know there's always a CampGirl troop selling cookies some-where? So I stocked up." Yeah, so I ordered five hundred boxes of ChocoMints. So what? If I make them last until this time next year that's only a little over a box a day. I think that's reasonable.

Tall's got this look of pure lust on his face. I hope I never have to see it again. "May I?" He holds up the box.

"Yeah, sure, go for it." He tears into it like a little kid on Christmas Day—which, really, would mean he'd snuck down last night, found the cookies, opened the box, ate half of them, then closed it back up, rewrapped it, put it back under the tree, and crept back upstairs until now, when he looks properly surprised. It got to the point where my parents would set booby traps to try keeping us kids away from the presents until the morning. Which just meant we spent all night trying to disarm or circumvent or otherwise outsmart those traps. I was never completely sure why they didn't just hide the damn presents until morning, but looking back I realize it was a great way to keep us out of trouble on Christmas Eve when most of our friends were out partying. And it made us use our heads for something other than hat racks. Turns out my parents are a lot more devious than I realized.

Tall tears open the packaging and stuffs three or four ChocoMints into his mouth at once. Then he gets this totally blessed-out look on his face, which is also something I hope never to see again. He slumps down a little, the couch shifting around him, and his eyes get glassy and his face goes kinda blank, and he's still chewing but real slow, like he's an old horse or something.

"Hey, you okay, man?" I ask, climbing to my feet. He doesn't answer. "Tall! Are you okay?"

"Of course—I'm fine." He doesn't sound right, though. The words come out all stiff, like one of those programs that speaks whatever you write. Which is a very dangerous thing to have, especially for a kid with too much time on his hands, and particularly when coupled with one of those untraceable burner phones and a faculty directory and a badly translated Turkish porn magazine. Hey, I'm just sayin'. But I know what a computerized voice sounds like, and Tall is edging way too close to that for comfort.

"Yo, Tall!" I step in close and grab him by both shoulders. The look he gives me as he slowly raises his head is utterly perplexed but not concerned, like he doesn't know how he got here or what he's doing but he trusts that it's all okay. That's definitely not a look I'd normally associate with Tall, who once harassed a delivery guy into showing us his route before Tall would accept the fact that our food got cold on the way over and that it wasn't some kind of plot to raise our cholesterol by making sure the fat was fully congealed before it arrived. He takes everything personally, yet I'm shaking him like a rag doll and he's totally relaxed about it. This is getting out of control.

"Snap out of it!" I practically shout in his face—and his eyes clear, then narrow as he reaches up and slides both arms up and out, knocking my hands free and forcing me to take a step back.

"What. Are. You. Doing?" he demands through clenched teeth.

"A better question," I reply, "is what're you doing? You went all zoned-out hippie in me again. How do you feel?"

"Fine." He stops and frowns. "A little lightheaded, actually. I probably just need to eat something." Suddenly his gaze drops to his lap, and the open box of ChocoMints. "Oh, right! You have CampGirl cookies!"

I snatch the box away before he can shove his great big hand into it. "Let's hold off on these for now," I warn him. "I'm not sure I want you eating any more of their cookies just yet. I'll get you some water, and something you can eat." I'm starting to think there's something funny with these cookies, and until I can figure out what I'm putting a moratorium on them. For me and for Tall, though I don't think they've messed me up any that I can tell. Then again, I've had plenty of nights out where I thought I wasn't messed up at all, and a whole lot of those ended with wrecked cars and shaved pets and incomprehensible tattoos, sometimes on the shaved pets, and lots of other weirdness, so maybe I'm not the best judge.

When I come back with some Turling beef cubes ("Like eating a slice of prime rib, but without all the mess!") and a bowl of cloud chips ("You'll swear they're as light and fluffy as a cloud—because that's exactly what they are!"), Tall's shaking his head so hard I can hear his brains rattling from across the room. "I feel like I've been asleep," he says, accepting some of the food and opening another can of beer to go with it. "Like when you have a hard time waking up, and everything seems foggy and your brain just isn't firing on all cylinders."

"Yeah, like when you can't tell the difference between dreams and reality and you try to fly, only to crash hard on the floor and almost crush your junk, and then you have to hobble to the john, cursing under your breath and wondering why it didn't work, and then your pee is rainbow-colored and you can't tell if that's real or not but it smells like apricots and lilacs?" He hits me with a Number Four. "What? Is that just me?"

"I can't imagine it being anybody else," he answers dryly,

and I relax a little. Looks like the real Tall is back in the house.

I do wonder, though, what address he was at a few minutes ago, and if there was anybody at home while he was out. He may need to get a better lock on his own thoughts, or the mental equivalent of a big dog, or at least some curtains.

Chapter Seven
It's like a tour of the stars—only with real stars!

". . . and this is the Matrix building."

I start, and sit up, clutching at a pillow, a bowl of chips, anything—I'm not sure if I'm planning to use them as a shield or a weapon or just a way to pry myself off the floor but I figure at least I'll have options. Then my eyes catch up to my ears and I see shadows approaching along the way from the front door, and then my brain finally joins the party to tell me, good news, it's just Tall.

Only he's clearly talking to someone else, and there're two shadows there, so I finish standing up and brushing myself off and kicking the couch back into shape—I was lounging on it and got tired, so I had it make itself into a mattress and fell asleep. What? It's a tough job, sitting around all day—most people can only manage it for a few days, a week at most.

Luckily, I'm a pro.

Tall comes into view, leading someone else, and my first thought is—well, this probably isn't very nice of me, but you know that movie? The one I always tease Tall about by saying things like "Hey, why don't you just go by your first initial, wouldn't that be cool?" and "when do you get a silver dildo that makes people forget their own names?" and "the really impressive thing is that somebody moved the Guggenheim so it's only a few blocks from Grand Central, and nobody noticed!"? Well, one of the things I like to give him trouble about is, "Hey, it could be worse—you could have a co-worker who's one of those little googly-eyed Jack Russells, in a suit and everything!" I've been hitting that one a lot since the whole "WiB" thing started.

So anyway, my first thought when they come into view is, "Screw me sideways and call me a wall hanging, they went and did it! They hired a Jack Russell! And got him a suit!" Then I realize that this would have to be one HUGE Jack Russell, since it's only a little shorter than Tall himself—probably about my height, I'm guessing. Then I realize that the proportions are all wrong on the body, this guy's walking upright, has shoulders and arms and hands and forward-facing knees, the whole bit, and I realize, hey, it's just a guy with the head of a Jack Russell!

What, you think I'm the only one out there? Trust me, I'm not. Turns out the Grays have a wicked sense of humor, or they're just insanely thorough, or maybe they're completists and were trying to work their way through the entire Audubon collection. Regardless, there's a bunch of us out there with partial mods like mine, only other animals. I've met dogs, cats, horses, elephants, parrots, eagles, snakes, rats, all sorts. We actually have a get-together once a year, out in Vegas—we figure nobody'll notice—so we can catch up and let our hair down, or our feathers or scales or whatever. The thing is, most of 'em have gotten plastic surgery to reduce the effects, or wear hoodies all the time along with sunglasses and those surgical face masks, or just live in a trailer or a cabin somewhere and order everything they need online and never let anyone get close enough to see them. Me, I'm the only one who flaunted what he had, or at least didn't bother to hide it. Which is how the MiBs found me in the first place, of course.

And yes, this means theoretically any of the others could've gotten themselves fully attuned by Ned and could've come out here, re-aligned the Matrix, and saved the galaxy. But they didn't. I did. So there.

Though I did consider enlisting them as Matrix babysitters. They'd be a better match than most people, and like I said, most of 'em are total shut-ins, so it's not like they'd mind sitting here instead of wherever they normally are. Besides, I get more cable channels than anybody this side of God. I haven't mentioned it to any of them yet, though. Dunno why, exactly, except that I like being important, I guess, and I'm not sure I really want to share.

But anyway, I think this is one of those guys, with the head of a dog and maybe fur instead of hair, and now he's apparently a MiB, which is certainly one way to hide in plain sight. Then they get even closer, and I finally realize, oh, crap, it's just a guy who looks a lot like a Jack Russell.

And then I notice the way the suit fits, and realize it isn't even a guy.

Oh, crap. Or did I say that already?

"And this," Tall says, waving a hand at me like he's showing off his prize possession, or at least a possession he's not entirely sorry to own from time to time, when he needs it or when someone asks to borrow it and as long as the local authorities aren't looking for it or anyone connected to it, "is DuckBob. DuckBob, this is"—I cringe, already guessing what's coming— "Agent Jones."

Yes, there could be more than one MiB named Jones. Hell, there probably is. But given my luck, and the timing, this has got to be Violet Jones, the MiBs' newest recruit. And the only woman they've had in forty years.

"Hey." I hold out my hand. "How's it going?"

The look she gives me is like the one you have when you open the fridge, hoping against hope to find a slice of left-over pizza or half a roast beef hoagie or some fried chicken or at least a few slices of cheese and instead you find a small Tupperware container you don't remember owning, containing something you can't recognize and don't remember ever eating, labeled with some scribble you can't possible read and are pretty sure isn't your handwriting. And yeah, that happens to me. A lot. I'm convinced somebody sneaks in at night and stashes those in my fridge just to screw with me, or maybe to hide them from the police. Either that, or there's some kind of space-warp just above the lettuce crisper. Which might explain how it keeps the lettuce so crisp, come to think of it.

So, right, no hearty handshake. No limp one, either.

"Tall, can I talk to you for a sec?" I grab his arm and steer him to the other side of the room without waiting for an answer. "What're you doing, man?" I whisper once we're out of earshot, or at least far enough that anyone with social graces will have to pretend they can't hear us. "Why'd you bring her here?"

He shrugs. "She'd heard of you, and about the mission to restart the Matrix," he explains. "She asked me what it was like, and I said it was amazing, but that I couldn't adequately describe it. Then she said she'd like to see it someday." He shrugs again. "So I brought her to see it."

I stare at him. "Dude, I thought you guys had classified the hell out've all this!" He'd once told me that only like three guys in the whole organization had the clearance to see the files on what we'd done. I asked if the President was one of them. Tall laughed for a good five minutes over that one.

"We did," he agrees. "It is classified Triple-Octagonal-Ultramarine-Uranium, which is as secret as it can get."

"Didn't she just start, like, a week or two ago?" I indicate Little Miss Friendly, who's currently eyeing my living room with so much disdain my mother would defend me if she saw it.

"Yes, Agent Jones has been with us for three weeks now," he answers. He seems awfully calm about all this, and I'm getting that worried tingle between my eyes again.

"And is she somehow cleared for this, all of a sudden?"

"No."

"So you brought her to a place she's not actually allowed to see?" I don't even want to ask how they got here, and how many classifications that violates.

He shrugs. "Yes."

"For the love of Pete's Dragon, why?" I swear, if I still had hair I'd be tearing it out by the handfuls right now. But feathers, it turns out, are both harder to grab and more deeply rooted. Wacky.

"She asked."

"That's it?" I stare at him—I can't help it. "She asked?"

"Yep."

Now I'm sure. I reach up and grab his face with both hands, squeezing like my Great-Aunt Matilda used to do every family get-together. Hard enough to leave marks. He doesn't react at all. "Tall," I say slowly, "snap out of it."

And there it goes—it's like watching the computer warm up and turn on, or the monitor clear, or the defrost finally kick in and clear the window, or all the alcohol burn off the bathtub. (What?) I can see his eyes clear, and then glare, and then he's pulling my hands off his cheeks.

"What the hell?" he demands. Then he glances up, sees Agent Jones standing there across the room trying to touch as little as possible and breathe as little as possible, and stiffens even more than usual. "What is she doing here?"

"You," I answer, jabbing him in the chest with my forefinger, "brought her here. Because she asked you to."

"What? That's ridiculous." But he stops, and closes his eyes, and then shakes his head. "Oh, God. I did, didn't I?"

"I need to ask you something." I study him closely. "Did you have any more CampGirl cookies right before this happened?"

Normally I'd expect a question like that to get Stare Number One, but he actually considers the question seriously. Then he nods. I knew it! "Yeah, I just took a box out of the freezer last night," he tells me. "I had a handful then for dessert, and brought a few into work this morning to snack on. Why?"

I rub the bridge of my beak. "Because it's looking like those things are seriously bad news," I answer. "Every time you've eaten them that I know of, you've turned into a zombie, basically. You talk and answer questions and all that, but you're not you. You're—nice. And mellow. And you pretty much do anything anybody tells you." I look over at Agent Jones again. "Including violating Triple-Ripple-Vanilla-Roadmonkey clearances."

"Triple-Octagonal-Ultramarine-Uranium," he corrects automatically, which more than anything tells he's back to normal. "You may be right," he admits, which worries me all over again. "I'll look into the cookies when I get back. And I won't eat any more of them, either." He rubs his jaw. "In the meantime, what are we going to do about her?"

"Oh, no!" I hold up my hands and back away. "That's your problem—you brought her here. You figure out how to get her back home again."

Tall sighs but doesn't argue. Instead he squares his shoulders, tenses his jaw, and walks over to her.

"I'm sorry, Agent Jones," he tells her—yeah, so I'm eavesdropping shamelessly, so what? It's my giant glittery skull, after all!—"but you're not cleared for any of this. I never should have brought you here."

"No, you shouldn't have," she agrees immediately, and it almost looks like she's pleased about it. Her voice matches her appearance, by the way. It's deep and husky, and not in a sexy-Lauren Bacall way—more like an overtired trucker way. "This is far above my clearance rating, as I'm sure you know.

So why did you bring me here?"

To his credit, Tall doesn't come up with some crazy excuse about aliens controlling his brain or the Jell-O at lunch leaving him a coded message or the fate of a thousand chorally trained tuna depending upon it. He just shakes his head. "I don't know. I believe my mind may have been clouded, as was my judgment, but I take full responsibility for my actions. Now let's get you back."

She just nods and turns to go, without even a backward glance or a cheery "thanks for letting me show up unannounced and wake you from a sound sleep, let's get a beer sometime!" or even a "harrumph, I hear you saved the entire galaxy, so thanks for that, I suppose." Nothing.

"Nice to meet you," I call out to her as they leave. "Maybe we'll run into each other again some day—in Hell. Or at the local dog run." What, I can't be a little rude back? "Give as good as you get," my Uncle Jack always said. Though that didn't work out so well for him the time somebody rear-ended his truck and he got out, grabbed the guy, dragged him out of his car, and dropkicked him into a nearby Dumpster. At least the judge thought it was funny, and he and Jack were drinking buddies anyway, so he went for the minimum sentence.

After they leave I think about going back to sleep, but of course I'm wide awake now. So I switch on that new game again and play it for a while. Right now it involves running around and making people's heads explode, which I do a lot in real life but not usually in the literal sense. There's supposed to be rules for who you want to explode and who you don't, I think, but I don't bother with those, I just explode everybody I meet. Again, kinda like real life. Hey, at least this way nobody can accuse me of favoritism. I do wonder, though, if everybody's heads explode, who's going to clean up the mess? Because I can tell you one thing, it ain't gonna be me.

Chapter Eight
Utili-kilts all around!

"**It is a** conundrum," Mary agreed a few days later. We were lounging on the couch, relaxing and recovering after a rousing game of Strip Mah Jong. What, you think poker's the only game you can play that way? Hell, no! Almost any game that lets you go head-to-head (heh!) and has a clear winner, you can do a strip version. I've played plenty of 'em, too. Geez, one time we even tried Strip Risk.

And let me tell you: That? Does not work. At all.

First off, it's just too damn slow. It's hours before a game ends, so unless you start everybody out in only a wifebeater and a utility kilt—a look that works on pretty much anyone, by the way—there's no way you're gonna get anywhere before people fall asleep from sheer boredom, usually either in the chips bowl or across the game board—or, in my case, both. Second, there's just something about Risk that's a little too combative. It must be because you're playing whole armies, but people get too entrenched in their little worldviews and their nationalistic roles and, well, they're not exactly interested in hooking up with what they consider foreign powers. Like I said, the one time we tried it I fell asleep partway through, but I do remember getting woken up by hearing one of the girls playing shouting about how there was no way she was gonna bow down to some socialist imperialist scum—which doesn't even make sense, when you think about it—and a guy yelling back about how she was nothing but a child of criminals anyway, and he wouldn't want to see her with her shirt off even if he could! Yeah, it got pretty ugly, though it did provide an excellent primer for my World Politics class.

But Strip Mah Jong? Brilliant stuff. It's nice and fast-paced, you can see the other player's tiles as they get laid out so you're constantly calculating your chance of winning, and there's lots of reaching across the board, which after the first game or two can get all kinds of distracting—in a good way.

It's exactly what a strip game should be—quick, fun, cutthroat but still friendly, with lots of jiggling. Because ultimately in a game like that, no matter who wins, everybody wins.

And yeah, I won. See above.

Anyway, we were catching our breath and debating a rematch—the biggest drawback being we'd have to get dressed all over again—and so while we were chilling I filled Mary in on the latest with Tall. Including both his new glassy-eyed behavior and his impromptu turn as a tour guide to the unpleasant Agent Jones. Which probably wasn't the best plan on my part, because now there's a furrow above those gorgeous blue eyes and a frown plastered across those lovely red lips. Yeah, my lady friend's a serious looker. Trust me, I know how lucky I am.

"Your hypothesis may be correct," she tells me, "regarding the cookies as at least a catalyst for Tall's unusual behavior, if not the outright cause." Yeah, she's a brain, too. I love the way she talks, like she's the world's hottest science teacher. Sign me up for extra credit! I am a little alarmed, though, at what she's saying. If both she and Tall think I could be right about the cookies, something's seriously wrong. "Yet you have had no adverse reaction to them?"

I shrug. "I got a ChocoMint stuck in my gullet at one point and spent the morning coughing up cookie bits until it finally dissolved enough for me to swallow the rest of the way, but other than that, no. Did you?"

She shakes her head, which sends those thick waves of glossy black hair flying. Did I mention how hot she is? I know, I just like to point it out whenever I can. "I did not observe any change in my mental acuity or my ability to withstand suggestion," she agrees, "though admittedly there were only a few cookies left for me by that point in time." She tosses me an arch look along with that comment, and I hang my head a bit. Yeah, I'd meant to save her half of that box from Tall, but what can I say? I got peckish while waiting. Also, I just can't resist the darned things. Hell, I was pleased that I left her any at all!

"But I've got tons more now," I point out, gesturing toward the stack of them over by the TV. "Pick a box and it's all yours—I'll even write your name on it so nobody else'll touch it. Including me," I add as she elbows me in the side. "Promise."

She considers for a second. "It would be advisable to sample them again," she says finally, "to confirm my earlier lack of reaction and to test for any unusual flavoring or contents." So saying, she hops up from the sofa—which sighs a little, 'cause it likes her almost as much as I do—and sashays across the room to select a box from the pile.

And no, she doesn't bother putting her clothes back on first.

Did I mention— yeah, yeah, fine.

I have no problem, however, just laying here and waiting for her to take her own sweet time returning.

No problem at all.

When she does plonk herself down next to me again— only, when she does it it's a lot more graceful, and a lot sexier, than it sounds—she opens the box, removes a sleeve of cookies, tears the end of the wrapping enough to extract them, and then selects one between thumb and forefinger. She holds the ChocoMint up like it was a lab specimen, and we both stare at it.

It looks exactly like a ChocoMint. I know, because I dream about them. A lot. It's a thin disk, sort of scalloped around the edges, a little rounded across the top but perfectly flat and with the CampGirl logo pressed in on the bottom, and the whole thing is coated in dark chocolate.

I'm practically drooling just looking at it.

And then there's the smell—you get the chocolate first, like a sledgehammer, then the mint sort of sneaks up on you and puts you in a chokehold while you're laying there, and then the sugary, bready scent of fresh cookie dough leans in and bops you right on the nose.

Wow, I hadn't realized, but CampGirl cookies are kinda violent!

"I do not see anything amiss," Mary says finally, and I nod. Looks like a regular ol' ChocoMint to me!

Then she parts those luscious lips and takes a dainty bite.

Is it bad that I could probably sit and watch her chew for hours?

She swallows—hey, now!—and studies the rest of the wafer. "I do not feel unusual," she tells me. "How long after ingestion did Tall show signs of altered behavior?"

"Pretty much the instant he chomped down," I answer, thinking back. "He shoved several in his mouth, chewed, swallowed, and—instant zombie. Nice-guy zombie. A zombie hippy."

Mary doesn't look like a zombie at all—I can tell her eyes are just as alert as ever. Not much gets past those peepers, which can be a damn shame when you're trying to surprise her with flowers and she sees you paying the delivery guy at the door and recognizes the florists' logo on the package.

"There is a flavor here," she remarks, "that I do not remember encountering in these cookies before. I cannot place it, and it is subtle, but it is there."

"Really?" I reach for a cookie. "May I?" She nods, and I pop it into my mouth. Hm. "Yeah, you're right," I say, and only think to raise a hand to my face after I've sprayed her with cookie crumbs. "Damn, sorry. Here, let me get those off you." I start trying to brush them off her, which may have to be round two of Strip Mah Jong from now on, and I pretty much forget what I was saying or doing or even thinking before then.

"What do you notice?" Mary prompts after a few seconds.

"Well, this dimple here is all kinds of hot," I answer, and she harrumphs and swats me on the arm. "Oh, right." I finish chewing. "Yeah, under the mint and the chocolate and general cookie-ness there's something else. It's kinda bitter, actually, maybe a little metallic? Like chewing tin foil, but so faint I didn't notice it before you said." Hey, I've got good taste buds, okay? It probably comes from having such a large mouth, plus I think the Grays sort of plugged in brand-new ones when they modified me, like when your mechanic changes the oil and pops in some new spark plugs, too.

"Metallic," she muses, absently finishing the rest of her cookie. And there's that chewing again. Damn. "Yes, you are correct. Some sort of vitamin complex, perhaps? I will need to test them in order to determine the exact ingredient. But there is certainly something here, which bolsters your theory further."

Ooh, now I'm getting bolstered. That sounds kinda rude—and kinky. But I get the gist.

"You think Tall's getting anywhere on his end?" I ask her, taking the box and setting it down on the floor out of our way so we can snuggle close again. "He said he was gonna look into it, too."

Mary's silent for a minute. "Perhaps," she decides after the pause. "But I would not count on it, not when he has already proven himself highly susceptible to whatever is occurring to him."

"Yeah, that makes sense." I sigh. "Unfortunately, it's not like I can go back to Earth and help him out. I'm pretty much stuck here. And you're too busy, what with all these assignments they've got you on. And who the hell knows where Ned is—he hasn't been by in over a month." Okay, maybe I'm feeling a little sorry for myself. I've got it pretty good, and I know it, but sometimes it strikes home that I'm stuck here—and I mean really stuck here, since without me around as its final element the whole Matrix grinds to a halt and its protective mojo drops and outsiders can pop in and invade us. Again. Normally I don't mind being housebound—especially since my house is the size of a football stadium, complete with its own dugouts and concession stands—but this is one of those times I really wish I could just hail a cab and get on out of here, at least for a little while.

"You are already helping him," Mary assures me, "and I will do what I can as well." She gives me that coy little smile of hers, the one she knows full well knocks me for a loop. "That is a matter for later, however. In the meantime, perhaps you would be up for another game?"

Did I mention— yeah, yeah.

Chapter Nine
Does this make me look fat?

"What is it?" Tall asks, squinting at the little box I've just handed him. And by "little," I mean about the size of my thumbnail. Which, admittedly, isn't as small as it could be, but hey, sometimes you just need a screwdriver that very second. Or a spackle knife. Or a spatula.

"Well, open it." I'm almost vibrating with excitement, though that could also be the Eargan Lightning Jelly I ordered online. Tastes like a cross between spearmint, pennies, mini-wheat cereal, and ginger marmalade, and wires you better than any ten shots of espresso ever could. Plus, you can produce static shocks from hell!

I am excited, though. I got the idea a few days after talking to Mary about everything, and spent the time since then scouring the Galactic Net for something that would fit the bill. That's how I happened across the Lightning Jelly, which I figured was worth trying, too. I'd almost given up on finding these when a set popped up on AuctionWorld. And I managed to snag them!

Tall opens the box and just sits there staring at what's inside. Finally I reach over and take the box from him, then remove half its contents to show him. "See, this is like the world's tiniest webcam," I tell him. And it is, too. It's barely the size of a dime, just as thin, and vaguely flesh-colored. "It's got a nonadhesive clingy back, like those plastic clingform pictures you can stick on glass, and it's breathable and waterproof so you put it somewhere like your forehead and just forget about it. The color'll shift once it's in place, matching perfectly to whatever's below it so it'll be completely invisible, and pretty much undetectable by any other method, too. But I've got the matching dongle installed and its specific frequency already logged in"—I pat my computer and almost get frostbite for my troubles—"so I can see everything it sees. And according to its specs and the little test I did the other day, this baby'll see just about everything." I admit, I'm proud of myself. "It's got a range measured in astronomical units and shown in scientific notation," I add, "and it's supposed to be able to cover from one end of reality to the other, so I figure we'll be fine."

"I don't get it. You want me to take pictures for you?" Wow, sometimes the big guy is seriously dense, and not just in muscle mass.

"No, doofus! Well, yes, but no. Okay, yes, but that's not the point." I'm not going to let him dampen my enthusiasm. "Look, I can't go anywhere, right?" I gesture at my "crown," the wired-up doohickey that connects me to the Matrix, and then toward the door in the general direction of the Matrix itself. Thank God for Ned's almost-infinitely-extensible cable! Otherwise I'd have to spend all day every day walking around the Matrix chamber with my head literally stuck in the gap. And let me tell you, with a head the size of mine, we're talking serious neck twinges!

"Right." Oh, good, he gets that much!

"But this way I can!" I'm bouncing again, so much so that the couch tries to turn itself into a trampoline. Not helpful, pal. But I do file that option away for the next time Mary's over. Rowr. "I can be right there with you, checking everything out, offering suggestions, pointing out things you missed—it'll be just like old times!" Except that I'll actually be halfway across the galaxy, most likely sitting with my feet in the lounging pool and a cold drink in my hand, checking my email, chatting with Mary, and probably watching a movie or playing online at the same time. But I leave that part out—I don't want him to feel like he's not getting my undivided attention.

Tall's still just staring at me, so I hold out my hand, the camera perched on my forefinger. "Take it, man."

He does.

"All right, now just stick it in the center of your forehead." He does, which surprises me, and it adheres at once. Then the coloration affect kicks in and it darkens and fades. If you really stare, and squint a lot, you can maybe just about tell that he's got a slight protrusion there, but only just. If they made them to match feathers I'd consider wearing it myself, just so I could scan back over footage at the end of the day and make sure there wasn't anything I missed, but apparently it has trouble mimicking texture. "Good, that should be that—for seeing what you see. Which just leaves hearing what you hear—and talking back and forth." I lift the rest of the box's contents out for him to admire. "State of the art wireless earbud and mike," I explain. It's even smaller than the camera, not much more than a centimeter long and also sort of but not quite flesh-colored. "It goes in your ear—it's supposed to be 'acoustically transparent,' meaning sound passes right through it, so it shouldn't mess with your hearing at all. Plus I can talk to you directly whenever I want. Y'know, offer suggestions, dating advice, whisper sweet nothings, stuff like that."

That should have gotten a big old glare, a frown, a "not a chance!"—something! Instead Tall just sits there like a statue.

Or, I realize, like someone who ate more CampGirl cookies again.

Only one way to find out.

I hand Tall the mike. "Put this in your right ear," I tell him.

And he does. Without a single word. No arguing, no blustering, no threatening anyone with grave bodily harm. Yep, definitely wrong.

As soon as his hand comes away from his face, I grab both cheeks and hold him steady. "Tall," I shout in his face. "Snap out of it, dude!"

At this point I'm almost used to the transformation that happens next, though it's still all kinds of creepy. He slumps a little, surprising the couch so much it parts and dumps him on the floor on his butt again, his eyes clearing and that vacant expression fading, instant zombie in reverse, then straightens and looks around before glaring my way. Number Seven, which is just fine by me. "How—?" he starts.

"—did you get here, and why didn't you bring any Cheetos like I asked?" I cut him off. "I'm guessing you either took the bus or had Ned or the Grays do the teleport thing. And you ate more CampGirl cookies, didn't you?"

Tall hangs his head. I can't always read his expressions or his body language, but this one's pretty easy. "I know, I know," he mutters after the silence stretches on over me. "I meant to avoid them, I did—but it was late at night and we'd been on a case and I hadn't had time to eat and then the cookies started calling to me."

"Whoa." I squint at him. "They're calling to you now? How'd they get your number, I thought it was unlisted? What language are they speaking? Is it one you understand, because I hate getting phone calls from people when I don't know what they're saying—unless they're relatives, in which case I hate it when I can understand them. Maybe there's some way to teach my entire extended family to speak Lower Estonian or something? We could tell them it makes barbeque taste better, that'd be all it takes, and then when they call and yammer at me at least I can just admire their fricatives and not worry about even trying to follow along." I force myself to focus—thoughts of my family always do that to me. Brrr. "But back to these other voices. What're they saying to you? And does any of it involve other instructions about other people, committing random acts of violence, or baby seals?" I actually threw that last one in there— I've found that a picture of anything small and cute like a baby seal helps break up the monotony and relieve any dark ooginess. But somehow Tall doesn't look like he wants any cheering up. Unless it also involves getting him someone or something to rip apart with his bare hands. And I am definitely not volunteering for that job, no sir!

It actually takes him a minute to gain enough control over himself to speak, or maybe that's just how much time he needs to winch his jaws apart enough for sound to escape. Fortunately I'm used to this from him. Sometimes I like to check messages while he's working on spitting those words out, but that usually just makes matters worse. "They don't actually talk," he grinds out, "but it feels like they do. Like they're sitting there saying, 'eat me, eat me.'" He hangs his head again. "And I do. I just can't help it."

I nod. If there's one thing I've seen a lot of in my life, it's chemical dependency. That and cheesy low-budget cable movies. And bad hair. And people who think their entire outfits should be all one color, which really only works if you're Johnny Sunshine or maybe Zorro the Gay Blade. But I've had way too many cousins go through addictions to booze, weed, Twinkies, and other controlled substances not to recognize the signs.

"You're hooked, bud," I inform Tall, sitting on the floor across from him. The couch decides it's being dissed and slinks off to sulk in the corner. "You're addicted to those cookies. That ain't good."

"I'm not the only one," he protests, "it's the whole office! There're ChocoMints and PB Sandwiches and Island Delights everywhere you look!"

That image makes my gut lurch, and not because that's a lot of cookies laying about and I haven't had lunch yet. "The whole office? All the MiBs? Come on, don't you have a few gluten-free health food types around somewhere?"

"We do," he agrees. "Agent Smith is gluten-free, and so are

a few of the others. But the Lemon Stripe cookies are gluten-free, and they ordered a whole case of those." A quick smile flits across his face, then vanishes like it doesn't want to get caught there. "My niece had so many sales she not only got the badge but also the T-shirt, the hat, the duffle bag, the scarf and gloves, the poster, the MP3 player, the camp chair, the razor scooter, the wading pool, and the luggage set." He shakes his head. "She was only a hundred boxes short of the pool table."

"Wow, CampGirl décor everywhere, huh?" I shudder at the thought—that's a lot of decorative flames. Then, going back to the problem at hand and what Tall was saying before he got distracted by the list o' loot, I scratch the top of my bill. "So everybody at work's been eating CampGirl cookies. And now the entire office's . . . nice?"

He thinks about that, frowning. "Yeah, I guess it is," he says eventually. "I hadn't really thought about it, but usually there's people shouting and yelling and throwing things at each other and at the walls—it's a high-pressure job. But lately, it's been . . . quiet. Friendly. Hell, I'm not even sure we've had an accidental shooting in weeks!"

"So these cookies are making all you MiBs nice and compli-ant." I think about that, and it gives me the willies. "I wonder if it's messing with anybody else, or just you guys?"

Tall levers himself to his feet. "I definitely need to find out."

"Yeah, you do that." I stand as well, which is a wonder since I don't exactly have a crane or some kind of pneumatic lift on hand. Hey, my bill's heavy, okay? "Just do me a favor—don't eat any more cookies! I mean it!"

"I'll try." For once he doesn't look smug or condescending or even arrogant. "Later, man. And I'll remember the Cheetos next time."

"Cool." For some reason, one of the only things I can't get out here? Cheetos, the proper turn-your-fingers-orange kind. I can get almost any other kind of chip, including ones that no one on Earth's ever seen, and a few that'd probably violate several local laws, a handful of church laws, and even a few natural laws if they got anywhere near the planet. But I just can't get Cheetos.

I wave Tall out, then sink into the chair in front of my computer desk. Hm, should I have maybe told him that I could now see and hear everything he does? Nah, why spoil the fun? Besides, this way he won't act all self-conscious like those people you can't even wave a camera near without them suddenly vamping and being "witty." He'll look and act completely natural.

And DuckBob the Tele-presence is on the case!

Chapter Ten
One heck of a commute

It takes Tall an entire afternoon to get back to Planet Earth. I had no idea—the only time I've made the trip was on the way out when we first got tasked with the whole "save the galaxy" thing, and we didn't exactly take the direct route. So I'm fascinated as I watch him hitch a ride on a pleasure yacht ("We're doing a tour of the supernovas, in descending order of magnitude, of course," the owner tells him. "We'd be happy to drop you off along the way, and in the meantime you can watch the show with us. Do you like puppies?" It isn't clear from the way he said it whether he's asking if Tall likes pets or whether he's hungry— or possibly both—so the big guy wisely demurs. I would've, too, but I would've been damn curious afterward).

The yacht drops him off at Red's, the intergalactic truck stop diner we visited on our way up, and I amuse myself watching Tall go inside and flirt with Delia, who'd been our waitress. I'd thought he was sweet on her from the way he kept staring, open-mouthed, every time she stopped by to top off our coffee, and the way he's acting now, all super-nice and ultra-polite like a little boy trying to impress his teacher, confirms it. So Tall's type is short, rounded and round-faced, and cheerful, huh? Good to know.

After a quick lunch—which I envy him, because even though Red's does deliver, and believe me I take advantage of that fact all the time, the food's never quite as good as when you get it piping-hot from the oven or off the grill—he hops the bus and takes that back home. When we'd all been on the bus, it had been a messy, bumpy, dangerous ride, owing to the fact that we'd been attacked along the way. Of course, crashing a car into it to sneak on board had probably started us off on the wrong foot anyway. This time, there isn't any trouble, and it's obvious Tall's done this a bunch of times before—he even has what looks like a rail card, only it's made of a green glow and projects from something I'd thought was an ink spot on the inside of his right wrist—and after showing that at the door the conductor lets him on. He picks a seat next to what looks a lot like a giant tangerine with a green-and-purple emo haircut flopping down over its face and a pair of overalls that seem to be made out of green lace, folds his arms over his chest, and puts his head down. I'm pretty sure he's closing his eyes at this point. I can tell Tall's a veteran of the New York subway system, because he immediately falls asleep and doesn't wake to any of the jostling around him, or any of the random sounds or, I assume, smells. In fact, he sleeps right up until the conductor announces that they're nearing Stop Number Twenty-two, Alpha Centauri. I vaguely remember Mary saying that the bus didn't stop at our solar system, so apparently this is the closest it gets. Tall straightens when he hears the announcement, and a second later he's hauling himself to his feet and heading toward the nearest door.

I wondered how he's planning to get from Alpha Centauri, four-point-two light years away (I Google it while he's in transit, though I do get distracted by some of the other things I find along the way—GalacticTube is a dangerous time-sink!), back to Earth. But Tall's a thorough guy, so I figure he's already got that part covered.

Sure enough, he gets out at the Alpha Centauri station—which looks a lot like a standard New York subway station if the stop itself was on acid, rolling around and shifting colors and patterns and curling in and around on itself like an inchworm exercising—and walks over to a small row of parking spaces.

And there, in one of them, is a black Ford POS sedan. With tinted windows. I'd say it was a sight for sore eyes except I have less than fond memories of that car, or one an awful lot like it.

That clearly doesn't bother Tall, but then he wasn't the one who got scooped out of his nice, boring, normal life and dragged into one of these exact same cars. No, he was one of the two doing the manhandling. Now he pulls a key fob from his pocket, walks around the car to make sure it's okay, unlocks the driver's side door, climbs in, starts her up—she does roar nicely, I'll give her that—and backs out of the space. Then he swings around, orients her with the stars or something else I don't know anything about and can't be bothered to learn, and hits the gas.

I will say this, that sedan may look boring and crappy and like something your grandfather would drive to the drugstore to stock up on Ensure, Depends, Twizzlers, Corn-nuts, and wine coolers, but man, she can move! The stars blur past, and it's only another hour before good old Sol comes into view. Tall slows down then, and it takes him another forty minutes to maneuver past Mercury and Venus to Earth.

Ah, Earth. I haven't been back in months, obviously, and that hits me full-force now as I watch Tall hovering behind the Moon, apparently waiting for the right spot. The planet looks amazing, with its swirl of clouds and its deep blue oceans against that green. I find myself homesick, and have to glance away for a second.

I guess I picked exactly the wrong time for that, because the next thing I know Tall's hit the gas again and he's barreling into the Earth's upper atmosphere. He cuts through that like a hot knife through butter, and I can see the car's hood starting to turn bright orange around the edges as the friction takes over. Fortunately that controlled fall only lasts maybe ten minutes before he hits the brakes again and our mad descent slows to a crawl.

Tall doesn't hesitate. He taps a button on the car's center console, which I hadn't really noticed before, and it displays a map of Manhattan, with both our destination and our current locations clearly marked. I'm happy to see we're pretty close already, and that's definitely Manhattan laid out below us, growing bigger by the second.

The front dash has all kinds of buttons and things, and now Tall leans across and flips a toggle switch, which makes the car shudder and whine for about ten seconds. Then the noise is gone, it's all perfectly quiet again—

—and I realize I can't see the car's hood through the windshield anymore.

It's not just a Ford POS, it's an invisible, flying Ford POS!

Tall deftly maneuvers the car as it enters Manhattan airspace, cutting around news copters and traffic copters and the occasional police helicopter or private one. As he guides the car toward someplace in particular, I wonder if the MiB headquarters is supposed be eyes-only and need-to-know and all that crap, in which case I'm probably not cleared to even know it exists, much less where. Then I wonder if I should tell Tall about the whole tele-presence thing now. But I decide against it.

For one thing, I don't want to startle him so much he loses control of the car.

For another, after saving the universe I really deserve a little respect—and a higher security clearance (it would be hard to get lower) to match.

And finally, I'll admit it—I'm just plain curious.

So I keep my massive bill shut and my eyes open as Tall finally reaches a particular building in midtown Manhattan, just a few blocks from Madison Park. He doesn't bother bringing the invisi-car all the way down to street level, though. Instead he circles around one more time—and parks on the roof. A roof I realize looks like a grade school blacktop, complete with painted-on marks for the court. There're two other POSs sitting there, both visible and looking perfectly normal if not for the fact that they're twenty stories aboveground, and Tall parks his beside one of them, shuts off the engine—which makes the car visible again and I can practically hear the car's battery sighing in relief and maybe crying a little—and pulls himself out. Then he spends several minutes checking things over, making sure the car hadn't hit a galactic pothole or something. Finally, after what seems like forever, he nods, locks up, walks across the roof to an elevator door housed in a little shack at the end, and pushes the DOWN button.

I'm all a-tingle. Seriously. Part of it's the vicarious thrill of it all—I'm like the ultimate voyeur, at least as far as watching a boring, slightly uptight, somewhat do-gooder-ish dude like Tall on his morning commute. Part of it's seeing Earth again, and not just Earth but Manhattan, which was my home for many a year. And part of it's the fact that I'm about to see MiB Headquarters! Me! And not only can they not stop me, they won't even know I'm here!

I don't think I've been this turned on by electrical doodads since a high school girlfriend showed me her "special, silvery little friend."

This is awesome!

Chapter Eleven
Duck's-eye view

Oh. My. God.

I want to put a pencil through my eye. No, a drill. Switched on.

Somebody save me.

This is horrible. It may well be the most hideous thing I've ever seen in my entire life, and that includes the time my cousin Vernon tried to win a bet by eating an entire Pizza Hut buffet all by himself—and the unsurprising aftermath. I couldn't touch barbeque pizza for years afterward.

But this is worse.

I don't see how Tall can stand it. He's got to be superhuman—or partially comatose. Still, I'm shuddering on his behalf. I mean, I expected it to be bad, but this?

It's sheer torture.

And yet, I just can't look away.

"Agent Thomas," someone says, and I shiver and drag my eyes toward the speaker just to escape the horror that surrounds them. It's a guy, big and bulky but kinda doughy, with a pudgy face and small features that look like they were just plopped on, or maybe thrown against his flesh like darts, or raisins in oatmeal. I remember him—he was the guy with Tall when they first grabbed me right out of my company's downstairs lobby. I always called him Potato Head. I'm guessing that's not his real name, though.

"Agent Howard," Tall replies, confirming my guess. "Any problems?"

Howard sighs, which makes his jowls shake. It's like watching a bulldog trying to do that "sexy girl tossing back her hair in a rain shower" thing. Scary, and I'm glad to only be watching—I can't get hit by the spatter. "Yeah, you could say that." His voice is still all deep and raspy, like a permanent smoker or just a big rock that's somehow learned how to talk. "We got a whole boatload of Polarians—literally, came on the galactic ferry—running around, and we've been trying to corral 'em. They didn't fill out their paperwork correctly, claim they never got the standard instructions, so now none of 'em have proper tourist visas and they're snapping pics of anything and everything and keep walking off with people's dogs and jewelry and hairpieces and a few of 'em've let themselves get spotted just 'cause they think it's funny—it's a zoo."

This time it's Tall doing the sighing. At least he doesn't shake his head when he does, otherwise I might get vertigo. "You set up a transmission void around the area?" he asks, and I'm impressed to see that Potato Head/Howard's face registers the same "huh?" I'm feeling. It's not just me! "It'll keep them from sending any pictures out," Tall explains, "and at the same time it'll stop anybody here from Tweeting about them or uploading photos or whatever. Everyone'll just think a cell tower went down or got overloaded, happens all the time."

"I'm on it." Before he's even finished speaking PH is up and out his chair, which looks wrung out from trying to contain him in the first place, and waddling off down the hall—hey, I happen to be an expert at waddling, thanks to my massive, webbed feet, and I can tell you, this is definitely a waddle. I put it right up there between the pregnant-lady waddle and the bowlegged sailor waddle for speed and grace, meaning he looks like he's a walking land mass in perpetual tectonic shift, or a living volcano trying to do the sidestep and failing miserably.

Meanwhile, Tall pulls out his own chair—pretty standard-looking office chair, all black fabric and metal, though it has more knobs and levers than a Nautilus machine so maybe it doubles as an espresso maker or something—and sinks into it. He sets both hands flat on his desk and stays like that for a long, deep breath, and I take advantage of that to look around again.

Nope, still terrifying.

Who in the world ever thought an open office plan was a good idea?

I mean, sure, I basically have one myself these days. But the difference is that I'm the only one here, so another way of looking at it is that I have a huge private office, bounded by the glittery pink walls that make up its exterior. I like that approach better.

Look, I did the whole cube-zombie thing for years. Pretty much as soon as I left college, not counting that brief stint in a salmon cannery up north or when I tried selling used cars or when I worked fast food. The rest of the time? Yep, cube farm after cube farm after cube farm. And each one got smaller and smaller. My first cubicle was big enough that I could literally stretch both arms out and spin around and get through three whole rotations before I ran into anything, a fact I demonstrated more than once in the short time I was there. My second cube was big enough for me to lean all the way back in my chair, stretch my arms up over my head and my feet out as far as they would go, and just about touch the walls on either side, which probably would have been okay if the boss hadn't walked up right then and harrumphed, causing me to bolt upright—and my chair to shoot out from under me, nail the boss in the shin and the Adam's apple, flip over him, crash down on top of the company v-p right behind him, roll end over end down the hall, and take out the company president's three kids who were waiting near the door to the lobby for their dad to finish his meetings and take them to ballet rehearsal. If it'd been in bowling, that would've counted as a definite strike. There, it turned out to be strike three, and my path out wasn't a whole lot more graceful than my chair's had been. Anyway, by the time I was at my last regular earthbound job I was in a cubicle so small I couldn't reach my arms out to either side without punching my fist through the one wall and sticking my hand out into the corridor on the other. There was just enough room to push my chair back from my desk and squeeze past it, and that was about it. I called that my cubelet because it clearly wanted to be a real cube when it grew up.

But even with all that? I'd take my cubelet over an open-plan office any day.

Yet that's exactly what Tall has going for him. I'm staring out at desk after desk after desk, with no walls between them, no privacy, no personal space, no solitude or silence. Each and every MiB in the place can look over and see what Tall's doing at any point in time. The ones behind him can see exactly what's on his computer screen. The ones all around him can hear anything he says on the phone. He can't pick his nose, fart, play Gemstone Blitz or that garden zombie game or the one with the birds and the catapults or even check his email or call his mom back without everyone around him knowing all about it.

I would have gone insane within two days.

But not Tall. He just sits there, switches on his monitor, logs into his work account—yes, I see his password, and no, I'm not telling you—and starts pulling up a bunch of really boring-looking files and reports. If he even notices that there're other people around, he doesn't let it bother him—he's sitting up straight, his typing is firm and clear and loud, he isn't hunched over his screen trying to keep anyone else from seeing what he's doing or who he's emailing or some cutesy little picture his niece sent him that he's taped up along the side. For how casual he's handling it, he could be alone in that office.

Until someone comes straight up to his desk and stands there, waiting to be acknowledged, that is.

"Agent Thomas." It's Agent Smith, the guy who got me into this whole mess in the first place. He was the one who sent Tall and Potato Head to fetch me and then introduced me to the Grays and basically shanghaied me into saving the galaxy. When I met him he was whip-thin with sharp features and glossy, slicked back black hair and a suit that'd obviously been tailored. He still looks exactly the same.

"Agent Smith." Tall shifts to face his superior.

"How fares our fine feathered friend?" It's clear from the sharp little smile on his face that Smith says this particular phrase a lot—I'm guessing every time Tall comes back from hanging with me. I doubt repetition makes it any funnier.

"He's fine," Tall replies. "And the Matrix is still running smoothly, no glitches and no further signs of intrusion. It'll all be in my regular status report."

"Good." Smith nods once, a sharp, crisp motion like cutting something with a single slice, and then turns on his heel and marches off.

Tall goes back to work, and I have the joy of watching as he files reports and turns in requisition requests and answers queries and scans logs and a whole host of other fun and exciting things. Funny, I'd always thought being a MiB would be damn cool and would involve a lot of battling aliens and chasing them through Flushing Meadows Park and rescuing people from their clutches and all that. I didn't expect it to look an awful lot like an accountant preparing a quarterly expense report. Ugh.

I practically die of excitement when Tall pushes back from his desk and rises to his feet. Gasp, movement! And then he turns and walks away from his desk and down the hall! Astounding!

And then he goes into the john. I close my eyes. Hey, every man deserves a little privacy when he pees, okay? It's only fair.

After—and I'm glad to see he does wash his hands, otherwise the memory of all the time we've both dug into a bucket of hot wings or a pizza together would make me yarf—he strides down the hall to what I quickly realize is a break room. There're cabinets against one wall, complete with a sink and a full-sized fridge and even a stove, and several small tables along the other side, each with four chairs around it. A coffee maker and a microwave sit on the counter, and there're actually several treats laid out there a well, including a pound cake and some home-made cookies and a bag of baby carrots—

—and several boxes of CampGirl cookies.

Crap.

I wish I could say I'm surprised when Tall zeroes in on those ChocoMints. Damn it, I knew there was no way he could with-stand the lure of that chocolaty, minty goodness. Sure enough, after pouring himself a cup of coffee from the pot there, Tall opens the cookie box and shakes a handful of ChocoMints out into his hand. Then he closes the box again, which is good, at least—I can't stand it when people open something and then just leave it out like that instead of putting it away properly because they simply can't be bothered to take that extra few steps back to the cabinet or pantry or wherever—carries the cup and the cookies over to one of the tables, and sits down.

And no, the table isn't empty.

"Agent Thomas." She looks exactly as unfriendly and unap-pealing as she did the last time I saw her, only this time at least she isn't so drastically out of place. Seriously, I've been in riots that were friendlier than this place, so surrounded by all that negativity and bottled-up hostility her barely restrained ani-mosity toward everything with a pulse hardly stands out at all.

"Agent Jones." Tall's voice is perfectly level, neither friendly nor nasty, just calm and professional and utterly disinterested. Like my shrinks always started out, before the inevitable screaming and crying and cursing-in-multiple-languages stage. I always felt so bad for them, but of course offering a hug only made it worse.

"Did you hear about the Palvotian ambassador?" she asks after a moment of his sipping his coffee and her crunching on some kind of cracker or something.

"I did," he replies. "Bad business, that, but there's a reason we warn them about the local cuisine and about what those chemicals and vitamins and additives could do to their foreign digestion. If they would just stick to the hot dog carts they'd be fine—that's why they're there!" He shakes his head. "Did they manage to get enough of him back to reconstitute him?"

"Almost enough," Jones answers. "He's a little shorter in one front feeler than the other, but apparently that's a sign of sexual prowess back on Palvotia II, so he's happy."

"Worked out, then," Tall says. That's followed by a long pause only slightly less awkward then my showing up to pick up my date for the high school prom and discovering that her father was none other than my proctologist—and her mother was my dentist. So both of them knew how to get under my skin, and how to probe me painfully. Good times.

"I had best return to my duties," Jones breaks into the silence eventually. "I'll see you around." How could you not, I wonder, with the open floor plan? It isn't like you could miss him—he looks like Godzilla or King Kong if you dropped one of them into the dessert with nothing around but a few low dunes, a handful of camels, and an oasis up ahead.

"Of course." Tall nods politely, judging by the way the camera bobs about. And he waits until Jones is gone before opening his hand to reveal the ChocoMints he's been concealing all this time. I'm a little surprised they're more than a chocolate smear along his palm but they look intact, other than a few fingerprints. He lifts the top cookie off with his other hand, holds it up and stares at it for several seconds, turning it this way and that—and then pops the entire thing right into his mouth.

I'm not actually there of course—I'm still safely at home—which is good because otherwise I'd be tempted to throttle him. Instead I can only watch as Tall seems to straighten slightly. Then he devours the other cookies, drinks the rest of his coffee, returns to the sink and rinses out his mug, and heads back down the hall toward his desk. All completely normal—

—except I'm pretty sure Tall's now a complete and utter zombie. Again.

So much for staying awake in the workplace.

Chapter Twelve
He's like a great big guppy—in a suit

Up to this point I've kept from saying anything directly to Tall, though, man, that has not been easy! I mean, let's face it, I was born to be a color commentator—I can sit there and kibbitz and snark and question and joke with the best of 'em. Hell, when I was in college *Mystery Science Theatre 3000* was still on, and we'd sit there and watch it and heckle right along with that one guy and those two wacky robots—until it got to the point where we were funnier than they were, and then we'd just turn off the sound and make up our own lines. And then we started just getting crappy movies and doing that without even turning on *MST3k*, and all our friends would come over to watch us eviscerate these movies, and they'd bring some of their friends, and they'd bring their friends—we started charging a buck or two a head, just to make some beer money, and wound up with enough to rent the back room in the local bar and hold the events there, with an open bar the whole time. Not too shabby for a couple of guys whose biggest talent was finding fault with everything right? Funny thing, I always wound up with the Crow T. Robot role—and he does look a bit duck-like. Just a coincidence or some kind of weird foreshadowing?

Anyway, I'd been itching to let loose with my usual snide comments, but figured this wasn't the best time, what with me hitching a ride on Tall without his knowledge or consent and basically spying on a top-secret government installation. But now, with Tall turned cookie-zombie, I decided I didn't really have much of a choice. I had to snap him out of it, and that meant talking to him. And, well, no time like the present.

"Yo, Tall," I say as he's walking down the hall. "Snap out of it, man."

Not surprisingly, he stops and looks around. "Who said that?" he asks.

"The ghost of Christmas Past," I answer. "No, Jiminy Cricket. No your Aunt Jemima. No, that weird-looking splotch on the wall. Who'd you think?"

He scratches the side of his nose. "DuckBob?"

"Got it in one—nice going, brainiac!" I'd slap him on the shoulder but I'm half a galaxy away—I make do with patting myself on the knee, which doesn't really have the same effect at all but does make me kick the computer monitor. Ow. "Now, snap out of it."

"Snap out of what? You want me to snap something?" This isn't a good sign. Every time before now, when I've told Tall to snap out of it, he does. Instantly. So why isn't it working now?

"You've been taken over by the evil cookie fairies again," I tell him. Then I get sidetracked for a second, imagining that there really are evil cookie fairies who go out and steal people's cookies or, worse yet, turn all them into those stale, dry, crumbly spice-cookie things you always find in your doddering maiden aunt's cupboard. Ugh. I swear, they're like sand that's been loosely pressed into discs and wrapped just to mess with people. Or maybe the evil cookie fairies are evil fairies actually made of cookies or from cookies, so you've got the Dread Snickerdoodle and the Sinister Humentaschen. They sound evil! And both of them are a bit on the dry and crumbly side, now that I think of it. The good cookie fairies would be things like ladyfingers and Florentine laces and of course sugar cookies. They could have whole battles, with cookie dough and powdered sugar and frosting going everywhere.

What was I doing again?

Oh, right. Tall. Cookie zombie. Got it. "Shake it off, pal," I order him. "You need to be your usual grumpy self again, pronto."

"I don't know what you mean," he answers, and starts walking again. "And how am I hearing you, anyway? I didn't call you—I don't even have my phone out."

"Oh, uh, this is a new phone system," I tell him. "It lets me call directly into your head. Pretty cool, huh?" Okay, no, I don't know why I didn't just tell him about the earpiece mike and the forehead camera. I should. This excuse just popped out instead. Sometimes I really have no control over what I'm saying. Maybe a lot of the time. Especially if I'm awake.

"It is cool," he agrees, which only proves he's not in his right mind. Tall just said something was cool? I'd better make sure the universe didn't just implode from utter shock. "What do you want?"

"I want you to stop acting weird," I answer as he reaches

his desk again and sits back down. "Or weirder. Or weird in a different and unsettling way. Your normal weird would be just fine."

"I am fine," he declares, and starts typing on the file already open on his screen. Apparently that's the end of that conversation. Maybe it's because he can't see me, and that's why the command didn't work? I'm not sure. But right now there's not a whole lot I can do about it.

So I get to sit and watch Tall work some more. Whee. I'd change the channel if I could only figure out how—maybe I could tap into some reality show's feed instead. Because this one's dead boring.

It's actually a relief when footsteps approach Tall's desk and stop alongside it, because Tall turns and looks over at the owner of those feet. It's Potato Head.

"I put up that transmission void, like you said," he informs Tall. "Looks like it's working—the Polarians are complaining that they can't get a signal to upload anything, and most of 'em are actually coming up to us voluntarily in the hope we can fix the problem." He grins. "I love dealing with stupid people."

Tall doesn't say anything. He doesn't look away either, though. I think he's just staring at Potato Head.

After a few seconds, Potato Head starts to fidget. "So, uh, you hungry?" he asks.

"I could eat," zombie-Tall replies. If he starts chewing on PH's head I'm gonna be sick.

"Cool." PH shifts from foot to foot. "You wanna grab a bite? Maybe Gray's Papaya?"

"Of course." And just like that, Tall's swiveling his chair around and pushing up to his feet. It's disconcerting having my view suddenly rise by at least three and probably more like four or five feet. It's like being in the world's smallest, smoothest glass elevator. "What would you like?"

Now, it's obvious from the way PH gapes at him that Tall never offers to buy him lunch. Which is almost a little sad. I mean, they're partners, right? Shouldn't they grab lunch together all the time? And wouldn't it make sense to trade off buying that lunch, just to make things easier and a little friendlier? Sure, Tall isn't always big on the social niceties, but hey, he and I hang out all the time over beers and pizza—especially Fernalian singing-cheese disco pies, which are awesome and come with platform shoes and big sunglasses every tenth pie— so I know he's capable of it. And PH doesn't seem all that awful once you get past the crumbling-stones grimace of a smile and the way the ground shakes when he walks and his suit jacket tears every time he moves. Sure, he's not the brightest bulb, but at least he's trying. And he looks so pathetically pleased at the fact that Tall's just agreed to lunch or dinner or whatever meal this is. Then Tall offers to buy him lunch? The big doughy guy's blown over.

"Uh, a Recession Special plus two chili dogs," he says finally. "And a diet cherry Coke."

Tall nods and heads for the door at the far end of this massive room. It isn't the way we first came in, I don't think, so this is probably the way down to the outside. I try to memorize it as he starts down some steps, then cuts to one side and flattens himself against the wall, then goes a few more steps before hiding again, and so on. Either somebody's after him or he's just always this paranoid. Given how well I know him, I've gotta say—the jury's still out on that one.

We're a few steps shy of a landing when another MiB appears around the corner, making his way up. Average height, average build, with an impressively full head of snow-white hair over a face so unlined it could be a balloon or a teenage boy's, he takes the stairs like an old man, slow and careful and never completely convinced they're not just gonna drop out from under him. Hey, happened to my Uncle Ralph once, though admittedly he was balancing on a bundle of fresh-cut logs at the time. We all knew he should've worn his cleats.

"Agent Thomas," he says as soon as he spies Tall. Which is when I realize he's got a plastic bag in one hand, marked with the ubiquitous "Have a Nice Day!" smiley face. Those things give me the creeps, especially since most of the time they're used by cheap-ass lunch carts or rundown corner bodegas. At least it's better than having bags showing some negative, glowering, frowning little demon-child saying "I hate you all and I wish this whole world would perish in flames." Those might be more honest but I doubt they'd sell well, unless death cults started having their own lunch carts. And I know I wouldn't eat at 'em! "I wonder if you wouldn't mind carrying this up to my desk for me?" the old dude asks. "I've got a meeting back downstairs in a few minutes." What he doesn't say but doesn't have to is that clearly he's gonna need that time just to make his way back down again, never mind going up and coming all the way back down. That's just crazy talk!

"Of course," zombie-Tall replies. He takes the bag, turns, and begins making his way back up the stairs, toward the main office space.

"Thank you," old-guy agent calls after him. Tall doesn't even glance back.

We get up there and Tall sets the bag down on some other desk in the hellish open-office space. Then he turns and starts toward his own desk again. I'm guessing he's now completely forgotten that he was supposed to be going to Gray's Papaya for lunch for him and PH. I guess, like with a guppy, there's only so much memory a zombie brain can handle. I wonder how long it'd take to reboot. I'm sure I saw an outlet around here somewhere.

We're almost back to his chair when a slender figure glides up alongside us. Oh, great.

"Agent Thomas."

"Agent Smith." I'm tempted to cry out, "Janet! Rocky! Biff! Uh!" but that probably wouldn't help us much.

"I was hoping to prevail upon you to deal with a small problem we seem to be having," Smith explains slowly, somehow making it sound like he's about to do Tall a big favor. "A Cervasite smokedancer is here for the festivities and got a little carried away. Unfortunately, it turns out he's also a shadowgrifter, a fact we had no way of knowing beforehand—he conveniently left that off his visa application." Smith sighed, doing his best to look put-upon and aggrieved and all that, and only succeeding in looking like any evil he'd caused might not have been entirely premeditated. "A few of our fellow agents were a bit . . . forceful in detaining him, and caused him to unleash those other talents upon them. Thus far he's absorbed about two dozen men's shadows, which would be problematic in and of itself. But as you know, each shadow adds to his power. He's absorbing them more frequently now, and his range keeps increasing. At this rate he'll be able to absorb the shadows of everyone on the Eastern Seaboard by noon tomorrow, and I don't even want to think about the mountain of paperwork that would cause!" Yeah, because obviously if someone's eating shadows we should be worried about which forms we have to fill out to report it! Give me a break! "We need to convince him to stop somehow, and to return those shadows he's already appropriated."

Tall sits down. "You want me to speak with him?"

Smith nods. "Yes, you're always so . . . persuasive, I'd hoped you could prevail upon him to behave reasonably."

Tall stands again—up down, up down, like a damn jack-in-the-box. Which, come to think of it, isn't a bad analogy. Now we just need to wind everybody else up so they should all pop more or less simultaneously. "Of course."

And he turns and walks away.

Great. We're gonna go talk to a Cervasite smokedancer now, whatever that is. And we have to be careful he doesn't try to steal our shadow, plus we need him to give back the ones he's already stolen.

It's like setting out to speak with Peter Pan, if Peter was a compulsive thief and, from the sound of it, a bit of a nasty customer. And on a bender. Plus somehow I don't think a needle and thread are really gonna help solve this whole damn question/case/whatever it is. And how do you convince some guy to give back the shadows he took, anyway?

Then I remember something else Smith said. "His range is increasing." And suddenly I get chills wondering what'd happen if his range was long enough to, say, reach to the Matrix. Could he take my shadow right through the little doohickey on Tall's head? Bad enough I've got the head of a duck, if I lose my shadow how'm I gonna cast Mount DuckBob and Mount Duckmore images across the kitchen floor?

Great.

Chapter Thirteen
Not a shadow of a chance

Tall goes downstairs—and when I say "downstairs," I mean it! He heads to the elevator, steps in, swipes his ID through a slot alongside the row of floor buttons, and causes a whole new row to slide down from those. These new ones are labeled "B1" through "B12," and he pushes "B11"—which makes me wonder, if we're dealing with a guy who treats shadows like Cookie Monster treats Oreos and he's only on B11, what kind of monsters do they reserve B12 for? Or maybe, just maybe, it's in ascending order, and they put the worst guys on B1 and the mildest on B12, in which case we're in for a cakewalk.

Yeah, right.

I don't for a second consider turning the camera and mic off and leaving Tall on his own, of course. Hey, the guy's a bud and I don't ditch my buds—unless there's cops from three different states involved, and we've got an expired hunting license and a sinking canoe and the daughter of a foreign dignitary, but, hell, it's not likely that's gonna happen to me a second time, right? I actually wish I could do more for the big lug, but since he's not exactly listening to me what can I do? I decide to try again, though, just in case it'll work better now that we've got actual wall around us.

"Hey, Tall!" I say in his ear.

"Yes?" He shakes his head. "DuckBob? Did you call again?"

"Uh, yeah. Listen, I need you to snap out of it."

"Snap out of what?" he shakes his head again, which makes me a bit dizzy. Darn shiny metal elevator walls!

Okay, still not getting anywhere. "Never mind." Since I've got him talking, though, I figure I might as well find out what I've gotten myself into. "So, what's a Cervasite smokedancer?"

He doesn't seem the least bit surprised that I've heard of them, which only goes to show how not-Tall he's being right now. "The Cervasites have the ability to warp air and light around themselves," he explains as we descend—judging by how fast the indicator's changing, this's got to be one of the fastest elevators ever built. I bet it's the kind that makes you feel like you're in zero-g right at the end, when it stops so suddenly you float for a second before gravity remembers to grab you again. I always loved those as a kid—I used to ride up and down in them for hours, just to feel that momentary weightlessness. Well, that and I discovered if I wore a little red cap and pushed buttons for people when they got on I could make pretty decent pocket change. But Tall's still talking: "They have an affinity for fire," he's saying, "and like to create shapes with it. A smokedancer is someone who's mastered that art and can weave the smoke and flames around him as he moves, creating a dance between himself and those elements."

"Huh. Okay, like one of those ribbon-dancers but with fire?"

"Exactly." I have no idea if he's looking amused at my

comparison or pleased that I got it at all or just stoic like usual.

"So what's a shadowgrifter?"

"Someone who can steal other people's shadows." Well, that makes sense. "They feed off the shadows, gaining strength from them."

"And this guy you're gonna go talk to now is both of those?"

"Exactly." Again he doesn't ask how I know that, which shows that being a cookie-zombie is messing with his head. Normally he'd be all over the question of how I'm getting my information.

I can't think of anything else to ask—other than "what the hell are you supposed to do about this guy?" which I figure isn't very helpful—so I stay quiet the rest of the way down. The indicator finally reads "B11," and the door slides open, letting Tall step back out.

I'm expecting a dark, dank dungeon, all cobwebs and damp walls and guttering torches. Or one of those high-tech prisons you see in movies, with everything gunmetal-grey and sharp-edged but with muted lighting to make it all a bit hazy.

Instead, it looks like—

A doctor's waiting room.

I kid you not. The walls are white and have stylized trees and flowers stenciled on them in bright colors. The floor's green rubber with raised dots for traction, and the ceiling is painted to look like a sunny day, all bright blue with fluffy clouds. There're big, comfy chairs and couches grouped to either side of the elevator, and a door in the wall straight ahead with a big window set in it. I'm surprised there's no receptionist with a big fake smile and a bowl of lollies for after, if you're good.

On reflection, though, the décor kind of makes sense. I mean, going to a doctor's sheer torture, so why not make a prison look like a doctor's office? It's like bringing back all the trauma all over again. Not that I've been to a regular doctor in a while, but vets' offices aren't much different except they have dog biscuits and cat treats and sunflower seeds instead of lollies. You want my advice, stick with the seeds—the biscuits're too dry and the cat treats taste like moldy tuna.

Tall doesn't waste time—he heads straight for the door, swipes his ID again, pulls it open, and heads on through. The rest still looks like a doctor's office, basically a long, wide hall with doors on either side, except that each door's got a card-swipe alongside the handle and a small window at eye level. Tall peeks in each one as he passes, and so do I.

I kinda wish I hadn't.

I've never seen sentient wood before. I kinda hope I don't ever again, because this one's a whole lot less than pleasant-looking—it's like somebody crossed a small redwood with a low-class thug and maybe threw in a rabid wolf while they were at it. He's all splinters and fangs and claws and beady yellow eyes surrounded by thick bark, and he must hear Tall or smell him because he turns and snaps at the door as we pass. Charming fellow.

The next cell's got a dog in it, a nice little beagle or spaniel or something, all big soft eyes and floppy ears and round little body. He's just sitting there, panting and looking like he wants to play, but then Tall's shadow falls across him and he changes.

Suddenly his head's five times bigger than his body, snarling and snapping, and there's another head alongside it, and a third one on the other side, all of 'em huge and hideous. What is this, Cerberus's pup or something? We don't stop, which is for the best. I'd hate to see this thing trying to play Fetch.

A few of the other cells—that's what they are, despite the cheery colors—are also occupied, and they range from people that look normal to things that I'm not even sure how to describe. In one of 'em there's a guy I can only explain as Cheese Factor Five—he's got a white polyester suit, a big glossy black hair-do, a black silk shirt open halfway down, gold chains, and white faux-leather loafers. Talk about a *Saturday Night Fever* flashback! The fact that his skin's blue and covered in what look almost like raised paisley polka-dots actually works pretty well with his whole Disco vibe. Wacky. But finally we come to one door and Tall peers in, then nods and swipes his ID to open it. He enters, and it's not like I have much of a choice—I go with him.

The room's not big, maybe eight by eight, with a bed against one side wall and a table and chair by the other and a sink and toilet and some other doodads that could be alien equivalents arrayed across the back. Tall shuts the door behind him and moves over to the one chair, because the bed's already occupied.

At first glance, this guy looks completely normal. Really tall and really skinny, with thin, jutting limbs and a long face and wildly curly black hair, but still normal.

Then I check out the shadow peeking out from over his shoulder.

And the one swaying to some invisible music at his feet.

And the pair fighting back and forth across the wall behind him.

And the other pair dancing along the far wall, their feet linked to his by a thin thread.

Yeah, this'd be the guy.

Tall sits down and stares but doesn't say anything. After a minute the guy concedes defeat and meets his gaze. "Hello," he says, his voice all soft and dark and a little raspy, just like you'd think smoke would sound. Or a shadow. 'I am Vijik'yin. Let me guess, you are the next one they've sent to torment me."

"My name is Agent Thomas," Tall answers. "Agent Smith asked me to speak with you, yes. We need you to return those shadows you took, and to promise that you won't try taking any more."

I guess that's funnier if you're there, because this guy throws back his head and laughs. But what's really creepy is all of his shadows do too, making this shadow-chorus you can just about hear as a cold echo if you really listen. "And why should I do that?" he asks. "What would I possibly gain from such behavior?"

"Right now, you're to be held indefinitely," Tall replies. "If you cooperate, I can reduce that sentence. You could get out of here before you're too old to dance, much less anything else."

This guy starts to say something in return, but I happen to glance down at Tall's feet and I can't help myself, I gasp. "Tall!" I say, hopefully not so loud that Creepy McShadows will hear me. "Check out your shadow, man!"

Tall does, and I can just about hear the sharp intake as he

sees what I just noticed. His shadow is stretching out in front him, impossibly long and narrow, right toward this smoke-dancer—who isn't moving as near as I can tell, but Tall's shadow's being absorbed into his, regardless.

"Cut that out!" Tall snaps, and this guy does a much more convincing "Hey, wasn't me" than Agent Smith. Then again, so does the dastardly villain in all those Saturday-morning cliffhangers, the one always walking around and twirling his mustache while chuckling maniacally, so that's not all that impressive.

"I'm sorry, is something wrong?" he says. Then he smirks, which kinda ruins it. "Oh, that. My apologies." And suddenly Tall's shadow stops looking like it's twelve feet long and has a pinhead, and goes back to being a more normal cast-off of his real self. "I'm afraid I have a hard time resisting one in such close proximity," the guy adds. Yeah, I tried that line a few times at various bars, telling chicks why I was groping each and every one of them as I passed by, and you know what? Didn't work then either.

"Are you prepared to be reasonable?" Tall asks him, and he sounds completely reasonable himself, which I think is at least partially due to his being zombified. Normally he'd sound like he was chewing nails and about to spit them at your eye blowgun-style.

The smokedancer—what'd he say his name was? Victor Din or something?—frowns. He's got one of those mouths that looks like you could probably bend the lips to make balloon animals, they're all thin and wide and ridiculously mobile. Though these days I'm jealous of just about anybody with lips, no matter what kind. Ned asked me once why I didn't just ask the Grays to give me lips back, if I wanted 'em so bad. I told him he was crazy. Can you picture a duck with lips? Yuck!

Anyway, he says, "Reasonable? I was being reasonable, my friend. I was here to enjoy an evening's entertainment, watching a display of acrobatics and aerial maneuvering and dance and music—I believe they call it a Circus of the Sun, or some such? The next thing I know, I'm being asked to leave by two large gentlemen dressed the same way you are. I did nothing wrong."

"Really? Nothing?" Tall folds his arms across his chest, which should make the seams in his jacket scream in protest. Honestly, I've often wondered if they use elastic instead of cotton or rayon or whatever it is most suits are made from these days, otherwise he'd just Hulk out of his shirts whenever he takes a deep breath. "I find that hard to believe—I heard you got carried away."

Vic waves that off—his fingers are so long they look like bendy straws sticking out of a monkey's paw. "Oh, I may have added to the festivities," he admits as casually as if it were nothing. "They were playing with fire, after all, and that is my forte. I thought they could handle it." I get sudden images of a bunch of acrobats who think they're doing tricks and flips and stuff over a nice little row of gas flames, only to have those suddenly flare up to bonfires, and shudder. "I am sorry if they were injured," he says, "but they seemed like professionals, so I assumed they knew the risks."

"You're a professional, too," Tall points out. "You should

know better than to interfere with someone else's act." Ooh, nice one! And I can see the mildly stated jab strike home, too, as Vic winces. "Regardless, you're here on Earth as a guest, and if an agent asks you to step outside or present your visa or anything else, you are expected to comply at once and without argument. You know that, it's in the entry rules."

"But they put hands on me!" Now he sounds like an irate six-year-old. "No one touches Vijik'yin without his express permission!"

"So you lost your temper and took their shadows, and now you're stuck in here," Tall concludes. "Which is exactly where you'll stay until you learn to behave. And you can start by giving back their shadows, and the others you stole."

"And if I don't?" For a second all those shadows mass behind the guy, bulking into a single big, scary one that makes it look like he's really nine feet tall and a couple hundred pounds of hulking muscle. There's spikes and barbs and horns and the whole Goth show, and I'm shuddering even though I'm just watching from a distance.

To his credit, Tall's not fazed at all. "You can take my shadow," he says, and he sounds completely calm about it. "You can take every shadow in the building, every shadow in the city, every shadow in the state, every shadow along the coast. But then what? I know they make you stronger, but will it be enough to bust out of here? Because you know we've held some pretty tough customers before. Even if you do get out, you'll face the entire organization, and this time they'll be looking to put you down instead of just lock you up. Can your shadows save you from that? If you get off-planet somehow, well, we have ties to several other galactic peacekeeping organizations, and we'd put out a bulletin about you. You'd be on the run, with everyone after you. Is that what you want? All because two agents were a little more hands-on than you'd like, and because they didn't want you burning down a performance?"

Vic glares at him for a minute, and I'm guessing they're locking gazes. I try to help by staring hard at his high forehead, but I doubt he notices. Still, he finally looks down at his hands and sighs, his shadow breaking apart into a small village again. "No, you are correct," he says softly. "I lost my temper, and I shouldn't have. Nor should I have overstepped my bounds, or the rule of professional courtesy. I apologize." He straightens up, chin high, and waves one hand. "I dismiss the shadows back to their true owners," he declares, and I watch as they flee like rats from an oncoming train, racing off in every direction and disappearing through cracks or into corners. All except one, the one behind him, which must be his real one.

Tall nods. "Good," he says as he stands up. "I'll make sure those two agents apologize for manhandling you, and I'll let my superiors know you regret your actions and vow to behave better in future. They'll probably ship you back immediately, I'm afraid, but at least you should be able to go home. And in time you can apply to return and see the rest of the performance."

"Thank you." Vic stands—damn, he's really tall!—and holds out one hand. "You seem more even-tempered than your compatriots." Wow, he has no idea who he's talking to! "I appreciate that."

"You're welcome." Tall shakes with him. "I'm sorry your

visit was cut short."

Vic laughs. "Oh, that's fine. I still enjoyed what I saw of the performance." He gets a slightly evil look on his face. "And human shadows are so much fun to play with!"

Tall leaves him there and heads back out into the hall, and I relax a bit, especially after checking my own shadow. Yep, still here and still duck-headed. Whew! That went a helluva lot better than I thought.

But just as Tall passes through the outer door back into the lobby, the elevator opens. Out come two MiBs, dragging a short guy between them who looks like a cross between Barney and a heavy metal rocker—he's covered in pink and purple dinosaur scales and has horns at his temples and a row of triangular spines running down his back, but he's wearing black leather and chains and has piercings all over, including most of those spines. He's struggling against them, and holding his own considering each agent has at least a foot in height over him, and he's cursing up a storm the whole time, too.

"Let me go, motherfuckers!" he's shouting as they half-drag, half-lift him toward the door. "You're just jealous 'cause I'm not bound by the Man! I can do what I like, when I like! When's the last time you did that?" Then he spots Tall, standing to the side to let them pass. "You! When'd you last cut loose, huh? Why don't you do it now? Go on, cut loose! Go stomp about! Go full-bore rampage through the streets!"

I swear, I can practically feel Tall go frozen-seal-stiff through the camera.

Uh-oh.

Chapter Fourteen
Godzilla with shades

"**Tall? Tall? You** still with me, man?" I'm practically yelling into the mic, for all the good it's doing me. He'd turned, after the death-rock-dino's rant, and gotten into the elevator. Not a word, not a sound. Pushed "L" for lobby, and now he's standing there as the doors slide shut, hands behind his back, feet slightly apart, looking in the reflection like the perfect model of a MiB—tall, stern, and utterly unmoved.

I'm not fooled for a second.

For one thing, I know Tall. I know him real well. In fact, now that I think about it, he may just be my best friend after Mary, and since she's my girlfriend that makes him my best friend anyway, by default—you can't be best friends with the person you're seeing, just because then who're you gonna talk to about your relationship? Ever tried talking to your significant other about them? See how well that works: "So I'm really into her—I mean, you—but there's this one thing she—I mean you—does that really drives me nuts. And I can't say anything about it to her—I mean you—because I know that'll just piss her—I mean you—off. So here it is." Yeah, I don't think you'll have to worry about the whole "best friend or girlfriend?" question very long.

Wow, so Tall's my best friend. Weird. I never would've pegged that. Neither would any of my old friends, especially my old frat buddies. Me, best friends with a MiB? Get out!

But anyway, the thing is I know him pretty well. I know all his facial tics, on account of I've caused half of 'em—I feel a certain sense of proprietary responsibility toward them. Which is why I can tell something right now that probably nobody else in the world can, except maybe his mom assuming Tall wasn't grown on a vat somewhere deep in the basement, which I've still got good odds on. But that thing? Yeah, here it is:

He's smiling.

It's almost unnoticeable. His lips are still pressed together like they're vacuum-sealed, and they're still as straight as a ruler. His brow's still slightly furrowed, with that crease just above his nose. His jaw's still solid enough to shatter boulders. But I know the signs. There's just the tiniest hint of an indentation along the outer edge of his eyes, peeking out from those shades. There's the barest bit of a shadow at the corners of his mouth. That crease isn't as long or as deep as usual.

Listen to me, I sound like a stalker. Or, worse yet, a fanboy. Ugh.

But I know what I'm seeing. Inside, Tall is smiling.

And it isn't a good smile. Oh, no. I've seen those too, usually when we're hanging out and his team trounces mine in whatever sporting event we're watching at the time. The actual Tall smile, when he's not trying to be a bad-ass and is almost human—not that I'm one to judge.

But this isn't that.

No, this is the kind of smile you see a guy get right before he pulls a pistol and starts opening up on everybody standing in line in front of him. Or before he floors it and smashes his massive SUV over and through all the other cars in his way. Or right before he sets foot on the ice in a pro hockey game. Or before he opens his mouth to tell you that your loan's been rejected, so sad too bad, kiss your great-grandma's house good-bye.

This is the smile of a man about to destroy people's lives.

I am so glad I'm all the way over here and Tall is all the way over there. Not that this guarantees my safety, but at least I should have a little advance warning.

It's not going to help all those unsuspecting people in midtown Manhattan, though. And I'm not sure what I can do about that.

I try again: "Tall!"

And this time he answers. "Yes, DuckBob?"

"You need to chill, man!" I tell him. "Just relax, okay? Go fill out some parking tickets or something—I know you enjoy that!"

"I am relaxed," he tells me, just as the elevator dings. "I am perfectly relaxed." The elevator doors part, revealing what looks like a normal office building lobby, just as he says, "I am about to cut loose."

Two guys, two MiBs, are standing waiting for the elevator. They kinda startle when he says that. I don't blame them. Too bad they don't startle enough. Neither of them does much more than grimace and look askance, which is why they're still in easy reach as Tall grabs their heads, one in each hand, and clonks them together. That's the sound they make, clonk!, like a pair of big coconuts. I can tell even through the sunglasses that their eyes've just rolled up in their heads, and they both drop to the floor. And Tall crouches beside them long enough to reach into their jackets and pull out a gun from each. Then, holding those aloft, he makes his way toward the front door and out onto the street.

Oh, man.

"Wa-hoo!" he shouts as he emerges from the building. "I am cutting loose! I am on a rampage!" And he levels both guns at a parked car right nearby. Yeah, I've always wanted to shoot those cars that think they can just park anywhere, too—there's a No Parking sign practically over this sleek sedan, but it's sitting there with its hazards on like, oh, that makes it all okay. There's nobody in it—thank God for small favors—and I'm betting it's been sitting there at least an hour, but of course nobody's touched it.

Well, that changes rapidly.

I don't know that I've ever seen Tall fire his gun before. No, that's not true, I'm almost sure he was shooting back at the Dinotropic Aesthetic Elite that time on the train, but I didn't stand around waiting to see if he hit anything. So this is the first time I see the result of him shooting something. I make a mental note to make sure he's unarmed the next time I piss him off, because both pistols don't fire regular slugs, of course—no, that'd be too mundane for the great and powerful MiB. No, they shoot what look like little tiny bursts of blue-white light, which speed toward the car, splash against it like water droplets, expand rapidly until the whole front end is covered in a fine spiderweb of glowing blue that I can see even in the broad daylight—

—and then the whole front end just disappears. Winks out like the Cheshire Cat taking a nap. Whole car one second, half a car the next.

The hazards on the back end stop blinking, too. No battery to power 'em, after all. Heh, that'd serve the owner right, to come back and find half his car missing AND a parking ticket!

"Uh, nice one," I tell Tall as he turns and starts marching down the sidewalk, both guns up at head-height. "Score one for you, and for responsible drivers everywhere. You can stop now."

"No," he replies, "I am on a rampage!" And he promptly obliterates a hot-dog cart, leaving the umbrella to crash to the ground and the condiments and sodas that had been sitting on top to go splashing and rolling everywhere.

Great.

Ever see that one movie, the one about aliens invading our planet even though they're deathly allergic to water—because, yeah, that makes sense! Do you have any idea how many planets there are out there that don't have freestanding water? And they couldn't pick one of those instead? That's like the guy with the peanut allergy so severe even peanut dust in the air makes him stop breathing deciding to break into and rob a Planters factory! Anyway, there's one really funny bit in the movie where the lead, who's a retired priest and still just as stiff and awkward as one, thinks there's somebody outside his house and decides to go outside and scare him off by running around acting crazy.

So he goes out and he starts stomping around shouting things like "I am filled with furious rage!" and "I'm insane with anger!" It's hysterical because he has no idea how to curse and shout and so it sounds ridiculous.

Yeah, put him in a suit and give him a pair of guns and that's about what you've got here.

Now, in his defense, I've heard Tall curse plenty of times. Usually at me. But this is cookie-zombie Tall, which means he's stuck in nicey-nice mode. Plus, Tall understands being pissed off easily enough, but Death-Barney told him to "cut loose." And letting loose? Not something Tall's good at. Or any of the MiBs, for that matter. To be fair, Tall may be better at it than most of them. I like to think some of that's my influence. I've shaken him loose from his shell a little bit.

But not enough for him to be able to act convincingly here.

So instead he's stomping around—because that's what he was told to do, after all—and shooting cars and carts and trash cans and street signs and so forth at random, and shouting things like "Whee!" and "Yahoo!" and "I am free and out of control!", all in a complete monotone.

It's the tamest rampage I've ever seen.

Unfortunately, it's still a rampage. He's still doing a ton of property damage. No personal damage, though—he isn't shooting a single person, not even the obviously snooty ones who possibly deserve a mild winging. No, he's only targeting inanimate objects—assuming he's targeting, and I've been on the receiving end of his tosses and pitches enough times to know he's got excellent aim.

I have no idea what'll happen if he starts shooting people too, and I'm not keen to find out.

Of course, the second I think that, someone shouts his name from behind him.

"Agent Thomas!" Tall swivels around to look, and there's two other MiBs there, both with their guns drawn but not pointed at him. Both of them look vaguely familiar—I think I saw them up in the office earlier.

"You need to put down the guns and come with us!" one of them orders. He's a little shorter than Tall, almost as broad in the shoulders but a lot wider in the gut, and his hair's a little wild under his hat—he almost looks more like a Blues Brother than a MiB. Maybe they've got a band?

The other one doesn't say anything, he just stands at the ready.

Thank God, I'm thinking. Now Tall can do what he says, and that'll be that.

Yeah, not so fast.

"I can't do that," Tall yell back. "I am on a rampage!"

And he shoots them both.

The blue lights hit them, spider web across them, and then flare flash-bright, but the MiBs don't disappear, at least. Instead they just stiffen and collapse on the sidewalk. So apparently these guns can disintegrate nonliving matter but just stun living creatures? That is so cool! I wonder how well they can distinguish. If there's a person in a car and Tall shoots the car, will it disappear and the person collapse on the ground, or will it just annihilate both of them? How does it deal with previously living matter? Would it make a tree disappear or just try to stun it? A log cabin? A package of luncheon meat? Moldy luncheon meat, which would technically be living again? What about a zombie, where would that fall on the scale?

But Tall's marching along again, shooting things, so I table the questions for later.

Except for one—why didn't he stop? The one MiB ordered him to, and so far he's done everything people tell him. At least, everything people right there tell him—he hasn't done bupkus of the things I've shouted in his ear.

Which is when two things hit me at once.

First, it's a presence issue. I'm not there, so Tall isn't obeying me. If I was standing right in front of him, he'd snap out of like every other time.

Second, the MiB screwed up. He said "You should." It was a suggestion, not a direct order. Yeah, that's splitting hairs, but Tall's always been a grammar Nazi, why should cookie-zombie Tall be any different? If the other agent'd just said "Put those down and come with us!" Tall would've done it.

Which begs the question—can I count on any of the other MiBs to be that direct?

And the immediate answer is no, I can't. One of them might be, but it's a serious longshot. After all, they're used to being deliberately vague and spooky. They talk double-talk all the time. Hell, half the time getting Tall to answer a simple question like "you want another beer?" gets me a sly look and "I'm considering it" or "I'll let you know" or "We'll come back to that."

A cop'd be direct, but I'm not sure how close any of them're gonna want to get once they see the kind of damage Tall can dish out. I wouldn't get within a city block of him. And I don't know if there's a range involved on the voice-command trick—so far every time someone's given him an order he's obeyed they've been within five feet, in which case we're screwed. Nobody around here's gonna be dumb enough, or suicidal enough, or just plain crazy or inattentive enough, to get that close.

But I think I know somebody who would.

Besides me, I mean. But I can't, damn it. So this'll have to do.

"Hang in there, buddy," I tell Tall as I turn away from the monitor. It's weird looking around at my real surroundings again, and it takes a minute for my eyes to adjust—one minute I'm staring at midtown Manhattan (and almost crying as Tall obliterates one of those halal carts because I'd kill for a good chicken-over-rice with indefinable white sauce) and the next I'm back in my living room, with the computer steaming in front of me and my couch oozing around somewhere behind.

Never mind all that right now, though. I grab my phone and hit one of the numbers I programmed into it a few months back.

"Hey, it's me," I say when it picks up. "Listen, drop whatever you're doing and head to Manhattan. I'll explain on the way."

I sure hope this works.

Chapter Fifteen
Cutting it close

"I can't believe I let you talk me into this," Ned says for like the fifty-thousandth time as he appears in midtown. "I must be crazy."

"You are," I agree. "Definitely crazy. But in a good way."

Ned was the only person I could think to call. Well, I could've called Mary, of course, but she's way too smart to go anywhere near Tall at a time like this. And Ned, well, he's a bright guy, of course, really good with gadgets and wiring and computers and stuff, but when it comes to everyday things—yeah. You know those stereotypical absent-minded professors, the ones who're brilliant in the lab but can't figure out how to button their shirts correctly, or remember to wear matching socks, or puzzle out which settings to use on the washing machine?

Ned's a lot like that.

Still, he did agree to go, which counts for a lot. I figured he would. He's buddies with Tall too, after all—the four of us, them and me and Mary, we saved the universe together. That kinda bonds you together. I don't see him as often as Tall, just because the Grays still send him on jobs all over the place, just like they do Mary, but he stops by at least once a month to check in on me and on the Matrix, and we hang out and order pizza and beer and watch a game or play foosball—yes, I have a foosball table, only it floats and spits out soap bubbles here and there and sometimes growls if you slam a shot home—or whatever. I don't think he and Tall get together separately, but when their trips coincide it's like old-home week and we all have a blast.

Besides, and this sounds terrible, I know, but I figured he wouldn't really register the danger. Not once I told him about the guns Tall was using. At least half his attention has been on theorizing how those things work, ever since.

"Okay, I'm here," he reports. "Now where—holy buttermint schnapps!"

"What? What? What's going on?" I'm looking all around, but of course all I see is my living room. Ned's got a hands-free phone, of course. Most people do, these days. Admittedly, most of the ones I know don't have versions that look like small metallic bees buzzing around your head thinking you're the world's biggest daisy and just looking for a place to hunker down, but that's Ned for you. He likes to tinker. The good news is, I can hear him perfectly, and he can hear me as well—something about a "sound-conducive dome" or something. Plus, that same dome cuts out most other noise, making it easier for an ADD champ like him to concentrate. Of course, it also means nobody who isn't pressed cheek-to-jowl with him can hear him or me, so it looks like he's muttering soundlessly to himself, but in most places nobody really notices that, or at least pretends not to. The bad news is, no video. Apparently the dome creates too much static for a clear picture, though Ned says he's working on something called "distributed image-intake" that might fix the problem. In the meantime, I can hear him but I can't see him, or what he's looking at. If only I could—wait! I tap my computer monitor to wake it back up, and sure enough when the image blossoms into view it's midtown Manhattan. I'm back on Channel Tall!

Only, some time between when I glanced away and now, it's turned into a horror movie. Or at least a post-apocalyptic tale.

Tall's still moving, and I see a familiar building up ahead. The Flatiron. Its triangular floor plan's hard to miss—I always thought it looked like a kid had shaped a tall office building out of clay but then it fell over and one side got squished in, or maybe it was supposed to be rectangular but there were budget cuts while they were still under construction, so they just decided to cut in half and call it a day. Anyway, it's right in his path, maybe two blocks away, which means he's covered about eight blocks since I left.

And by the look of things, what he's covered them in is rubble. And despair.

The streets around him are almost completely empty, because by this point everyone's heard about the big, burly guy in the suit whose guns make things disappear, and nobody wants to stick around and see firsthand how that works. A few oddly well-dressed shadows off to the sides mean Tall's fellow MiBs are nearby but laying low. Flashing lights reflected from around corners and through windows show that the cops are out as well, but they're hanging back, too. Nobody wants to get close enough to see what those guns'd do to normal flesh and blood. Can't say I blame them—Tall's pretty much the best of the best when it comes to a MiB, I think, the stereotypical "worth ten ordinary men" type, and well, even with nine other guys alongside who wants to risk those odds? I guess everyone's waiting in the hopes somebody else'll show up with a clear dozen and try their luck.

Except Ned. "Nice!" he says softly, and I suspect those sensory organs sprouting from his temples right over his ears—the ones I always think look like he's glued on horns made of broccoli, or at least asparagus—are wriggling with delight. "Full material disintegration! That's awesome!"

"How is that awesome?" I demand. "He's probably single-handedly wiped out half the food trucks in midtown! He's set the New York street-cuisine culture back at least a decade, dooming yuppies all over the city to boring lunches of pizza and subs and sushi. And you think that's cool?" Not to mention that all those cart owners are now out of work, and a ton of people are suddenly no longer car owners, either.

"Yeah, but think about it," is Ned's answer. "These guns he's using, they can distinguish between living and nonliving matter, probably by gauging the electrical current present and seeing whether it's constant enough and low-grade enough to qualify as brainwaves. That's amazingly sophisticated!" Yes, I know, it's weird—Ned looks like some plumber from Brooklyn, not counting the skin color and the hair and those broccoli horns and the way his face is perfectly flat like it was smashed into an anvil, but sometimes he talks like some hoity-toity college professor. Then he follows up this min-lecture with a deep, sustained burp, the kind you couldn't do in most states or major cities without clearances for both the noise level and the air pollution. Yep, that's Ned in a nutshell.

"I'm thrilled you're happy," I tell him. "Can we focus on capturing him for now, and you can geek out over the hardware later?" I figure if this works the MiBs won't object to parting with a few things, like one of those guns. Seems like a small price to pay to keep the Big Apple from becoming the Big Empty.

"Sure, sure." There's a pause, and I'm guessing Ned's looking around. "I'm at the corner of Thirty-fourth and Fifth," he says after a minute.

"Got it." I picture midtown in my head, and try to ignore the smell of fresh bagels and hot pizza and cannoli all mixed together. Sometimes having a really strong olfactory memory isn't the blessing you'd expect. "Okay, just head straight down Fifth," I tell him. "Tall's at Twenty-third Street."

"Right, nine blocks to go." And Ned starts walking. And chattering like a squirrel who's just found that one last acorn he needs to finish his collection. It's like listening to an audiobook while you drive to work, only he's the one moving and I'm sitting still. I'm not sure what that makes it—a moving story? A walking soundtrack? Whatever it is, it's annoying, especially since I'm still looking through Tall's eyes and trying not to get disoriented from hearing one thing and seeing another.

". . . why is it, do ya think, that the signs are set up the way they are?" Ned's asking me or himself or the air or invisible hovering gods or some such as he crossed from Thirty-fourth to Thirty-third. "I can't tell which street is which, half the time—is it the one the sign parallels, or the one it faces? Why can't the signs be shaped like arrows and point the way they mean? That'd make a lot more sense. Another thing . . ."

It occurs to me that I talk a lot. Okay, an awful lot. And that I'm usually more than happy to speak my mind, even if all my mind's saying at the moment is "hubba hubba" or "I'm tired. Is there pie?" So is this what I sound like to other people? If so, I may never talk again.

Or at least not until I get bored.

Tall's still rampaging, of course. He's nothing if not methodical, and that little hairy dude didn't give him a time limit or anything, and nobody's dared to get close enough to give him a command to counter that first one. Yet. "Hey, Tall, do you hear me, buddy?" I say into the mic, and I see him slow to a stop and glance around.

"DuckBob?" he asks. "Where are you?"

"Costa Rica—the weather's so good the only umbrellas you'll ever need are the ones in your drinks," I answer. "Come on down, we'll do Mai Tais."

"No thank you," he replies. "I am on a rampage right now."

"Yeah, about that. Wanna knock it off? I think it's always best to leave 'em wanting more, don't you?"

The camera wobbles, so he must be shaking his head. "I don't understand," he admits, "but that is not unusual with you." And he shoots a newspaper rack. That's fine, though—it was just the *Post*. If it'd been the *Onion*, then we'd have to have words.

"Listen, help's on the way, okay?" I tell him. "Ned just wants to talk to you. Don't shoot him, all right?"

"I will do my best not to," Tall assures me. "But if he is the path of my rampage, I cannot guarantee it."

"Understood." To Ned I say, "slight change of plans. You need to come in from behind him, so cut over to Sixth in a block or two and then just head straight down Twenty-third." And hope he doesn't hear you coming and turn around, I add silently. But I figure why burden Ned with constant proof of my negativity?

"Roger that." Which is immediately followed by: "Why Roger? What about Hank, or Billy, or Ted, or Andrew, or any of the others? Why is it always Roger?"

That's actually something I've wondered myself, in the past. I've never been able to figure it out either. My best guess is it's an homage to either Mr. Rogers or Roger Daltry or maybe Buck Rogers, but I'm not convinced.

"I'm at Twenty-fifth," Ned reports a few blessedly quiet minutes later. "Where is he now?"

I glance up at the monitor. "Still right by the Flatiron, Twenty-third and fifth."

"Okay, cool." He sounds amazingly calm, considering he's about to do the same or better than staying someplace that's now all vegans and others who've thrown in together to free the world of its "tyranny of dead flesh" and accidentally wearing your "All meat is good meat" T-shirt to breakfast. Not that I've done that, of course. Much. Let's just say, lack of proper protein? Makes some people really cranky.

He hits 23rd and turns onto it, then half-walks, half-ambles, half-jogs—yeah, I'm not the only one around here who's good at creative math—the block from Sixth to Fifth. Now he and Tall are within a block of each other. I used to frequent this area a lot, and it's really weird seeing it on the monitor. Especially since I don't know if I'll ever be able to go back.

Or, at this rate, if there'll be a "back" left for me to return to.

"I see him!" Ned whispers into his phone a couple of minutes later. "He's not looking at me!"

"Great! Go for it!" I wonder if this plan could actually work.

Then Tall turns around.

I see Ned clearly in the monitor, in all his alien-plumber-mojo glory, so there's no way Tall misses him, and sure enough a second later both pistols are aimed his way. "Uh, I'd stop there, if I were you," I warn Ned.

He skids to a halt in reply, and starts to hide behind a trash-can, changes his mind—which is for the best, because it wasn't really adequate coverage for him anyway—and just straightens up and faces Tall boldly. That was the other reason I thought Ned might be able to help. He's got moxy.

"Hang on, switching phone to loudspeaker mode," he warns, and I hear a beep. "You might want to cover your ears." Uh, sure, but how'm I gonna hear anything then? And if the phone is under my hand so I can hear, how is covering them gonna help?

"Hey, Tall!" he shouts. Yes, Ned and Mary both call him that. What can I say? When I give people nicknames, they stick. Go ask "Crawdad" Fowler if you don't believe me. "It's me, Ned!" The sound reverberates through my phone, making me wince, but it's bearable. Of course, I'm also hearing it echoed through the mic I've got on Tall, and there's a nanosecond delay, so that's just odd.

My camera-view bobs. "Hello, Ned. Why are you here? I am on a rampage." Yes, he seems to have misplaced his contractions. And his ability to string together complex sentences. I swear, talking to cookie-zombie Tall is like dealing with a small child, just one with monstrous destructive capabilities. "Oh, yes he disassembled my Stradivarius and wrote with marker on my first printing of *The Hobbit*, but he was so polite about it! No, dearest, I'm not going to explain what 'eviscerate' means. Go look it up."

"Uh, yeah, about that," Ned says. He moves a little closer. I'd say he's probably forty feet away. Too far, I'm thinking. "Can we talk?"

More bobbing, but the guns stay steady. Damn. "Certainly," Tall replies. "But please don't interfere with my rampage." It's like he's got this on his to-do calendar now: "Rampage from 1pm to 7pm," and as long as he's allowed to continue that, he's fine. I hate to think what kind of fit he'll throw if it gets thwarted, though. And as if to prove my point, he takes a few steps forward and obliterates a mailbox. Not the real kind, though—one of those weird green ones that doesn't have a slot for mail, doesn't have a Post Office sticker or logo, and nobody seems to use in any way. I've always wondered what those're for, actually, and especially since meeting Tall I've been curious as to whether they were MiB devices of some sort. Guess I won't find out from this one, since it does the whole blue-glowing-spider-web thing and then slumps like its metal turned to putty and it's been in the sun too long. Which means it must be organic. Gross.

"I won't," Ned promises. "But can I walk with you? I'll stay out of your way." Smart man! Especially since Tall nods again, and now as Ned slides around to his side the guns switch to targeting other objects in his path, one of those little electric cars and a chained-up bike in this case. There's literally nobody else in sight, not counting that creepy unconscious mailbox thing. It's like the end of the world has come and gone, and all that's left of humanity is a plumber and a government agent. And the plumber isn't even human to begin with!

"Okay, now what?" Ned asks, and after a second I realize from the lowered tone that he's talking to me, not Tall.

"You need to get within five feet, just to be safe," I tell him. "Then tell him to stop the rampage and put down the guns."

"Right. And how do I get that close without him deciding I *am* interfering, and shooting me next?"

"Oh, come on, you're doing great!" I assure him. "Just, I don't know, make polite conversation or something."

"Have you ever known Tall to make polite conversation?"

"Well, no," I admit. "But this is cookie-zombie Tall. He's a whole different breed. Try it. Say something nice."

"Nice. Right." But Ned tries. He's only ten feet from Tall now, maybe less, and off to his side. "So, how's the rampage going?" he asks, and takes advantage of talking to sidle a little closer. Nine feet.

"Good, I think," Tall answers. Another mailbox goes poof— the regular blue one this time, and I feel bad for anybody who had their letters in there. Or their bills. Would any company really take "a crazed-zombie government agent shot the mailbox and disintegrated it and all the mail in it, including my check" as a valid excuse? I have to remember to try that.

"Yeah? You enjoying yourself?" Eight feet.

"Oh, yes. I am cutting loose. Wa-hoo." All of that's delivered with the same lack of enthusiasm a ninety-year-old wracked with arthritis might offer when told he's just won free rumba lessons.

"Cool, cool. So, how long's the rampage for, anyway?" Seven feet.

"I have no definite end in sight." That's not good—I was really hoping it was on a timer. "Why?" Uh-oh—careful, Ned!

But he shrugs. "Oh, no reason. Just wondered if maybe you wanted to grab some lunch after." Six feet. And his question's completely believable, too. I've never seen anyone as perpetually hungry as Ned, not even the goat we stole from a rival college once. He can put away a breakfast fit for three and still claim to be "a bit peckish" an hour later, enough to demolish an entire Super Bowl party's worth of chips. Trust me, I've seen it happen. I've learned to stock enough food for an army any time I know he's stopping by. That usually lasts long enough for me to order more.

"Lunch sounds nice," Tall admits, destroying a scooter and a street sign. "But it will have to wait until I am done with my rampage."

"Oh, sure, sure." Five feet. "Know any good places around here? For lunch, I mean."

"Get a little closer, just to be safe," I whisper to Ned. I resist the urge to add "now don't be shy," but it ain't easy. "Then hit him with the orders."

"Right," he whispers back.

Tall seems to be considering Ned's last question. "Yes," he says finally. "I know several good restaurants within easy walking distance. What sort of food would you prefer?"

Ned scratches his chin and steps a little closer still. Four feet. Definitely within range—if I'm right. I really hope I am—do you have any idea how hard it is to find a good tech guy these days? Especially one who makes house calls? "Oh, you know me," he answers. "I'll eat just about anything." And he grins—if I was there, I'd be worried about him trying to gnaw on my femur right about now. Not that he looks mean or angry. Just hungry.

"We can discuss it more after my rampage," Tall offers, shooting that little glass dome above the subway entrance that's supposed to be green if it's open and red if it's closed but is usually so murky and dirty you wouldn't know if there was a small glowing pixie trapped inside. Which just makes me wonder again.

"Yeah, about that." Ned's only a few feet away from Tall now. Perfect. "Hey, Tall?"

Tall swivels around to look right at him. "Yes, Ned?"

Ned takes a deep breath. "Stop the rampage and put down the guns."

I hold my breath. So does Ned—I'm not sure how he managed to say that without exhaling, actually.

"All right." Tall just lets the guns fall—they clatter on the ground, and I'm just glad neither of them goes off by accident. Whew!

"Whew!" Ned says, letting that breath out in a whoosh now and wiping his forehead. "You had me worried there, big guy!"

Me too, I think. But that's not what I say. "Tell him to snap out of it!" I instruct Ned.

"Oh, right. Snap out of it!" he says. I could get used to this whole give-orders-and-people-carry-them-out thing. I can see why generals love wars, too. It's kinda fun, having other people do your dirty work. Which also explains why people love to order food for delivery. It's basically another way of saying, "fetch me my turkey pot-pie, bitch!"

I can't see Tall, of course, but I'm sure he's doing the whole "eyes clearing" thing right about now. Sure enough, a second later he says, "Ned? What're you doing here?" Then he looks around. "What'm I doing out here? And where is everyone? Last I remember I was in—hold on, are those PMDU Mark IVs?" He's looking down at the guns at his feet.

"Uh, yeah, well, the thing is . . ." Ned rubs the back of his neck. Poor guy! I'm not sure how the hell he's gonna explain all this.

So maybe it's for the best that he gets shouldered aside as at least six MiBs charge past him and tackle Tall to the ground.

Or maybe not.

Chapter Sixteen
Looking for an open bar

"**How did I** get myself into this mess?"

That's what Tall mumbles into his hands, which are cupping his head, which is down near his knees as he leans over. He's sitting on a bed that looks remarkably familiar, or maybe it isn't all that impressive since I just saw one exactly like it less than two hours ago. We're in one of the holding cells down in B11, or maybe we're on B10 or B12 or Riboflavin or something, I wasn't paying all that much attention when they brought him in. I was too busy talking to Ned, the two of us trying to figure out how to keep Tall out of trouble.

As you can tell, that didn't go so well.

When we finally gave up and backed off—after the MiB who seemed to be in charge had threatened to arrest Ned as well, and then to deport him permanently—and I switched back to Channel Tall, he was already in one of the holding cells. They'd taken off the restraints, at least, leaving him free to pace or stomp about or slam his fist against the door. Tall didn't go for any of that, though. He just sat there, without a sound.

It was driving me nuts.

"Well," Tall tells himself after another minute, wiping at his face with both hands like he can scrub away all memory of what happened, "that's probably the end of that career. Time to look for something else, I guess." He glances around. Same spartan design as we saw in Victor Din, Shadowmaster's room before all this went south in a big way.

"Oh, knock it off," I mutter, and then gulp as he glances all around.

"Who said that?"

Hm, come clean or let him think he's crazy?

It's a tough call.

Not really, though, which is why I answer him a second later. "Yeah, it's me. DuckBob. Hey."

"DuckBob?" He's scanning the room again, and I'm tempted to point out that there's no way I could be hiding in there. Hell, my head's practically too big to fit in that room all on its own, never mind the rest of me! But of course he's gotta be thorough. "Where are you?" he asks while he's still looking around.

"Same answer as always," I tell him. "Full-on matrix action here, twenty-four seven."

"Then how am I hearing you?" Yeah, not much gets by him.

"It's—" I start to roll out the storyline I created as my cover when he asked the last time, but I stop. Why should I lie about it again? Especially to Tall? Real Tall, not cookie-zombie Tall. The guy who saved my bacon—duck bacon, in this case—more than once. Damn. "I planted a camera and a mic on you the last time you visited," I say instead. Then I pause to let him absorb that, wondering if I should've worded that more carefully, worked up to it maybe. This whole "honesty" thing? Still kinda a work in progress.

"You bugged me?" That's not a good start. "How did I let you get away with that?"

That is the million-dollar question, and again I debate making something up versus explaining the even weirder real-life events. But he's gotta learn the truth sometime—better it comes from me than from one those fortune cookies or ouja boards. "You weren't exactly yourself at the time," I explain slowly. Man, I really don't want to have to do this! "You turned into a zombie or something."

"A zombie? Uh-huh." Yeah, I wouldn't believe it either. But still . . .

"It's true, man. The past few months you've been turning into a zombie—not the shambling-about-eating-live-people version but definitely more laid back, to the point that you basically did anything people told you." I scratch at my bill. "You saw the way midtown looked? That was all you, dude. And all because this one furry little alien ordered you to 'cut loose' and 'go on a rampage.'"

Tall shakes his head. "Never happened. If I was a zombie, I think I'd know."

"Yeah? How?" I decide to try a different tack. "Listen, what's the last thing you remember? Before finding yourself facing the Flatiron with a pair of smoking guns at your feet and Ned practically in your face?"

"Hm." I can almost feel his brow furrowing—any deeper and he'd crease the lens. "I was at work. I took a break, got some coffee . . ." He trails off, and I fill in the rest for him.

"—and you had a few ChocoMints. I know. That was over an hour ago, dude. You zombied out, same as you've done every time you've had them, except this time I wasn't there to tell you to snap out of it. So I had to send Ned to do it instead."

"So you're saying the cookies did something to me?" he asks. "Took away my ability to reason, turned me into a mindless drone?"

"Uh, not exactly. You still think, I think. You answer questions, speak in complete sentences, fill out paperwork—if anything, I think your typing speed actually went up, which only goes to show there's some things you shouldn't overthink in life, and that being conscious at work isn't always the best solution. It's just that, any time anybody told you directly to do something, you did it. No argument, no questioning, no nothing. Oh, and you were . . . nice. To everybody."

"Nice? Me?" Hey, at least he knows himself.

"Yeah." I sigh. "Even to Agent Jones."

I'm pretty sure his eyes've gotta be bugging out by now. "I was nice to Agent Jones?"

"Yeah. You two . . . chatted." Just thinking about the awkward cloaking that brief conversation gives me the shudders. Ugh. Like trying to watch one of those comedies where they equate incredibly uncomfortable with funny, so you gotta watch some schlub you can't help but feel sorry for getting stuck in some awful situation and sit there cringing as he fumbles his way around all flushed and flustered and embarrassed. Oh yeah, that's high comedy for you.

Now, at least, Tall rises to his feet. And starts pacing like a lion in a cage, one who scents fresh meat just beyond the bars. This is more like it! "Somebody drugged me," he says as he walks. "That's what you're saying?"

"Exactly. Through the cookies."

"Why hasn't it affected anyone else?"

I don't know. "I don't know." See, no filter—I think it, I say it. At least people know what they're getting from me. None of those "yeah, but what does he really mean?" looks around here. But something occurs to me. "Are you sure it hasn't? Who else's eaten those cookies at work?"

"Everybody." That was the answer I was afraid of. "Well, almost everybody. Agent Jones is borderline diabetic—she can't touch processed sugar. And I don't think Agent Smith has, either. He's gluten-free anyway, but he made a big stink when I first passed around the order forms—he said something when they showed up in the break room about 'the laxity of allowing such frivolous comestibles into the workplace,' and how the endorphins released by chocolate could have a deleterious effect on judgment and efficiency."

"Yeah, that doesn't mean much," I tell him. "Half the time, the guy saying alcohol's the devil is the same one doing shots at two in the afternoon and adding a slug of Jaegermeister to his coffee every time he brews a cup. I'll bet you dollars to donuts Smith's got a box or two stashed in his desk, maybe not ChocoMints but Lemon Stripes for sure. That's probably how he justifies it to himself, too—'these aren't chocolate so it's not the same!' Trust me, I know the type." Hey, what can I say? I'm an expert at explaining away one's own bad behavior. I used to rationalize jumping the turnstiles as 'not giving in to authority' and stealing waiters' tips off tables as 'freeing them from the dilemma of reporting their under-the-table pay.' Heck, when I was in the frat we used to 'bump into' beer trucks until kegs fell out the back, then claim those as ground-scores. I don't do that kind of thing anymore, of course—for one thing, I'm way too easy to pick out of a lineup—but it's easy enough to remember how to think along those lines.

"Okay, so let's assume the whole office is a goner," I say, returning to our current problem. "Think back. Did you tell anybody to do something and have them argue with you? Anybody at all? Even something as simple as changing the coffee filter or washing their hands after they peed or putting down another buck to help cover the bill?"

Another pause. "No," he admits finally. "Nobody. We haven't had any arguments in weeks—maybe months. And everybody I tell to do something, they do it." Something kind of like a laugh, only raspier, escapes his lips. "Of course, most people jump when I talk, anyway."

"Sure, but they usually grumble about it afterward, right?" I don't really need his nod to know the answer to that. "And nobody's complained in a while, I'm guessing. They still do what you say, but now they do it willingly. Right?" Another nod. I'm getting whiplash out of sympathy. "Yeah. All cookie-zombies. Great."

Tall stops near the door. "We need to do something about this. We need to find out who's behind this, how they're doing it, what they want, and put a stop to it. Now."

"Uh huh. And how do you expect to do that, bright guy? Hm? You're in jail, in case you hadn't noticed. Your jail, MiB jail. And I'm guessing you guys were pretty thorough at making it so people couldn't just come and go as they pleased."

He starts to answer, but gets interrupted by another noise. The click of a doorknob. His doorknob.

Tall steps back as the door swings open. And there, not quite filling it and trying to look menacing anyway, is Agent Smith. He's got two other MiBs behind him, both the bulky type, but they wait there as he enters.

"Agent Thomas," he starts. Does this guy ever just say "hi?" Probably not.

"Agent Smith." Tall stands aside and lets him walk in, close the door, and then take the single chair. They don't exactly provide space for parties in here, do they?

Smith steeples his fingers, which I know is supposed to make him look all stern and serious and thoughtful but really just makes me expect him to flip his hands over and show us "all the people." Then again, he probably never went to summer camp as a kid. I did, though, pretty much every summer—it was a good excuse to get out of the house, and sharing a cabin with nine other boys my age is nothing compared to dealing with all my siblings. And hey, I can still tie a slipknot! "I trust you have an explanation for your recent behavior?" Smith asks Tall.

"Yes, sir." Tall doesn't bother to sit. "I was not in full control of myself, sir. I was operating under an impairment that clouded my judgment and made me susceptible to commands from others." Personally, I think "I was a cookie-zombie" is a lot shorter but really covers the same ground.

"I see." Smith taps his index fingers against his lips. Maybe he's checking to see if they're real. I'd love to know the answer to that, because they look more like wax from here. "And do you have any proof of this interference?"

"Not yet," Tall tells him. "But I intend to."

"Of course." Ever seen a piranha smile, right before it does the Ginsu-death-shred on your right leg? That's the look that appears on Smith's face. If I were Tall, I'd back away slowly. "Unfortunately, without such proof, there is no way I can exonerate you for your actions."

"I understand." I'm glad one of us does!

Smith stands and leans on the chair back. "For now, I am suspending you from active duty. You will be held here while we conduct a full investigation into what happened and why, at which point we will decide whether to release you, rehabilitate you, or punish you, and to what degree." He steps over to the door and grasps the knob in one hand. "Did you have any final questions, anything you wished to add?"

"Yes." Tall only takes one stride but it's enough to put him right next to Smith, and it's only because I'm in his ear that I hear what he whispers next:

"Sleep now."

If I were Tall, I'd let Smith crumple to the floor like a cheap suit. He catches his boss instead, carrying him over to the bed and laying him down across it almost gently. A helluva lot nicer than I'd be right now.

Then Tall opens the door. The two MiBs there both startle

upon seeing him, and they're already reaching for their guns when Tall says, "Sleep now" to both of them as well, and they topple over, already unconscious. He doesn't make any effort to catch them. I guess he likes Smith more.

"That was awesome!" I tell him as he rifles through their pockets. He comes up with their pistols, their IDs, a set of car keys, two sets of house keys, a pair of cell phones, a half-empty container of TicTacs, a condom (Ew!), some cash, some change, and a ballpoint pen. He takes all of it. Then he drags both of them into the cell and shuts the door on them. Neither of them wake up during this process. "How'd you know that would work?" I ask while he starts down the hall, toward the door out.

"You said we all did anything anyone told us to," he answers sharply. This is the Tall I know, terse and surly and in charge. I hadn't realized how much I missed him until now. "I figured I could tell them to let me go but they'd just come after me again. This was easier."

"They'll still come after you," I point out as he reaches the door, swipes one of the agents' IDs through it, and pulls it open. "Once they wake up."

"Absolutely, but that'll take time." He crosses the lobby and hits the elevator button up. "By that time, I'll be long gone."

"Got it. Where're you going?" It's amazing that he can smirk and I can hear it through the mic. "Ah. Right. Well, I'll try to tidy up before you get here."

"Good. And call Ned and Mary," he instructs as he gets into the elevator. "It's time we took the fight to them."

Take the fight to Ned and Mary? I think as Tall heads up

toward the roof and the MiB-mobiles. Why would I want to fight either of them? I'm so confused.

Chapter Seventeen
I love you, you make me sick

I hate cleaning. I'll just state that right here and now. Cleaning and I? We're not friends. Not even friendly acquaintances, not even nodding ones—if we had the same commute every day for years, taking the same busses and subways at the same time, pressed shoulder-to-shoulder half the time, we'd still ignore each other the whole way.

Not that I like filth, mind you. I'm not a pig or anything—ducks are surprisingly clean, really, and I wasn't much of a wallower even before the change. I prefer to have things clean and tidy and all that.

I just hate having to be the one to do it.

Before I left Earth, I shared an apartment with two other guys. In New York, you pretty much have to have roommates unless you're rich or you had an old relative leave you their rent-controlled loft in the village or you're willing to live in a shoebox. Since I wasn't any of those, I had roommates. We had a decent enough place, a three-bedroom apartment in an old building out in Sunnyside, just a few blocks off Queens Boulevard and the 7 train.

My one roommate, Nathan, he was a total slob. Guy would

take food into his room, eat half of it, fall asleep or get stoned or just get distracted, and leave the rest sitting somewhere near his bed or his desk or on his dresser or whatever. For weeks. The good news was, we didn't have bugs in the rest of the apartment because they all made a beeline for his room. The bad news was, you didn't want to walk barefoot in there. The floor moved.

My other roommate, Greg, was practically the opposite. Not that he was completely anal—I know because when I moved the cereal boxes around so they weren't in order of ascending height, he didn't shuffle them back right away, and if I turned my toothbrush so it wasn't facing the same way as the others, it might stay that way for a couple of days. But Greg did like the place neat and clean, and Nate and I quickly learned that, if we left a mess for long enough, Greg would clean it. Nate didn't really care, himself—he left messes not because he wanted Greg to clean them but because he just couldn't bother with them himself. If nobody had touched them and the ants and roaches had eventually formed a coalition and informed him that they had claimed his room as their own, he probably would've just shrugged and told them they were responsible for the rent.

Me, however, I did take advantage of Greg's neatnik tendencies. Mercilessly. It was horrible of me, and I admit it, but I would let dishes pile up in the sink just to see how long he could stand to leave them that way. The answer? Four days. Then he'd break down and wash them, dry them, put them away, the whole bit. It was like having a live-in maid.

Admittedly, I tried to make up for it. I never let Greg pay for a single beer the whole time we lived together, and I always covered him when we ordered food, too. I figured that was only fair.

Besides, even though we had three bedrooms our place wasn't exactly huge. We each had our own rooms, yeah, but they were New York-sized, which means there was enough space for beds and dressers and small desks and the occupant to shimmy through them. The kitchen could fit the three of us at one time, barely. The living room was the largest room in the place, and when we had parties and more than eight people showed up we had to spill over into the hall. Or, more likely, up on the roof. Provided it wasn't raining, and sometimes even when it was.

So when I took over as Guardian of the Matrix, and it came with this huge, sparkly crystal-skull hangout that looks like a cross between Skeletor's fortress and someplace My Little Ponies might live, I was thrilled to have so much space all to myself. That was my first reaction, "Oh wow, look at all this room!" My second reaction was, "Crap, who's gonna keep this place clean?" I considered calling Greg and seeing if he wanted to relocate, but I figured he wouldn't appreciate the commute.

And no, I didn't think about calling Nate.

The first week or two, I just didn't bother cleaning at all. Hey, I'd just saved the universe, I figured I deserved a little break. Plus my whole life had just changed—new job, new living situation, new restrictions, new girlfriend. It takes time to adjust.

But after a little while I started noticing the smell. Not me—I always bathe regularly, or at least walk through a mister or something. The rooms. The ones I was using—and a few I wasn't.

I think I mentioned that the last Guardian had, as near as we could tell, been zapped by the invaders, leaving nothing behind but a small pile of ash on the ground in the big Matrix chamber.

What I probably haven't said is that it looks like he didn't live here alone. We have no idea who or what they were, whether they were his friends or his family or his marketing staff or what. All we know is, there were other piles in other rooms.

And a few that weren't completely ash.

Those were the ones that were starting to stink.

Finally Mary, Ned, and Tall all sat me down and read me the riot act. "You're the Guardian," they said, "and this is your place now. You need to keep it clean." Then, because that's the kind of people they are, they pitched in to help.

It took us a week to clean, top to bottom, front to back, side to side, inside and out. There was all kinds of stuff scattered around, and a lot of it we had no idea what it was, food or clothing or refuse or some kind of interstellar stamp collection. Anything we couldn't identify, we tossed. Clothes got tossed too, except a few pieces I kept—hey, who doesn't need a tracksuit that looks like it's made of dominoes, or a Hawaiian shirt picturing volcanoes that actually explode? Food all went away, too—I was all in favor of trying them first, until Ned pointed out that we had no idea how long any of it had been here, whether any of it was still good, and whether the invaders had poisoned any of it, just to be sure they took out my predecessor. It was that last one that finally decided me. I was willing to risk the expired thing; I do that all the time. I figure those dates on the packages are just guidelines, really.

Anyway, when we'd finished the entire place was spic n' span. I hadn't exactly brought much with me—not even a change of clothes—and although I did manage to send for most of my stuff there wasn't a lot of it. I've never been much of a packrat. I set up a closet, and the pantry, and the kitchen, and the living room, and that was about that.

I've added a few things since then, though. Discovering there're over twenty different shopping networks, and all of them will deliver to the Galactic Core? Probably not the best thing, especially when you've got a few thousand races kicking in toward a monthly stipend for you—I'm basically loaded now. And it's amazing how many things look like something you absolutely can't live without at three in the morning. I bought clothes, weapons, gadgets, books, exotic foods, stuff that fit in two or more of those categories at once, all kinds of things. I figured, what the heck, I had plenty of room.

Except that I never remembered to carry any of it to any of those other rooms. I just opened each package in the living room, and the stuff stayed there.

Which led to the second intervention. Followed by the second bout of cleaning. A lot of the stuff I'd bought went away— did I really need a rotating pan-flute that created its own atmospheric light show but required three mouths and fourteen sets of lungs to play properly? Probably not. And how many synaptic conducer-arrays ("Fry an egg with the power of your mind!") did anyone really need? The answer, it turned out, was two— one for every day and one for company.

Now I try not to buy as much, and the things I do buy I try to remember to put in the rooms I've designated for different belongings. And I try to remember to pick my dirty clothes up off the floor and all that. It's a good thing I don't have a pet, though in a way I guess my couch kind of qualifies. Which is actually one reason I don't have a regular pet, because I'm afraid the couch would eat it. I suppose that's only fair, since I've had pets in the past that ate the furniture—it might just be the furniture's turn now. But then I'd worry about it getting a taste for flesh and demanding more pets, and then it would turn into a Broadway musical and I'd have to find a singing dentist and it would just go from there.

Anyway, the point is, when Tall arrived the next day—I hadn't bothered to watch his progress except here and there to make sure the MiBs hadn't dragged him back—the place wasn't any more messy than usual. Or any more tidy, either. Which Tall definitely noticed, judging by the way he scowled and turned his nose up a bit. Shame he never made it home while I was watching, because I've long suspected he's got a decontamination shower just inside the front door, and doesn't let anyone bring shoes or weapons or body hair inside. Now I may never know.

"I thought you were going to tidy up?" he says as he drops onto the couch, after first giving it a glare that makes it sulk and stay put for him. He's definitely got the thing trained. Me, I let it have a little fun and surprise me.

I look around. "What? It's clean . . . ish." I kick a Red's delivery bag out of the way.

"Whatever." He frowns. "Where're Mary and Ned? You did call them, right?"

"Of course I called them! They're in the other room. Come on." And I lead the way through the main Matrix chamber to an alcove I've never really used before. Ned and Mary are waiting there, all set up with a table and a chair. And a couch for me to observe from. I have good friends.

"What's all this?" Tall asks, eying the arrangement and especially the helmet Ned's holding. It looks like a stainless steel colander that somehow flowered after a bad acid trip.

"This is the behavioral realignment accelerated design," Ned says proudly. "Brad for short." He proffers it. "Here, put it on."

"What?" Tall's eyeing it like it just sprouted eyes and winked saucily at him—which, given all the wires and circuit boards and tubes and so forth jutting out of it, it just might. "We don't have time for this. We need to figure out what's going with the CampGirl cookies."

"Yes," Mary agrees, calm and cool as ever. "But before that can happen, we must be sure you have been freed from their influence. Otherwise—" She's had one hand behind her back, and now she brings it around—to reveal the box of ChocoMints she was hiding. Tall stiffens at the sight of them. Ever watch a man who's sworn off drinking when he winds up in a bar or at a party where there's booze, upon seeing that first bottle or glass go past? That look of worship and need mixed with self-loathing? That's the exact look that flashes across Tall now. He actually reaches out, possibly without realizing he is, and I grab his wrist, which gets me a glare. Number Two.

"Chill, dude," I tell him. "You wanna take down whoever's behind this? That means no more cookie-zombie for you."

After a second he nods and yanks his arm free, but he doesn't flatten me or toss me across the room or anything like that, so I figure we're cool. So do Mary and Ned, I guess, because Ned offers him the hat again.

This time, Tall takes it.

"You've heard of aversion therapy, right?" Ned asks as he gestures Tall toward the one chair and then starts fiddling with his diagnostic tools, which always looks to me like a guy air-drumming with high-tech chopsticks. "Where you get exposed to some kind of negative stimulus at the same time as something you like but shouldn't have, like cigarettes or booze? The idea is to associate the two in your head, so whenever you think of cigarettes you see a dead baby or smell wet dog or whatever." Tall nods. "Well, that's exactly how Brad works, only he hits you with five to ten different negatives all at once. And he projects those sensations directly into your cerebellum, so they're half-stuck right from the get-go. Normally this kind of therapy takes weeks to months." He beams. "With Brad, it takes about ten minutes."

Tall nods. He has the helmet strapped on, its built-in visor covering his eyes and nose, pieces on the side covering his ears. "Do it," is all he says, and I can tell he's already got his jaw clenched. But we need this to work—we can't risk him derailing every time he sees a box of CampGirl cookies.

Mary's helping Ned with the sensory inputs so I shuffle on

over to the couch and make myself comfortable. It's the normal, boring kind, doesn't move or anything, and after a few minutes I stop trying to talk to it. It probably doesn't have anything to say, anyway.

She and Ned confer a minute more, and Ned fidgets with his doohickeys, and then they flip a switch on the helmet and it lights up and starts whirring and clanking like Frankenstein's beanie. Tall hasn't moved a muscle since giving the go-ahead, and there's no big crazy display, no laser-light show sprouting from his eyes. He just sits there, and the helmet whirrs on.

Boring.

Ten minutes go by. Then another five. Finally Ned shuts off the helmet, and he and Mary approach Tall again. I'm close enough to hear what they're saying, plus I'm eavesdropping shamelessly. Yeah, yeah, I'm nosy—hey, this is the only way I can still say that and be right.

Anyway, Mary says, "Tall? How do you feel?"

"Fine," he replies. Could be a little terse, but usually it's more than that. He's still got the helmet on so I can't read his expression. "We done?"

"Perhaps." Mary picks up the cookie box again and waves it between her and Tall. "Would you care for a cookie?"

"Cookie?" The way he says that one word, all rushed and breathy and almost lilting, sends shivers up my spine. If I still had hair, it'd be standing up on the back of my neck. Too bad feathers don't work the same way, but even without that I can hear the naked want in Tall's voice.

"Maybe later," Ned says, patting Tall on the arm even as he

fiddles with the settings again. "Here, let's try this."

This time it's twenty minutes before they shut Brad down and offer Tall cookies again.

And again he practically lights up at the mention of CampGirl cookies. Nope.

Take three. Thirty minutes this time, over an hour total. I shift around a bit on the couch. They zap Tall. Then Mary offers him cookies.

"No, thanks," he manages, and I can tell he's clenching his jaw. She holds up the box and he resists for a second, then lunges for them. I'm halfway off the couch in an instant, but of course Mary can take care of herself. She sidesteps Tall's rush and slams her hand hard, edge down, at his neck. He slumps across the table, and now Mary steps back a bit. She and Ned share a glance and shake their heads.

Just our luck, the one time we need Tall to be susceptible and he's hard as rock.

"Sorry about that," Tall says as he recovers enough to move back to his seat. "Couldn't help myself."

"Which is exactly why we're doing this," Ned points out. "I've upped the intensity a little more. You ready?" Tall nods, and Ned throws another switch. This time I'm pretty sure I see his back arc as Brad assaults his mind, like he's being electrocuted.

Which, in a way, he is.

Chapter Eighteen
Results cloudy, try again later

It takes three hours before Brad is finally able to break Tall. Three hours. Halfway through, I get bored and wander away to check email. When I come back, munching on some popcorn, they're finally taking the helmet off. I'm pretty sure I see imprints from it burned into his hair and maybe even seared into his scalp. Ugh, pan-seared Tall. I put the popcorn down.

"Tall, would you like a cookie?" Mary asks, and I can hear the weariness in her voice. After all, this is like the tenth time she's had to ask that particular question. It's like being a kindergarten teacher, but without the fun of warping young minds. Just one older one.

"Get that thing out of my face," Tall snarls, knocking the box away, and Ned breaks into a smile. Mary just nods.

"I knew Brad would work!" Ned exults. "I knew it!"

"Yeah, after three whole hours," I point out. "Not quite as advertised, bub."

Ned frowns and pats the helmet as if its feelings might get hurt. Then again, for all I know maybe they could. I've had to console my couch a few times before, when I moved too quickly and startled it, or swept up something it was planning to ingest.

Pets, I tell ya—your work is never done. They're like kids, only without the ability to do chores. "It's not Brad's fault," he says protectively. "Tall has exceptional willpower."

I snort, but Tall just nods. "All MiBs do," he says, rising to his feet and stretching. He's been sitting in the same chair the whole time, and I don't envy him that. "It's part of our training."

"Okay, so now that you're cookie-proof," I say, "what do we do next?" I look at Ned. "You think you can build an industrial-sized Brad to run the whole MiB headquarters through at once? Because if we've gotta deprogram them one at a time, that's gonna take a while. And I'm gonna need to set up some cots or something."

Tall scowls, though it isn't at me for once. "That's not going to work," he declares, and he doesn't look too happy about it. "It'd take too long, and we don't know what's really going on here?"

"You mean besides making all of you guys look like blithering idiots?" I offer. That earns me a classic number two death stare from him. Ah, good old Tall. So predictable.

"Yes, besides that," he grinds out. I swear, he must regrow his teeth at night, or replace them with a new set when nobody's looking. I'm surprised he isn't spitting ground-up tooth dust when he talks. "Whoever's behind this, they've got something bigger planned. Incapacitating us is just the first step."

Ned interrupts his paranoid musing. "What makes you so sure it's about you at all?" he asks, and somehow his flat face is completely devoid of sarcasm or snark. How does he do that? If I could deliver such a line straight-faced, I'd consider going back into customer service, preferably someplace like a bank or a restaurant where you see them face to face, just so I could watch people's veins pop out and their eyes bulge as they tried to figure out if I was messing with them or not. Exactly like Tall's doing right now.

"No, seriously," Ned continues, which kinda ruins it for me, "maybe it isn't about the MiBs at all. Are other people being affected by the cookies? Or is it just the cookies that went to your office?"

That's actually a really good question, but I already know the answer. "It's not just his office," I tell them. "Tall brought me the first box but I ordered the rest myself, from different CampGirl troops around the U.S.—shipping charges were a bitch!—and all of them had the same effect on him."

Mary nods. "I noticed a strange aftertaste in the cookies when we tried them recently, and that was one of the boxes you ordered separately."

Tall studies her for a second, his eyes narrowed until they're just beady little dots between his brow and his cheekbones. "Why didn't it do anything to you?" he asks. That glare switches to me. "Or you? I saw you down an entire sleeve in one sitting"— that earns me a quirked eyebrow from Mary, and I suspect I'll hear about my diet later—"and it didn't make you any more . . ."

"Sweet? Friendly? Delightful?" I flutter my eyelashes at him, or would if I had any—instead I flutter my nictating membranes, which has a similar effect but probably a little creepier. "But I'm already so sweet!" Tall snorts at that, Ned guffaws, and even Mary giggles. Yep, I still got it.

"I believe I can answer that," Mary offers, amusement still clear in her voice. When we first met I thought she didn't even have emotions, and was basically a supercomputer brain in a sexpot body. But the more time we spent together, the more I realized she had a big heart. She just keeps it hidden most of the time because her scary intellect overshadows it. Her emotional responses tend to be on the subtle side as a result. Luckily I can be real observant when I want to be. "DuckBob and I were both augmented by the Grays," she explains. "Although most of his changes center on his avian morphology, and the majority of mine involve cerebral enhancement, I suspect the Grays made other minor adjustments as well. One of those seems to be in the realm of taste. I find I have a much broader and more discerning palate now than I did before." She taps the cookie box with one crimson nail. "If these were designed to alter a normal human brain, and to gain access through the normal human suite of taste buds, our alterations could prevent those changes from taking hold."

"Yeah, I can taste something a little different to the cookies from what I remember," I add. "It's almost metallic, a little bitter, and I can't place it but I don't think anybody regular's gonna notice at all."

Tall glances over at Ned, who shrugs and raises his hands. "Don't look at me, I'm not even human to start with!" he protests. Which always throws me for a loop—how does a guy from a small planet near Betelgeuse look and sound so much like he was born and raised in the Bronx? What'd they, have the mother of all foreign exchange programs?

"We need to find out who's behind this," Tall says again, pounding one hand into the other. I was never comfortable with that gesture—I know sometimes the left hand doesn't know what the right hand's doing, but does it really have to come to blows? "Then we can force them to tell us their evil plans." And how does he know they're really evil? What if they're just misdirected, or confused, or slightly malicious? He's jumping to some awfully big conclusions.

"Do you think it's the CampGirls?" I ask him. "I've never really trusted them, with their little badges and their vests and their caps and their handbooks and their campfire songs. They're like a nationwide cult, only they're knee-high."

Tall frowns. "It could be," he admits, "though I hope not. I get their newsletter—I helped with some of the activities for my niece's troop once or twice, so they put me on the email list—and it's always looked innocuous enough." You've gotta get inoculations just to be on their email list? Whoa, talk about strict! "I can look into it, though, find out who's in charge these days and pay them a visit." Somehow I don't think that would wind up involving tea and cookies. Especially not now.

"If we could identify whatever is changing the cookies' taste and altering the brain chemistry of whoever eats them, we might be able to track that back to the person responsible," Mary points out. "I ran an analysis on a ChocoMint the other day, but the results were inconclusive. The ingredients were too muddled together for me to pick out anything particularly alarming or out of place. I suspect some peculiarity in the baking process may have something to do with that, though there could also be something about the additives we seek that allows them to mask themselves—I have encountered a few such naturally camoflagued elements in the past, in different contexts. It would help if I had an uncontaminated sample to compare them to, such as a box of cookies from before all this trouble began, but it seems no one is capable of keeping them for very long." Yeah, there was a mercifully brief glare directed my way at that one, but I catch Tall looking a little guilty, as well. So there, Mister I've-got-the-willpower-of-a-saint-I-freeze-them-and-only-eat-a-box-a-month! Guess being a cookie zombie kinda killed that, huh?

"Well, somebody's gotta know, right?" I offer. "Somebody's putting whatever it is into those cookies."

Tall's eyes get all wide, and he hits me with a No. Six stare: "So your brain does sometimes work after all!" That's the same look he always gives me when I get something right or come up with a brilliant plan, so I'm not all that surprised when he says, "That's it! We've got to investigate this at the source!"

"I thought we didn't know the source?" But he waves my question aside.

"Not who's behind it," he says, "but where they've done it. And there's only one place that makes sense—on the factory floor."

"So we're going to a CampGirl cookie factory?" I can't believe it. It's like I've died and gone to Heaven. I'm pretty sure they have choirs of angels up in the factory's rafters, singing hymns as people walk underneath and stop at the free cookie stations, cookie slides, cookie contraptions, and cookie fountains. Oh, the bliss!

My spirits deflate when the three of them all give me a Number One. "You can't go anywhere, remember?" Ned asks me. "Guardian of the Matrix, constantly plugged in, deliriously happy?"

"I'm not so sure about the happy part," I grouse, kicking the wall. Again Mary does the quirked-eyebrow thing. I've already figured out I have absolutely no defense against that. "Oh, all right, yes, my life is awesome. Most of the time. But come on, you're going to a CampGirl cookie factory and I can't go along? That's so cruel!"

"You know we would rather have you with us if we could," Mary assures me.

"And you can still see and hear everything that goes on," Tall reminds me sharply. Then, when Ned and Mary look confused, he explains about the camera and the mic. And looks even more annoyed when he realizes from their lack of reaction that they both already knew.

"It's not the same," I complain, banging the wall again. But it was just wishful thinking on my part.

"We should go right away," Tall urges. "They may already suspect I'm on to them, and I don't want to give them time to plan."

Mary nods and then her face gets that weird "listening to the voices in my head" look and I know she's speaking with the Grays. Tall was annoyed when I claimed I'd called directly into his head—I can only imagine what Mary has to put up with from those little guys. It gives me the willies.

"They will transport us," she announces after she's done. "Where exactly are we going?"

Tall nods. "There're only two official CampGirl cookie factories," he answers. "One's in Louisville, Kentucky. The other's in Richmond, Virginia."

"Does it matter which one we try first?" Ned asks.

"They're supposed to use the same recipes," Tall tells him, "but it's possible one's involved and the other isn't. We can check the control numbers on the boxes, to make sure, but since I think they each service different regions, we should only be dealing with one of the factories here." He frowns. "Actually, there's an easy way to be sure—they have different names for some of the cookies. Not ChocoMints, but a few of the others. It's a trademark thing."

"You said you had Island Delights and PB Sandwiches at work," I remember. I have a really good memory for sweets—I still remember the candy bars I stole from Dooley Jenkins in the third grade. "Which factory is that?"

Tall closes his eyes for a second. Then they pop back open, and he smirks. "Alphabet Bakery," he answers. "Just outside Richmond, Virginia."

Mary nods. "Then that is where we shall go." She steps over and gives me a warm smile and a quick kiss on the cheek. "We will return shortly."

"I'll be here." I tug absently on the cord from my crown. Where the hell else'm I gonna be? "I'll watch, and let you know if I spot anything you don't," I add, both because I want to be useful and because at least this way I get to see Tall scowl again right before the three of them start to shimmer. The shimmering grows, covering more and more of them and getting brighter and brighter until I can't look at it directly. Then it just vanishes, all the light and warmth, and Ned and Tall and Mary are gone with it.

"Back to the computer," I mutter to myself, and turn to make my way back toward my living room. En route I grab the half-empty bag of popcorn. Hey, it's brain food, okay?

Chapter Nineteen
C is for Cookie

"So that's a cookie factory, huh?" I ask as I plop down in my chair. They've already materialized, of course—it only takes a minute or two to cover the distance from what I now think of as "Brad's room" to my living room, but the Grays' matter transporter doohickey is instantaneous, as near as I can tell, so they win that particular race. Which is probably for the best— I'm not sure I'd want to see what was going on around Tall when he was being broken apart into component atoms and beamed halfway across the galaxy, or whether my brain could handle it if I did. For that matter, if the camera was scattered into bits too, I wouldn't have seen anything regardless. Oh well.

But now they're back in one piece—I mean each of them is in one piece, not they're all muddled together into one big piece, which would be gross and a serious invasion of privacy— and they're standing there looking over at . . . an office building. Because that's what it looks like to me. A big, white brick office building, two stories tall but really wide, with a solid band of windows around the upper floor and a matching one around the ground floor and a big overhang jutting out from the front like it was a hotel and they wanted you to pull your car around there for the valet. Across the front of that overhang are the words "Alphabet Bakery" and their logo, and that's the only decoration I see anywhere, not counting the American flag waving out front, but there's a nice green lawn that spreads out around the building and glossy dark green bushes just under the windows and small trees in big pots on either side of the sliding glass doors. It all looks very bland and very friendly and not at all like the kind of place where they'd have mind-control drugs they were using to captivate most of the country. I guess that's the sort of thing they don't want to put on a big banner across the front.

"There're loading docks around back," Tall says as he stalks up the circular drive toward those front doors. "We could go in that way, might draw less attention at first, but it'd take longer to work our way through and get to the CEO or somebody else high up enough to answer our questions. I'm for the direct route." Of course he is. He's like a big angry bull, and those doors are a red flag. I'm almost surprised I don't hear him snort, though I do think the suit and sunglasses are a better choice for him than black leather and a nose ring.

"I'll go around back," Ned offers. "I can start scanning for any nonterrestrial tech, work my way up and in, see if I can find anything out that way."

Mary nods. "I will go with Tall," she says, "in case he encounters any of those same elements."

Ned turns away, and I lean forward and grab my mic. "Uh," I say, "nobody else thinks it could be a problem to send the goofy little green guy with the broccoli horns off by himself?

You don't think people'll notice him?"

"I doubt it," Tall answers as he resumes his trek toward the front doors. "Ned looks human enough, if you just get a quick glimpse at him." Yeah, and you're colorblind, I don't say out loud. "And he sounds completely normal. I've found that makes a lot more difference. Act like you belong and everyone will just assume you do." Really? I have to try that the next time I "accidentally" wander into an all-female steam bath. I'm sure nobody'll notice.

He reaches the front doors, which slide open to reveal a nice lobby, friendly but understated, and a big wide reception desk just in front of the back wall. A young woman stands there, wearing typical business-casual clothing, and she gives Tall a big smile as he approaches her. I see her big green eyes slide over to Mary for just a second, then flick away, and I've got to say, I'm impressed. Guys, when we see another guy who's better built than we are or better looking or just richer and more successful, we tend to glower for a second and then move on to trying to drink him under the table or beat him at pool or talk over the punchlines to all his jokes. Women, though, tend to be a lot more cutthroat. I've seen hot chicks at a party when another, hotter chick walks in—they go rigid for a second, fiery death shooting from their eyes like molten lava, the temperature around them paradoxically dropping twenty degrees from the brittle cold they exude, and you can just about hear the sound of claws being sharpened on a big ol' whetstone. Then they're suddenly all smiles again, and call her over and act all nice and friendly, all the while circling her like a pack of hyenas, darting in whenever there's an opening to jab and snap and bite, twirling little poisoned daggers and looking for places to plant the blades. And naturally Mary would get the worst of that sort of treatment, as she's not only the hottest woman since Eve (who only has her beat because she set the standard) or maybe Helen of Troy (who got entire countries to die over her beauty, which isn't what I'd normally call a ringing endorsement but what the hell), she's also a bonafide supergenius. Which is why I'm impressed that this little lady gives her one quick sizing-her-up glance and then ignores her—sure, there's a little spite there, but it's a lot less nasty than I'd expect, more of an "I can't compete so I'm not even gonna try" than a "I will ignore your very existence while I contemplate the most effective way to dispose of you."

"Hi, and welcome to Alphabet Bakery," the lady in question offers, her voice loud and cheery and filled with the soft twang of Virginia. "What can I help you with today?" Her gaze stays on Tall, but he is a big, rugged guy, so I guess I can understand that. Mary doesn't complain, either—she's letting Tall do the talking, which is probably a wise move here.

"I need to speak with your CEO," Tall informs the young woman as he reaches the desk and peers down at her. "Right away."

She frowns, but it's one of those cute-girl "I'm so sorry" frowns, not a real big "well, isn't that a pisser" look. "Ms. Daniels-Axland is real busy, I'm afraid," she says slowly. "I don't know that she's got any time right now to see anybody unless you've already got yourself an appointment."

A shadow falls across her, this big, looming thing full of menace, and I see her smile falter and her eyes go wide. For a second I think that smokedancer, Vic whatever, has somehow shown up here. Then I realize it's just Tall, plying his "big spooky MiB" mojo.

"It wasn't a request," he tells her, and his voice has dropped at least three octaves and maybe a subbasement or two. It's also doing the whole rocks-grinding-against-each-other thing, though I happen to know that's just his teeth. "Get her. Now."

The girl gulps and picks up the phone. "Hello, Wendy?" she says after a second. "It's Kelly. There's a guy here to see Ms. Daniels-Axland." She gulps again, and lowers her voice, turning away a little bit. I can still hear her just fine, though, which makes me wonder just how powerful these mics really are. I have to remember to keep mine well away from the bathroom. "I don't know, he didn't give one," she whispers, "but he's big and scary and looks like a Fed or something. Yeah." She nods and looks a little relieved. "Okay, thanks." Then she hangs up the phone and turns back to Tall and Mary. "Ms. Daniels-Axland is on her way down," she tells them.

Tall just nods, but Mary says, "Thank you." The girl— Kelly—nods back but her eyes don't leave Tall. She's like a deer watching a dozing lion, knowing he's quiet now but could wake and decide he wants a late-afternoon snack at any second.

Fortunately it's only a minute before the door to the side of the desk opens and a woman steps through. At first glance I think it's Mrs. Claus, only she's got herself a nice power suit. She's not too tall, plump, with a wide, friendly face and white hair pulled back in a slightly messy bun. Her eyes are sharp but look kind, and she has a smile on her face as she approaches. "I hear y'all have something you need to speak with me about," she says, and her accent's just as pronounced as Kelly's. Guess Alphabet likes to hire locally. "I'm Robinette Daniels-Axland, but y'all can call me Rosie, everybody does." She offers her hand, which looks just as friendly as the rest of her, and I can't help but mentally superimpose a flowery apron atop her business attire. She looks like everybody's favorite grandma. Well, not mine, exactly—Grandma Spinowitz was a little fireplug of a woman who could spit tobacco farther and more accurately than anyone I ever saw and liked to belt out show tunes in her native Polish and taught me to bake and to fight and to curse, usually all at the same time. But you get the picture.

"A pleasure." Tall shakes her hand but doesn't introduce himself, and I can see a tiny furrow appear between her eyes for just a second as she absorbs that fact, along with his black suit and sunglasses and towering presence. "Is there someplace where we can speak more privately?"

"Of course." Rosie gives Kelly a little "I'll take it from here, sweetie" wave and opens the door again, holding it for them. "We'll head on up to my office. And I didn't catch your names," she adds as Tall stomps past her, with Mary presumably right behind him."

"Mary," I hear my girlfriend answer. "And this is Agent Thomas." Tall growls a little at that—guess it's in the MiB handbook not to give your name unless you have to, or maybe it's just a little informal competition between agents to see who can withhold that info the longest, but he doesn't try to deny it. Rosie sidles past him and leads the way, which is good because Tall's just stopped dead—and I can see why.

The building's a shell, really. It's two stories tall because there're offices arranged around the outer edge of the second floor, with stairs here and there leading up to that level. But the whole rest of the place is one big, open space. Filled with people and machines and boxes and crates and sacks—

Of cookies.

And Tall's just been made to hate cookies with every fiber of his being. Now here he is, staring at literally hundreds of thousands of them, all in one place.

This could be bad.

"Focus, Tall," I hear Mary whisper to him. "Remember why we're here."

He nods sharply—I almost get whiplash—and follows Rosie, who's already halfway up the stairs. His longer strides catch up easily, though, and he's right behind her when she opens a glass door onto a nice big office.

It's funny how much you can tell about a person from the way they keep and decorate their office. You can see if somebody's messy or neat, organized or scattered, silly or serious, a family guy or a loner or a wolf on the prowl. My old office spaces were always filled with action figures and cartoons and beer paraphernalia and of course the duck-related *tchotchkes* co-workers thought it was hilarious to give me, duck whistles and duck-hunting caps and Donald Duck figures and so on. I've seen Tall's desk and it's pristine, no pictures or frivolous items of any kind, just his computer and an In box and an Out box and one of those little magnetic holders for paperclips and a pen holder with some pens and a mug with the Yankees logo on it, which is the most personal thing he's got there. Mary doesn't have an office anywhere—near as I can tell, she basically beams her mental reports directly to the Grays, like an internal fax machine—but if she did I imagine it'd be scrupulously neat and pretty spare, but with framed photos of some of the cooler places she's been and the crystal travel mug I got her (refracts light so it can actually reheat your beverage if you set it somewhere sunny for a few minutes, which I thought was cool because I hate it when you're drinking your coffee or your chai or your hot chocolate and it's steaming hot for the first few gulps and nicely warm for the next few but barely lukewarm after that and almost cold by the time you reach the bottom) and maybe, I flatter myself, a picture of me somewhere, too.

Rosie's office looks like a cross between a knitting circle and a Fortune 500 executive suite. The furniture is all polished wood, very high-end power suit variety, except the couch looks comfy and there's a wooden rocking chair next to it and both have what're obviously handmade throws over them. There's a fancy-schmancy computer on the desk, and an all-in-one printer-fax-copier on the credenza behind it, but the monitor's got one of those bulletin board frames around it with pictures and Post-its all over the place and there's a spider plant sitting next to the printer with its tendrils wrapped around like it's about to confide something big and the mug next to the computer says "#1 Grandma" and has that lopsided look you can only get when a little kid tries to make something themselves. The diplomas and awards on the wall vie with photos of Rosie with kids, most of them in CampGirl uniforms, and the different uniforms make it clear these were taken over a decade or two at least, though she looks exactly the same in all of them. Okay, her suits've changed a little in style, but not much. Two of the walls're mostly windows—the outer one, which looks out over the lawn and the driveway to the street beyond, and the inner one, which looks out on the factory floor. This's definitely a woman who likes to keep her eye on things, just like a grandma who's always watching but not getting in the way because she'd rather let you screw up and learn for yourself as long as it's not gonna cost you an eye or a limb.

"Now," Rosie says as she moves over to the little seating area and settles into her rocking chair, gesturing Tall and Mary toward the couch. "What can I do for you two?" Then she reaches over to the little table beside her, retrieves something, and turns back to them. My heart almost stops when I realize it's an all-too-familiar, brightly colored box, already opened, and I swear I can practically smell the chocolate and mint wafting from it as she waves the box toward Tall. "Would y'all like a cookie?"

Oh, boy.

Chapter Twenty
Fortunately not Pamplona

That's gotta be at least a 3.5 on the Richter scale, the grinding coming from Tall's jaws, and I actually see Rosie flinch a little and pull the box back like she's afraid she might wind up with nothing but a bloody stump where her hand was. She's right to worry about that, too, but not for the reason she thinks.

"No, thanks," Tall manages to grate out, and I can just see Mary shaking her head at the edge of my screen—this camera's got great peripherals. "We're actually here to talk to you about those cookies, ma'am."

She sets the box down, though they're still tantalizingly within reach, and nods. "I'd figured," she says, rocking in her chair a little, and I half expect her to produce a pile of knitting from somewhere. "After all, that's what we do here." The smile she gives them is pleased as punch, and under normal circumstances I can understand why. She makes CampGirl cookies. That's like being the guy in charge of producing all the Easter eggs, or being the head elf at Santa's workshop. She's practically the Willy Wonka of the cookie industry! "So, what do y'all need to know?"

Mary leans forward—I'm guessing she's realized, just as I

have, that Tall's using all his willpower not to start breaking things from the sight of that cookie box. "You recently changed your cookie recipe," she states. "We wish to know what the alteration is, and who authorized it, and who supplies you with the new ingredients."

But Rosie's frowning now. "Oh, no, dear," she says. "We haven't altered our cookie recipes in over forty years. The packaging's changed some"—she gestures behind her, and I can see well enough from this angle to realize that what looked like a series of small framed collages is actually a row of framed cookie boxes. It's the ChocoMint box, and I recognize the ones I've been chowing down from lately, the ones I used to swipe off kids when I was in college, and the ones my sisters used to bring home when I was a kid. She's got the entire history of the ChocoMint box there on her wall. That's actually pretty cool.

She's currently sighing, though. "We did have to alter the size a little bit," she says, and it's obvious she isn't happy about that, unless she's a damn good actor. "The cost of flour, sugar, everything has gone up. We had to change the packaging so the boxes didn't hold quite so many cookies anymore, and make the cookies themselves a little smaller, in order to survive. I've got lots of mouths to feed here, y'know." She shakes her head. "But the recipe, no, that's the same as it's always been."

Tall leans forward. "Ma'am, that's just not true." He growls it out a bit, but he's calmed down some already, so I don't think she's in immediate danger. "This year's cookies are having dangerous effects on people. Something's been done to them, and we need to know what that is if we're going to have any chance of correcting it."

"Nonsense!" She's got that whole indignant-old-lady thing going on now, and I wouldn't be surprised if she produced a ruler and thwacked Tall across the knuckles with it. "I'm telling you, these are the same cookies we've always made! And I certainly haven't had any complaints from any of the troops, or heard anything personally from any parents or their children." She peers at Tall, a little of her laidback attitude gone. "Which agency did y'all say you worked for again?"

"Have you tried the recent batch of cookies yourself?" Mary asks, countering her question. Nice one, babe! But Rosie shakes her head.

"I'm diabetic, I'm afraid," she says, and laughs—a slightly bitter laugh, to my ears. And I know a lot about bitter laughter—try spending a few years having to pretend every duck joke in the world is hilarious and you'll understand why. "I know, it's funny, the head of a cookie factory and I can't eat cookies myself."

I feel for the lady, I do. Imagine being surrounded by yummy food day after day and not being able to eat any of it. The closest I've come to that is working fast food in high school, smelling the fries and burgers and shakes constantly but only being able to scarf some down on my breaks. Of course, I took a lot of breaks. Pretty much one an hour, actually. Which is probably why, after two weeks, instead of a paycheck I got a termination notice and a bill.

That doesn't help us here, though. The one person who could tell us what's going on, and she claims she doesn't know—and there's no way we can prove to her that the cookies taste funny or affect people oddly, because she might keel over dead as a result.

But she's not the only person around, I realize.

"Tall," I say into the mic. "The one at the front desk—Kelly—when she called up here, she didn't talk to the head honcho directly. There was a secretary or something. She's gotta be nearby."

"Yeah? So what?" Wow, he's good—he's got the whole subvocalizing thing down cold! Must be from playing with mics like this on covert ops, or maybe it's just from swallowing half his snide comments, but I can hear his rumbling loud and clear even though it's obvious from her face that Rosie didn't at all.

"So," I tell him, "I bet her secretary isn't diabetic."

There's a pause, and I wish I had a mirror because I'm betting I'd see Stare No. Six right now. Especially since the next thing he says to Rosie is, "You have an executive secretary, don't you, ma'am?"

She nods, though I can see she has no idea where this is going. "Yes, of course. Wendy is right next door. Why?"

"Could you ask her to come in here, please?" Tall's showing admirable restraint. He sounds perfectly calm and professional, if you ignore the faint bass growl below his words. It's like watching the Beast, the Disney version, only he's got a black suit on and he's talking bureaucrat-ese.

I don't know if she's scared of him or just curious, but Rosie complies. "Wendy!" she calls out, and a second later the office door opens and a woman sticks her head in.

"Yes, ma'am?" Wendy's not bad-looking, curvy edging toward plump with a nice face and long, curly black hair. She's not as good at hiding dislike as Kelly was, and I see the daggers come out as her eyes rake across Mary. There's nothing but curiosity and maybe a little admiration as they study Tall. I can still drink him under the table, though.

"Could you come in here, please, ma'am?" Tall asks her, and after a quick glance at Rosie she complies. She steps in and approaches them, then sits on the other couch after a gesture from Tall. "We just need your help with something." He reaches for the cookie box but stops and balls his hand into a fist, which he then plants slowly and deliberately on the coffee table. That had to take a helluva lot of control! I could tell he just wanted to smash the thing to pieces instead. "Would you please have a cookie?"

Now Wendy's looking completely baffled, and I don't blame her. Her boss calls for her, and when she comes in there's this stunning woman and this rugged guy in a suit, and they want her to eat cookies? That's gotta be like the weirdest kink ever. But it's harmless enough, and Rosie's nodding for her to play along, so Wendy takes the box, extracts a ChocoMint, and takes a dainty bite.

Almost instantly we see her eyes glaze over. She sits up a little straighter and finishes the cookie, then goes for the box again, but Tall gets there first. He doesn't bother to be nice about it, though—instead his arm lashes out and the box goes flying, crumpled by the force of his hand slapping into it.

"Mind your manners, young man!" Rosie snaps at him, but

a look from Tall shushes her.

"Wendy, can you hear me?" Tall asks. "How do you feel?"

"Fine," the secretary answers. "I feel fine. Can I have another cookie?" Yep, definite cookie-zombie. I recognize all the signs.

"Maybe in a minute." Tall turns back to Rosie. "This is what your cookies are doing to people," he accuses. "Go on, tell her to do something. Something she wouldn't normally do."

"What? Oh, I . . . ." Rosie wrings her hands together, staring at her secretary, who just sits there on the couch, looking straight ahead. "I wouldn't—"

Mary's apparently tired of waiting. "Wendy," she says, "stand up." Wendy stands at once. "Hop on your right foot." Wendy lifts her left leg at the knee and starts hopping. "Now bawk like a chicken." Wendy starts bawking, still hopping, and still staring straight ahead. "Stand perfectly quiet and still." Wendy becomes a statue. "This is what the cookies do," Mary informs Rosie, who's been gawking at her secretary through the whole command performance. "We have come to you to discover how and why."

"I don't know," Rosie tells her, and the poor lady looks like she's close to tears. I hate seeing grandmas cry. Especially since, whenever mine did, it usually meant she was gonna go for her gun next. "We haven't changed the recipes, I tell you!"

Tall stands up—suddenly Rosie and Mary and even Wendy who's standing look like ants to me—and stalks over to the window, the inner one that looks out on the factory floor. "Maybe the recipe's the same," he states after a second, "but something new's been added. And if you didn't authorize it, it's going on behind your back."

Rosie stands now as well, and closes the distance to Tall. "Well, if someone's been messing with my cookies," she declares, "I want to know who! We pride ourselves on the quality of our cookies, and I'm not about to let someone ruin that for us!" Yeah, good for you, Grandma, I cheer in my head. You go out there and break a few heads!

I'm guessing Tall's impressed with her gumption, too, because his voice isn't quite as gruff when he responds. "We're happy to have the help," he tells her. "Where should we start?"

"The mixing room," Rosie replies at once. "Since it's not the recipe that's at fault, it's gotta be added right at the source." She reaches for the door, but stops and looks back at Wendy, who's still doing her best impression of a monument. "What about her? Will this wear off?"

"I don't know," Tall admits. "But we can fix it." He nods to Mary, who's on her feet as well but still standing beside the couch—and besides Wendy.

"Wendy," Mary says to the other woman. "Snap out of it."

It's still just as creepy watching the zombie effect fade as it is seeing it appear. It's like the dawn spreading across the sky, only this dawn is the light of self-awareness and self-control. And as it filters through her eyes and her face I see Wendy go from perfectly stoic to confused and a little frightened. "What happened?" she asks. "I was sitting down a second ago."

"You are unharmed," Mary assures her. "Your mind must have wandered." Yeah, to Peoria and back, I think, with maybe a little pause to gawk at Albuquerque, but Wendy nods absently and looks a little reassured. Oh, to be that easily convinced! I've always been too skeptical for my own good—or at least so I've been told, but I'm not sure I believe it.

I do notice, though, that Mary surreptitiously slides that box of cookies behind her back, and then drops them in the trashcan on the far side of the couch. Smart move—if Tall's any indication, whatever's in those cookies definitely leaves you wanting more, and we don't need Wendy going zombie on us again the minute we walk away.

"Hey," I think to ask Tall then, "what about just checking the security tapes? Since we know whatever's going on is happening in the mixing room, can't you just scan the footage from a few months back and peg whoever's doing it from the comfort of Rosie's office?" Well away from all those cookies, I add in my head.

But Tall shakes his head. "Wouldn't work," he replies under his breath. "If somebody's just been adding this mystery ingredient on the sly, how would we be able to tell from a tape? They'd just look like they were doing their job. Besides"—and now he sounds slightly disgusted, and even a little personally offended—"the security here is a joke. The cameras I saw on our way up are practically antiques, with crap for zoom or fine detail. We'd be able to make out blurry images and not a whole lot more."

"Ah. Right." Damn. I was really hoping to keep him off the factory floor if possible. "Sorry."

"No worries," he assures me. "It was a good thought." And he doesn't even sound like he's kidding. "Let's go," he urges the others, now back to full barking-out-loud mode, and Rosie only glances back at her secretary once more before nodding and opening the door. She leads Tall and Mary out, and of course I'm with them like a silent ghost as we all traipse back down the stairs. I'm a little worried, though. Tall managed to restrain himself in the office, but that was just one box of cookies. We're about to go out onto the factory floor, where CampGirl cookies'll literally surround us, thousands of them as far as the eye can see. For most people, me included, that'd be just one step shy of heaven—no dancing girls or alcohol. But for Tall those cookies are now on par with the devil. And I'm not sure even his MiB willpower is going to be enough to keep him from going berserk with the enemy closing in on ever side.

Chapter Twenty-one
Mixing it up

Okay, it's official. When I die, I want to wake up in a cookie factory. Or at least a cross between a cookie factory and a strip club. But this place is flat-out awesome!

We come down the stairs—I really feel like I'm there, like this is the best VR tour ever because the picture's so clear and I can hear everything and I've got the lights dimmed in my living room and my feet up and I'm comfy in my ergonomic desk chair, all I need are wraparound goggles with speakers by each ear and I could let my imagination fill in the scents and textures and I'd pretty much be Johnny-on-the-Spot—and the whole factory is spread out before us. Like I said, one big open space. And all of it, and everybody there, is all about one thing, and one thing only—

—making cookies.

You remember how it smelled when your mom made cookies at home when you were a kid? Okay, with my mom that involved Pop'n'Fresh and the microwave and a beer, but my grandma actually made them from scratch, grumbling to herself in Polish the whole time and the way the whole kitchen was filled with warmth and that rich, sweet, salty smell of cookie dough and fresh-baked cookies—yeah. That's pretty much my definition of security and affection at home.

And you know how a garage—a proper mechanic's garage, not some creepy parking garage with mould all over the walls and standing water in the corners—has a certain smell to it too, all grease and motor oil and electricity, kinda dirty and grimy but in a good way, a way that says "I'm fixing something here, doing real work with real tools and when I'm done this car's gonna fly like a rocket and look like a movie star"?

Well, take those two memories and mush 'em together. Because that's what Alphabet Bakery looks like to me, and I'm willing to bet that's what it smells like, too—it's got hot, fresh cookies and all the ingredients individually, mixed in with the smell of machinery and hard work, and all bound together by bright lights and cheerful music and that hubbub of easy chatter that says either the boss is gone for the week or you're lucky enough to work in one of those places where they really don't mind you gabbing with your mates as long as you're getting the work done.

It's amazing.

I can tell Mary thinks so, too, because at the landing halfway down the stairs she stops to take it all in and says softly, "What a beautiful juxtaposition of the comfort of sweets and the productivity of a well-run workplace!" That's my girl.

Tall, however, just grunts. "Too loud, too bright, and it smells like yeast," he grumbles as he moves past her, practically stomping on the backs of Rosie's feet in his hurry to reach the ground floor. Well, the whole cookie thing's getting to him, of course, so it's understandable if he's even testier than usual—and his usual level of "testy" would beat out a whole high school at SAT time.

Rosie, bless her, completely ignores his complaints but does take the time to turn and beam at Mary. "I think so too, dear," she says proudly. "We all love what we do here, and I think it shows!"

"Well, somebody here loves turning people into brainless automatons," Tall snaps, cutting off her happiness midstream. "So let's focus on that, okay?"

The look she gives him, I remember it myself from the few times any of us ever dared to interrupt Grandma during one of her stories. It's the "if you weren't my own flesh and blood I'd carve you up like a prize steer and turn you into blood sausage and tripes" look, and I shiver just getting it secondhand. I have no idea if it fazes Tall at all.

"Oh, I'm focused," she promises him, though. "I just can't believe one of my people would do such a thing, though." She turns and leads the way through the maze of machinery and boxes and barrels and sacks and so forth. "Mixing room's this way."

Everybody says hi to Rosie as she passes, and throws questioning looks at Tall and lustful or jealous looks at Mary—or sometimes the other way around. She always says hi back, I notice, and calls each person by name, stopping for a few seconds to exchange pleasantries before moving on. It's clear her employees think she's the bee's knees, and I can already see why. I've never had a boss like her myself, but it's obvious she's one of the good ones.

The only problem is, her stop-and-go approach is turning this would-be charge into a crawl. And that leaves more time for Tall to be exposed to cookies, cookies, cookies.

I can already hear him breathing in great big gulps, and the way the camera's view keeps shifting he's gotta be turning his head side to side like a caged beast desperate to break free. Not good.

"Yo, Tall," I tell him, "chill, okay? Just let the nice lady lead us there so we can get some answers, and then you can get out of there."

"I'm . . . having a hard time of it," he admits to me through that subvocal trick of his, and I'm kinda amazed. I mean, Tall never says he's having trouble with anything! "I can feel the cookies out there," he continues, "it's like a constant itch just under my skin, all over. My teeth are practically buzzing, my head is throbbing, my vision's starting to strobe, and with the way the light's stabbing into me I'm pretty sure my pupils are dilated. I'm going into full-on panic mode here, and if that happens, people could get hurt."

"Ah . . ." Crap. I have no idea what to tell him. I mean, what should he do? Get the hell out of there and leave it to Mary to sort things out? I don't know that'd work, though—I love Mary to pieces, and she's awesome, but interrogation isn't exactly her thing, and for all her brains there could be stuff someone who isn't trained might miss. Have him close his eyes until they get to the mixing room? He'd just run into something, and that might set him off even worse. Find a way for him to blow off some steam now, before he hits full meltdown? Hey, that's not a bad idea! "Listen," I say quickly, "ask Rosie if there's a place they put all the substandard cookies, damaged boxes, and so on. Someplace with nothing anybody would miss."

Tall nods sharply. "Yeah, good idea." I pretend not to hear the surprise in his tone. "Thanks." He reverts to actually speaking. "Ma'am, where do you keep all your damaged goods? The cookies that didn't turn out right, the boxes that got damaged in packing, things like that?"

"Hm?" They were just cutting past a pallet stacked high with sacks of flour, and Rosie stops to study him for a second. "Oh, that'd be the reject room. It's right over there, next to the loading bay." She gestures ahead and to the right. "We like to donate those to shelters and orphanages—no reason those folks can't still enjoy them. Why?"

"I . . . have a hunch I want to check out," Tall manages to reply, and I'm impressed that he only sounds a little more homicidal than normal. "Where's the mixing room from there, exactly? I'll meet you two over there."

"Oh, that's easy. From the rejects you just head straight down the pantry, where we keep all our ingredients, until you hit the second support beam. Then turn right and you're there." Rosie studies him for a second. "You sure you don't want me to come with you?"

"No no, that's fine." He's starting to sound a little desperate. "Mary, you go with Rosie. I'll be back in a minute." I'm not sure Mary knows what he's up to but she obviously realizes something's going on because she doesn't argue or ask for more detail—and this is the gal who likes to see the full ingredient list when I make her dinner! You know how hard it is to manage a culinary surprise with someone like that? It's not like she's allergic to anything, and any side effects've worn off within a day most times, plus I thought the fire-breathing thing was actually kind of cool, and worked out great with the s'mores. Anyway, she just nods and sets a hand on Rosie's arm, asking her something to distract her as Tall wheels about and hurries away.

The minute he's out of the ladies' sight he breaks into a sprint, and everything zooms past in a blur of metal and burlap and paper. I see a wide-open space at the far end of the building that has to be the loading bay, and as we close in on that Tall veers right a few degrees. We clear the last of the machinery, nothing but a wide open corridor here, bare concrete floors and whitewashed walls, with the bay to our left and a big storage room to the right. Tall makes a beeline for the set of double doors, and slams them open—

—and we're in the CampGirl cookie version of a thrift store. There're boxes of cookies here piled from floor to ceiling all around, stacked on shelves and heaped on the floor, plus whole giant bins of loose cookies, all varieties just mixed in together. Everything in here is a little dented, a little dinged up, a little damaged.

It's perfect.

Tall shuts the doors carefully behind him. Then he draws his gun, one of the two he took off those agents who were holding him. I think it's the same kind he was waving about in midtown, and when I see him shoot a stack of boxes and make them glow blue and then disappear, I know I'm right. He pulls the other gun then, and starts shooting with both hands, making cookies sizzle and vanish left and right.

That goes on for a good few minutes, but I can tell it's not enough because eventually he tucks both guns away again— I don't actually know where he's keeping them or how, and I don't really want to ask but I have this horrible image of Tall just clutching them in his armpits and I need something to scrub it out of my head, stat!—and starts whaling on cookies with his fists instead.

Wham! A pile of cookie boxes flies into the air, smashed by his punch.

Whallop! He backhands another stack, demolishing them and sending shreds of cardboard and bits of cookie everywhere. It's like the most colorful—and tasty—snowfall ever.

Thwack! He kicks a shelf, sending boxes raining down on his head, and smashes each one out of his way as it falls.

After a few minutes Tall pauses and backs up to lean against the doorframe, panting. The room now looks like the Tasmanian Devil decided to come in here for his midday snack.

"Feel any better?" I ask. I have to admit, it actually looked like fun.

"Yes, actually," he answers, and straightens, brushing any remnants off his jacket. "Thanks—that was exactly what I needed."

"Cool. Back to work, then." I'm pretty pleased with myself as Tall exits the now-substantially-less-full rejects room and starts down the row of ingredients. Hey, this is why I got the tele-presence setup in the first place, so I could lend a hand even if I'm stuck here with the Matrix. And not so I could gather blackmail material on not only my friends but their coworkers and relatives. Nuh-uh, thought never crossed my mind.

Tall's got ridiculously long legs and he still doesn't want to be here any longer than he has to, so I'm not surprised when he turns the corner and stops only a minute or two later. This must be the mixing room, and it isn't quite what I expected. I guess I figured it'd be an old-fashioned kitchen, with long wooden tables white from flour and all sorts of pots and pans and measuring cups hanging from an iron rack overhead and maybe a sturdy wooden cart to wheel away the cups once they're full of the properly measured and mixed ingredients.

Instead, what I see is a mass of pipes that looks like a plumber's wet dream, all snaking about and twisting around and past each other. There's hoses and nozzles attached in various places, and valves and spouts too, and right in the middle is a heavy-duty computer workstation with four different monitors all linked together and two chairs in front of them.

It's like looking at a Mad Scientist chemistry set, only grown to industrial size.

Mary and Rosie are talking to a pair of workers when we arrive. One of them's a tall, skinny woman with a long, bony face and straw hair who's blinking almost nonstop, as if there's something caught in her Anime-huge brown eyes. The other's a guy, a little heavy but who'm I to judge, shock wheat-brown hair up top but receded a bit from his wide, jowly red face. I feel like I'm looking at Jack Sprat and his wife's opposite halves.

"Did your hunch pan out?" Rosie asks by way of greeting as Tall joins them.

"Doesn't look like it, no," he answers, and yeah, he's definitely a lot calmer now. "But thanks." He swivels to study the pair. "And who're you?"

Both of them start at his bluntness, but after a beat or two the woman answers. "I'm Winona, and this is Reg. We're the daytime mixing crew."

"Winona was just saying that she knows nothing of any alterations to the cookies," Mary told Tall—and me, too. "She claims they have mixed nothing beyond the usual ingredients, and in the standard ratios."

"Oh, yeah." Winona's nodding so fast she's practically a metronome. "We'd never mess with the cookies, you know that, ma'am! We're very conscientious about it, aren't we, Reg?"

"Absolutely," he agrees, but there's something about the way he says it that sets off my radar. Is he lying? He does meet Tall's gaze for a second, which is more than a lot of people can say, and I feel like he wouldn't be able to do that if he was lying completely, so maybe it's a lie by omission, something like that?

Or, it occurs to me, maybe he's lying but doesn't know it but somehow does?

I think that made sense, at least to me.

"Listen, Tall," I say quietly, "I just had a thought—"

"Good for you," he responds. "Keep trying, the second time's easier."

"Oh, ha ha, I had no idea you were a comedian." I am glad he's messing with me again, though. That's more like the Tall

I know. "Anyway, what if these two're pouring in those other ingredients but they don't know it? Like, what if they were told to do it, and then told to forget all about it? That way whoever's behind this wouldn't have to worry about them slipping up and telling anybody about it—or about them saying anything if they ever got questioned."

He's quiet for a second, then two, then three. Finally he sighs. "You could've been one hell of a field agent," he tells me. I think he means that as a good thing.

"Yeah, well, I'm more of a pond and stream kinda guy," I tell him, "but thanks."

He's tapping his fingers against his cheek. "That would make sense," he adds. "I may even have to recommend that we institute similar measures—assuming we deal with this situation and're all still standing afterward." Then he turns back to the Mismatched Twins. "Where do you keep all the ingredients? You funnel them in through these tubes, right? But each one's got a reservoir or something, which you refill as needed?"

Both of them nod but this time Winona actually lets Reg answer. "it's these canisters right over here." He leads them to the far side of the workstation, where the tubes seem to end—or begin—at a row of larger containers, each clearly labeled: salt, sugar, shortening, chocolate, and so on.

All except the last container. It doesn't have a label.

"What's in this one?" Tall asks. Each container has a big airlock-like valve on the front, complete with an old-fashioned wheel you have to turn to cycle the door open. Tall reaches out and grabs the wheel with one hand, and I can tell he's waiting for a reply even if his tone says he's not really expecting one.

"I . . . don't know," Reg says. He looks totally bamboozled, poor guy. "That one's usually empty in case we need a spare or have overflow." He looks over at Winona. "Did you put anything in there?"

"Me? I didn't touch it!" she squawks. "But let's find out what's in this."

Everyone turns to Rosie, who nods once. "Open 'er up," she orders. "Let's find out what's really going on here."

Tall complies, hauling on the wheel and then swinging the door open. The container is half-full of something that looks like a coarse powder and is an exciting but somehow relaxing orangish-pink. It doesn't make my eyes bleed from looking at it, or start putting strange thoughts in my head, though admittedly I might have a hard time telling the difference there. It also doesn't shape itself into feet and start running around going crazy shouting "I'm alive!", which is definitely a good thing.

Though I wouldn't object to a knockoff of me. Then at least I'd have someone to play Scrabble with me, even if we keep coming up with the same words over and over.

Everybody's staring at the powder. "What is that?" Rosie asks anybody at all. "And how'n the hell'd it get here, 'cause I'll be damned if we ever put anything like that in any of our cookies!"

Mary steps over beside Tall and sniffs delicately at the open container. "It has a mildly bitter, metallic odor," she confirms, and I'm pretty sure that's at least partially for my benefit, since it's not like I can smell through this thing. That's the first thing going in my review, too. "I believe this is the mystery ingredient we detected." She produces what looks like a funky penlight and dips it into the powder, then taps a sequence of tiny buttons on the handle, making the penlight's tip glow blue. "This will give us a chemical analysis of the substance, and identify its origin if possible."

Tall turns his attention back to the CEO and her two mixers, which sounds almost like some kind of old-fogy rap group. "Next question," he grates. "Who put it here?" I can tell by the way they're quailing that he's giving Winona and Reg the hairy eyeball. "I'm betting it's one of you two." They both start sputtering protests, and Tall holds up a hand. They both stop like he stole their voices, which would be even more useful than taking people's shadows, I bet. And a lot nicer on the subway. "I know, neither of you've ever seen this before," he says. Then he sighs. "Mary," he tells my gal quietly, "we're going to need"—he shudders just a little, making the camera twitch—"a few cookies."

She hesitates for a second, then nods and turns away, leaving the penlight where it is. I watch her approach Rosie and whisper something to her, then Rosie disappears back around a corner. When she returns a few seconds later, she's got a box of Island Delights in her hand.

"Here, have a few of these, they'll calm your nerves," she tells her two employees, though she doesn't look entirely thrilled about the prospect. Both of them are happy to comply, though, and a second later they're chowing down on the caramel-coconut-chocolate yumminess—

—and, a second after that, they're chomping their way

straight into zombieland.

Once it's clear they've gone zombie, Tall tells them, "remember the first time you saw this powder, even if you were told to forget it." Both of them nod. "When was that?"

"A few minutes ago, when you opened the canister," Winona answers. But at the same time, Reg says, "six months ago, when the woman brought it to me."

Tall ignores Winona and bears down on Reg, leaning in so close I can count the poor guy's pores. Someone really ought to tell him about moisturizing cream. "Tell me about the woman."

"She introduced herself one Wednesday while I was having lunch at the Waffle House," Reg answers. "She said her grandson had given her a candy bar but she couldn't eat it because it had nuts and would I like it? Then she told me to add the powder to the cookies but not tell anyone about it, and to forget I'd done it or that it was there."

"What did she look like?" Tall asks, but Reg frowns.

"Older but still nice-looking," he replies after a second. "White hair in a bun. She had big, strong hands."

"What was her name?" The way the camera's jittering ever so slightly like a dog desperately wanting to run but ordered to sit still, Tall's gotta be quivering with anticipation. Just like those dogs.

Unfortunately, Reg shakes his head. "She never told me her name."

"Do you have any way to contact her?" Tall asks, but I can tell by his tone that he already knows the answer to that one.

Sure enough, Reg shakes his head. "Whenever I'm running

low on the powder, she somehow knows and comes to find me with more."

"Right." Tall sighs. "No name, no method of contact, a vague description—she's holding all the cards."

There's a muffled beep behind him, and Mary smiles. "Not all of them, perhaps," she argues as she sashays over to the container and retrieves her penlight doohickey. Then she holds it up right in front of her face and, I swear to God, shines the damn thing straight into her right eye! Holy crap!

It doesn't seem to hurt her any, though. And a second later she lowers the light and smiles. "It is called Jorbinate Sublimate," she explains. "It is a variant of Jorbinate, a mineral most often used in the refinement cells of certain supralight fuel cells. And according to my database there is only one place in the entire galaxy where Jorbinate can be found—the Joribau Mines."

Why do I get the feeling that's next on our whirlwind tour?

Chapter Twenty-two
Picking up the spare

"**Okay, explain to** me again why the Grays can't just beam you there?"

Tall shakes his head, dislodging a leaf that had stuck to his right temple after he sat down. The leaf apologizes and drifts away, probably looking for some other sucker to perch on. Which is good, because it was blocking part of my view. "These mines aren't anywhere they've been," he replies, using that subvocal trick again. I've got to learn how to do that, if for no other reason than it'd probably be a good idea to subvocalize most of the things I want to say to people. Instead of, y'know, just coming out and saying them like I do now. On the plus side, I rarely get wrong-number calls from the same person twice. "They can only program in a location if they've been there before."

"So they've been to the Alphabet Cookie Factory?" Somehow, that doesn't really surprise me—I can just picture the Grays bouncing around out in space, piloting their little spherical space saucers with one hand and gobbling down ChocoMints and Lemon Stripes with the other.

The sound of Tall grinding his teeth comes through the headset loud and clear. "No, they haven't been to the factory," he answers, and the good thing about him talking in his throat like this is his grinding doesn't interfere at all. "But it's on Earth, and they've been to Earth plenty of times. One planet is small enough, on a galactic scale, that tweaking the settings to put down somewhere else on it is easy."

I nod, even though I know he can't see me. Or get vertigo from my motion, which would totally serve him right. At this rate, the next time I see him in person and he starts to nod I'll probably flinch. I might even throw up my arms to brace myself for collision. "So like when you give a friend directions to your house but then it turns out you're over at another buddy's playing air hockey and you tell him to just meet you there instead and since it's only two blocks away from your house it's easy for him to adjust the directions, provided you gave him the right bus number in the first place?" True story. Who knew one bus went straight onto the LIE and kept going all the way through Manhattan and out to the Jersey Turnpike? Good thing it had a bathroom, that's all I'm saying—six hours without a potty break is a bit much for anybody, let alone some poor teenager who's sucking on a Big Gulp.

"Exactly." Tall goes quiet, and I amuse myself for a while watching the other people on the bus. Gawking is a lot easier when they can't see you staring at them, or hear you wondering how their limbs can bend like that and where those clothes fasten exactly and what they would do if confronted with a large block of Limburger and a handful of crackers. Y'know, the usual sorts of questions.

I can only stay quiet for so long, though—at least, without

the aid of some duct tape. As my kindergarten teacher quickly discovered. "Why didn't Mary and Ned come with you?" Ned had turned up right after Mary's revelation about the powder, only to admit that there wasn't any alien tech anywhere in the building. It's all completely genuine and 100% human, which feels like it's getting rarer and rarer. Anyway, when Tall announced his next stop was to investigate the mines and speak to whomever he could find, maybe get a better ID on this mystery woman, Ned and Mary had both agreed that was a good idea. But neither of them had offered to come with him, and here he was alone on the bus again.

Well, alone except for me, of course.

"They both have things of their own to do," Tall says, and he sounds almost petulant. Then he crosses his arms over his thick chest. Aw, I wonder if he's pouting, too! "I'm fully capable of handling a reconnaissance and interrogation mission on my own, you know," he says, his usually gruff voice sounding a little whiny. "I am a trained and experienced field agent, with dozens of successful cases under my belt. I don't need hand-holding!"

Yep, definitely pouting.

My initial, knee-jerk reaction is to say, "Yeah, but you aren't exactly an agent right now, are you?" I successfully manage to quash that one before it can leave my lips. Hey, look at me, thinking about what I'm saying! That definitely calls for something to drink.

My second thought is, "Sure, we know, you're top-notch. As long as there aren't any cookies around. Then you become a raving lunatic." Again, not my most helpful.

Finally I settle on an old classic:

"Okay."

Tried and true, simple but effective.

And it seems to work, because Tall stops griping. I'd still rather Ned and Mary were here, though.

Eventually the train conductor gets on the horn—not literally, his chair's actually more like a small wardrobe with clear sides all around, which I guess makes sense, since the conductor himself looks like his father was a wide-mouthed bass and his mother was an issue of *TV Guide*. The digest version. Good thing he's apparently waterproof! Anyway, his voice suddenly echoes through the train:

"We are now arriving at Galactic Center. This is the last stop on this bus. Please wait until we have come to a full and complete stop before disembarking, and make sure to check for any valuables or loved ones you might have left behind." It's nice of them to remind people like that—my Aunt Jerry used to forget my Uncle Tom on trains and buses and things all the time. At least, that's what Tom always claimed, but I always thought Aunt Jerry took an awful lot of rides, and it seemed like she'd get up and leave without him every single time. Sometimes before they'd even left the station.

When the train stops and the faint vibration fades—I know this because the camera's been shaking ever so slightly for hours, and it's been driving me crazy!—Tall rises to his feet. Slowly. No sense in rushing, after all, not with the madhouse erupting all around him. It's not like the train is going anywhere else until it turns back around.

"Okay, where to now?" I ask as Tall finally joins the thinning crowd and makes his way through the doors and out onto the platform. "Is there another bus or something?" If so, this won't be as bad as I thought.

Unfortunately, he shakes his head. "No busses—too dense." That's right, I forgot about the first time we came out, how we had to find a ship not only willing to take us to the Matrix or tough enough and powerful "We'll have to hitch a ride."

Oh, good—one disgraced MiB and one telecommuting partial duck. Who wouldn't stop for a pair like us?

Tall doesn't seem deterred, however. He marches right up to this one couple that look like somebody tried to do balloon animals using a bunch of sentient tennis balls. "Excuse me," he calls out as he closes the last few feet, "I was wondering if I could possibly get a lift? I'm heading to a place called Meribau, and my friend was supposed to come pick me up but he wound up having to work." I heard Mary tell Tall right before he left—the Grays teleported him to the Alpha Centauri train station, which helped, at least—that nobody went to Joribau, it was supposedly shut down decades back, but Meribau still maintained an active tourist trade, mostly for its summer squash, which were filled with hot lava and basically cooked themselves from the inside out, plus offered a runoff liquid that I'm told lets you breathe fire for a few minutes. I know plenty of friends' in-laws who must have a secret stash of the stuff.

The tennis balls swivel toward each other for a second, then back around to Tall. Gee, it's like staring down the barrel of an automatic server—there are just so many of them! Anyway, they all start to twist from side to side, is both fascinating and a little unnerving. I'm not sure any of my body has that much mobility, let alone all of it!

"We're only heading as far north as Epheseus V," one of them answers, the sound coming from each tennis ball at once like the world's smallest, roundest, yellowest chorus. "Afraid that's in the opposite direction. Good luck, though."

"Thanks." Tall turns away and accosts someone else, a floating flatscreen or tablet or some such. Is that a real person, or just their form of a telepresence, I wonder. Is there more of them somewhere else? If so, why send a whole tablet, and why on the bus? Why not just ship a monitor and a mic wherever they need and be done with it? And what would the telepresence of a tablet look like, anyway? Would it just be a little tablet icon on a screen somewhere? Or would the double negative somehow refract them into a real boy?

Tall clearly isn't worried about such deep philosophical questions as he asks the tablet for a lift. I'm pretty sure the sudden ringing like wind chimes is it's version of laughter, as it explains to him that even if it was going in that direction, he would never fit in its conveyance. "Though your companion might," it adds, and I swear its little camera lens swivels to focus directly on me. Eep!

Tall tries several more "people"—definite points for persistence—but each one either isn't going that way or can't fit him or is in too much of a hurry to even stop and reply politely. We're starting to run out of options—he's already exhausted the possibilities at the bus stop itself, and now he's wandered over to Red's and is asking random people in the parking lot there instead. A part of me wonders if this is such a good idea—I was always warned against hitchhiking when I was a kid, and this is hitching on an intergalactic scale, which even somebody as big and competent and scary as Tall might need to be careful about—but that part is safely sitting here watching all this from a distance and munching on some Golastian light-fries ("a tasty treat you can watch work its way through your system!"), so if he wants to stick his neck out, who'm I to argue?

"I can give you a lift out that way," a voice cuts into my inspection of the fries' progress (the feathers make them harder to see) and I glance back up at my monitor—and nearly cough up the glowing repast from sheer surprise. Because I'm looking at—

A bowling ball.

Not just any bowling ball, though. No, this one is floating at about the height of Tall's shoulder, though it quickly adjusts and ascends until it's eye level. It's one of those swirling, iridescent patterns, green but with hints of silver and blue and even purple, and as I watch I see something small and bright dart into view, like a lizard's tongue flicking out to taste the air except this nearly breaches the surface of the globe. There's a faint glow to it as well, and I don't think I'm imagining the sound of a single musical note, like the whole thing's been struck with a tuning fork. I'm pretty sure I saw this thing in a movie or three once, only it was smaller and more silvery and there were several of them and they kept popping out these nasty-looking blades and ramming into people at high speed. Less like a glowing bowling ball and more like a bunch of flying circular saw blades with artistic pretensions.

I guess Tall hasn't seen those movies, though, or he just doesn't care, because he says, "Great! Thanks! I'm Tall."

"I can see that," the Glowing Ball o' Doom agrees. "Most folks call me Heidi."

"Heidi?" Tall repeats.

"Well, high B, really, but I don't like to brag." The evil sphere chuckles at its own joke, which makes its surface turn more yellowish and causes the swirls to accelerate. "Come on."

Why is it, I wonder as Tall follows the clearly demonic globe across the parking lot, that a lot of the aliens we've met have what I'd consider to be Southern or Midwestern accents? Is it because all our old TV shows got broadcast out into space, so all of these aliens have seen shows like *Gunsmoke* and *Bonanza* and *Maverick* and use those as references when dealing with humans? Is it just my ear, translating their actual dialogue into something I can understand and using the old movies and TV shows I watched as a kid for a guide? Or is Dixie really some kind of universal language?

And another thing—why do the smallest people, things, recreational equipment, whatever always have the largest vehicles? I wonder this as "Heidi" stops beside what I at first think is some kind of small fortress, or maybe the biggest, most impressively fortified valet station ever built. And then he spins counterclockwise, brightens through a series of lights like a one-ball Simple Simon, and the giant iron-black edifice beeps and a section of it slides open. Heidi doesn't hesitate, it just floats up and in.

It's like the intergalactic equivalent of the tiny little old lady driving the mammoth pickup truck and barely being able to see over the steering wheel. Which always allows a real clear view of the shotguns and hunting rifles mounted on the rack across the truck cab's rear window. There's a reason everybody waves politely and gets out of the way when Granny Deerstalker comes barreling through.

"You sure this is a good idea?" I ask Tall as he grabs a hand-hold along the side—which looks an awful lot like the kind of heavy manacle you see in medieval dungeons in all those "knights and adventurers battle evil wizards and demons and the Devil" sorts of movies—and begins to haul himself up. "Climbing into a death machine the size of a small planet with a crazed bowling ball you barely know?"

"He offered me a ride," Tall replies under his breath, saving most of his energy for the climb. "Besides, I can take care of myself."

Sure, I think as he reaches the opening and maneuvers through it, the camera showing me nothing but blackness within. So could the Old Man in the Sea. He still got swallowed by a whale.

Or was that Jonah? Or Geppetto? I get them all mixed up.

Chapter Twenty-three
Traveling light . . . speed, that is!

"So," Heidi asks once Tall's strapped in. "What's taking you all the way out to Meribau?" Now that the camera's had a chance to adjust I can see that this oversized ship isn't just a big empty shell containing some kind of deep, dark void. Tall's sitting next to Heidi in an actual cabin or cockpit or whatever you call that part of the ship, and it's . . . nice.

If you like black velvet.

Which Heidi the Chatty Bowling Ball apparently does.

Seriously, I feel like I've been transported to an 80s disco lounge. Or a 70s strip club. And why is it that's the second time something else has made me think of strip clubs? I've got a girl-friend, damn it! Maybe it's just a holdover from the fact that I was pretty much banned from every club in Manhattan, and a few in the outer boroughs, as well. The official reason is because my noggin's so big it blocks everybody else's view. Personally, I think they're still pissed about that one guy, but he kept shoving past me to stuff bills into Lindsay's G-string and she kept tell-ing him to back off and he was seriously annoying me, and it's not like his arm didn't heal eventually, even if it hangs a little crooked now. Serves him right, anyway, for telling me "Back off,

Donald, or I find Daisy and turn her into a Peking dish" when I told him he was bothering Lindsay.

Anyway, the cabin's not big, maybe the size of my living room, ceiling's maybe seven feet up, the chairs are more like zero-g lounge chairs, there are panels and screens and displays and stuff all along the front, and everything except the actual monitors and buttons and gauges is covered in black velvet.

I feel like I'm sitting in a giant Victorian waistcoat.

Tall, of course, doesn't sound the least bit concerned as he replies, "I hear they've got a killer summer squash." Dude, if you try eating one of those and melt your internal organs you're on your own. I am all in favor of new culinary experiences, but being turned into a convection oven? I'll pass.

"Yeah, it's good stuff," Heidi agrees. "Great for those cold nights, too, really warms you up." It swivels toward Tall and there's a second of silence. "You, you might wanna give it a few minutes to cool down before you try it. Poke a hole in the top to let the steam out—that's one of the best parts, but you'd do yourself some serious damage if you tried inhaling that."

Wait, what? Is Heidi the Wrecking Ball is now giving food advice? He/she/it doesn't even have a mouth! What's he do, squash it flat—yeah, yeah—and then roll around on top of it like a pig wallowing in its mud or a dog who's found something good and stinky?

Sometimes, despite what anybody else might suggest, I think I think too much.

Yuck.

"Thanks, I'll keep that in mind," Tall replies, and damned

if he doesn't sound like he's seriously grateful for the tip. Then again, I've seen Tall eat—if anybody's gonna go trying to actually consume a miniature volcano disguised as a harvest vegetable, it'd be him. "You've actually been there, then? Can you drop me at Meribau itself, or just somewhere nearby? Either way, I appreciate it." This is about the most un-gruff I've ever seen Tall—or at least heard him, since the only reflective surfaces in here are Heidi itself and the various consoles and screens, and all that dark upholstery and dim lighting is making everything really muted and distorted—and I can't tell if it's just because he's tired or because he's playing along or because he's suspended and so definitely not on the job, or some combination thereof. Or maybe he's just happier talking to people who don't have their own faces. Or hands. Or clavicles. I don't know.

"Sure, I can take you to Meribau," Heidi says. "You'll want Meribau City, I'm guessing, that's where most of the tourist trade is." Its surface suddenly shades a bit darker, and more purplish. "Now, you'd better hang onto something."

And then the whole disco lounge . . . shimmies. That's about the only way I can describe it. There's a low hum, like a growl but more pleasant, maybe a big dog warming up, and the entire cabin sort of blurs and seems to shift a little to the right. And keeps shifting. It's like it's always just a little to the right of where I'm looking, somehow, like a pencil that keeps rolling just out of reach, or a little kid hiding in your shadow and stepping back fast enough that you never quite catch a glimpse of him as you turn, but you almost see an afterimage of him a few times. This is a whole lot like that, actually, including being just as maddening.

The Bowling Ball O' Doom is obviously used to this, however. It's the only thing in the place that isn't blurry right now, and it's glowing mostly blue. I can't help thinking that means it's content. Or maybe just moody. "Should be to Meribau in about an hour, the way you judge things," it says. "You are human, right?"

"I am." I can tell from his voice that Tall's having trouble adjusting to the weird shimmying, too.

"Right. And judging from your suit, I'm betting I know who you work for." Tall hasn't exactly had time to change his clothes since busting out of MiB prison. Then again, I'm not entirely he owns anything but black suits. I think I may have seen him in a charcoal pinstripe once, but I could've been hallucinating. Or maybe it was laundry day. "So what's a MiB want with Meribau? And don't tell me it's 'cause you're suddenly a wee bit peckish."

"Ah." Tall clears his throat, coughs, clears his throat again. Damn. The guy may be an incredibly competent field agent, like he said, and Lord knows he's saved my butt any number of times, and not just because I keep almost sticking my tongue into various electrical outlets, but one thing he's not good at? Lying.

Me, on the other hand, I'm an expert. I once convinced an entire group of freshmen that my name was Joe, or Fred, or Brad, or Bill, or Mike, or Brady, or Nick—I told each kid it was something different, and then answered to that name for them from then on. Kept that going for about two weeks before I ran into several of them at once, the predictable chaos ensued, and the gig was up. It was worth it for the looks on their faces when they started arguing over my name, and the awe when they realized I'd kept twelve names straight for that long. Yet somehow I can never remember the right temperature settings for my laundry. Go figure.

"Tell him you're investigating a suspicious message," I urge Tall. "Tell him somebody threatened to blow up the Earth, and you tracked it back to Meribau, and that's why they sent you. Tell him that!"

Tall clears his throat again, but before he can speak the floating death-globe cuts him off. "That's a swell story, and I'd sure love to hear how it plays out," it says, strobing in purple again, "but how's about you try the real deal? And without any help this time?" And that flickering shape within it darts into view again, making the whole sphere look like a great big eyeball—looking right at me.

"Oh . . . uh . . . hi," I say, since it's obvious this thing can hear me, or pick up my frequency, or sense my presence, or whatever.

"And who might you be?" It asks. Yep, it can hear me.

"They call me DuckBob," I answer, and I can't help injecting a little John Wayne into that. Hey, the Duke never would've let a bowling ball stare him down!

"Heidi, nice to meetcha," it says back. "And you're just along for the ride? What, to keep this big fella out of trouble? You his boss?"

"Boss, no," I answer hurriedly, before Tall can reach through the camera and choke me. Trust me, he'd find a way to do it. "Just his bud, looking out for him. It's a big bad universe out there."

"Sure is," Heidi says. "So, you wanna tell me the honest truth, this time?"

Tall takes a deep breath, and I just know what he's gonna say before he says it. Sure enough, the next thing I hear is: "You want the truth? Fine. I'm not actually going to Meribau at all. I'm going to Joribau."

Heidi goes purple again—I'm starting to think that means it's laughing. "Well, why didn't you say so in the first place? Hang on!" It turns a quick sequence of colors and the whole room spins. Literally. Then it's shimmying again, but now a little less to the right and a little more back toward the corner. "There, that's fixed it. So, what's on Joribau? Can't say's I've ever been there—didn't think anyone had, anymore."

"I need to get to the Joribau Mines," Tall tells him, and at least he sounds like his old take-charge-but-no-prisoners self again. "Someone's been messing around there, and I'm going to find out who they are and what they've been up to."

"Righty-ho." Heidi's surface shifts back to mostly blue. "Well, thanks for being honest with me. And I'm tickled, to be truthful—like I said, ain't never been to Joribau, so I'm eager to see what all the fuss's about."

They settle into silence then for a bit, which would drive me nuts if not for the fact that I can sit and play a video game while I'm waiting for something to happen to Tall or because of him. Right now I'm doing a first-person shooter, except that you "shoot" descriptive phrases and whatever you hit, it takes on that quality—so, for example, when I need to get through a wall

I "load" the word "ephemeral" and fire it, and then I just walk on through. The game's called Empirical Override. It's nice to know all those big words I learned from reading comic books are finally paying off.

Eventually, Tall breaks the silence, which surprises me— usually he's the one who sits there stoically, and I'm the one who says pretty much anything that pops into my head just to fill that awful gap. Of course, that's pretty much me all of the time. And usually that's after like two minutes, three if I get distracted by something shiny. Hey, I come from a big family—if it's quiet that means somebody's up to no good and probably messing with my stuff. This has been about half an hour, which I guess is Tall's limit or maybe he just figures he should make polite conversation. Either way, good to know.

"So, what do you do, exactly?" he asks Heidi. Wow, way to make a casual question sound like an interrogation, big guy! What's next, you gonna ask him where he was on the night in question, and whether anybody can corroborate his story?

But Heidi doesn't seem offended by the question. At least, his color doesn't change any. "I'm a trucker," he answers—I don't know at what point he went from an "it" to a "he" in my head, but somehow he has, and now it's stuck and I can't think of him as anything else. Weird. "Long hauls, mostly, though I'll do short runs if the pay's good enough."

"Really? What sort of cargo?" Again, I'm picturing Tall recording this for analysis later, or at least jotting down notes on a little pad. If this is casual conversation for him, it's no wonder he doesn't make a lot of friends outside work! I shudder to think what his pickup lines are like: "You there, what's your dress size, your favorite food, your astrological sign, and your mother's maiden name? Stat!" I'm sure that works wonders—though it might explain why Jones was chatting him up so awkwardly. Ew.

"Oh, anything and everything," Heidi says. "I've hauled food an' booze an' livestock an' furniture an' medical supplies an' ship parts an' stuff I'd've said was plain ol' junk 'cept the client was payin' good money for it. I draw the line at drugs, firearms, basically anything that might be illegal wherever I'm takin' it—that just ain't worth the trouble. As long as it's legal, though, I'm happy to take it from Point A to Point B."

"Wow, you're a regular connect-the-dots," I mutter, and then curse under my breath when he swivels around to "look" at me again. He's flickering violet, though, so I'm guessing he's more amused than offended. Phew! Not that he could do anything to me anyway, but I don't much like the idea of him getting annoyed and jettisoning Tall as a result. Midflight.

"That doesn't sound so bad," Tall admits, and there's a wistfulness to his voice that I've only ever heard before when he's wondered what his life would have been like if he'd never met me. "I bet you get to see a lot of different places and people."

"Oh, you betcha." I swear, Heidi's accent is shifting faster than his color scheme. "And I work when I want, for as long as I want—if I decide to take a break, I do, until I'm bored or broke or both. I'm my own boss, and that suits me just fine."

Tall nods and starts to say something, I think, but he gets interrupted as a loud noise blares through the cabin and all the monitors go bright red. "What's going on?"

"I'll tell you what's going on!" Heidi snaps back, turning chartreuse for half a second, and the biggest monitor right in front clears and shows a section of space filled with stars and with a single solar system expanding toward us rapidly. There's only two planets swimming around an anemic-looking little star, and one of 'em's got a series of concentric circles superimposed on it—I'm guessing that's Joribau.

It's also the one that's got something shooting away from it and heading right for us.

"We're under attack!" Heidi shouts. "Looks like whoever you're looking for, they know we're comin', and they ain't too keen on visitors!"

Great, I think as I watch those glittering shapes zoom closer on the monitor. Just once, couldn't we meet the intergalactic equivalent of my old Aunt Sadie? Some harmless little alien who offers us pickled herring and crackers and matzo ball soup whenever we knock on the door? Though, admittedly, Sadie's herring was sometimes lethal. Each of her three husbands never knew what hit him. And the third one disappeared mysteriously, right around pickling season. We stopped visiting Aunt Sadie right after that, or least we always claimed we'd just eaten and couldn't manage another bite.

Chapter Twenty-four
I'll swallow you whole!

"You got any weapons on this rig?" Tall demands, and I can't help thinking of that scene in *Star Wars*, where the Tie Fighters are after the *Millennium Falcon* and Han and Luke each head to one of the gun turrets and start picking them off. I bet Tall's hoping for something like that, too—I happen to know that under that stuffed shirt and cheap suit beats the heart of a true-blue fanboy. That's gotta be at least one of the reasons he became a MiB in the first place, the chance to play with alien ray guns and ride in spaceships. And, y'know, write off sunglasses as a work expense.

Unfortunately for him, it seems Heidi never saw that movie. "'Course I got weapons," he snaps, going a splotchy red for a second. "What'd you think, you were dealing with some green-horn?" Greenhorn? Really? Does Heidi even know what that term means? Hell, I'm not entirely sure I know what it means, or at least where it came from, and I rock at Scrabble. Mainly because I still maintain that onomatopoeia is completely legit. "Thwppt" for the win! Regardless, Heidi flashes through a rapid sequence of colors, and then there's a whooshing sound from the back of the cabin as a panel opens, and out come—

—more bowling balls.

Seriously, for a second I feel like I took a wrong turn somewhere and wound up in a ball return. Which I've done a few times, back in my college days, but never completely sober.

Though, admittedly, the bowling balls never floated in midair the way these do. Except that one time, and we were *really* wasted then.

My first thought, after reassuring myself that I'm not just having flashbacks, is that Heidi's called in reinforcements and teleported in a whole bunch of siblings and cousins. They're all the same size he is, after all, and they all have that same glow about them, and the swirly patterning. But then I realize the glow on these is a lot dimmer, and the colors don't change and shift the way he does.

And none of them seem to have a giant armored slug or whatever that is living inside.

"So, what, you've got spares?" I ask. I'm not even sure how that'd work, to be honest, mainly because I have no idea how he works. Is he the bowling ball himself, or just what's inside it?

"Something like that," he confirms, and he's shaded a pale pink. Am I crazy, or is the bowling ball blushing? "These're old shells," he says less boisterously than anything else I've heard from him so far. "They can only take the pressure and the heat for so long afore they start getting unresponsive, so then I've got to change out to a fresh one." Now he's a brighter pink. "I meant to toss these, but just keep forgetting."

"So, wait, you want to fling your discards at them?" I shake my head—it's getting so I keep forgetting I'm not in the cabin with them and they can't actually see me. "This is eerily like flicking toenail clippings at somebody, which is taking me all the way back to junior high." Hey, at least I used clippers—some of the other guys weren't so considerate. Or so tidy. "And how's this gonna help, exactly? I don't think whoever's shooting at us—at you—is in the mood for a swap meet."

The pink turns purple. "Oh, trust me, they're about to get a whole lot more than they bargained for." He whistles, and the main monitor closes in on those fast-approaching objects. Which, now that we can see them better, look an awful lot like lawn darts. Only I'm guessing they're probably a bit bigger, and moving a lot faster. And trust me, getting pelted with a regular old lawn dart hurts plenty!

"I count five, that look right?" Heidi asks, and I study the screen. So does Tall, I guess, because he answers before me.

"Five it is." Show off. He knows numbers aren't my strong suit.

"Right, then!" If Heidi had hands, he'd be rubbing them together right now. Instead he whistles, and clicks, and five of those other spheres converge on him. They ring around him, each one touching his own shell, and then—

Okay, this is gonna sound weird.

I mean, weirder than floating bowling balls and zombie-inducing cookies.

But it looks, for just a second, like the thing inside Heidi— which I'm beginning to suspect *is* Heidi—taps the glass against each of those other globes in turn—

—and, well, *breathes* on them.

I can actually hear the exhalation each time, like somebody blowing out heavily. But in each case, when it happens, the colors swirl within that other sphere and the glow around it brightens.

Almost like he's actually breathing *into* them, through both his globe and that one.

Like I said, weird.

It works, though, because when he's done the five other globes line up in front of Heidi, and it's clear they're more responsive now.

Then he flickers some more—it makes sense that he'd have rigged his ship controls to be color-sensitive, and I'm already starting to get used to it—and another panel slides open, this one in the front just below the main console. The globes head for that, and file in one by one. When the last one's in the panel shuts again, and all's quiet.

Until we hear a *whump*.

Shit, they got hit! But no, the monitor's still showing five dart-like missiles streaking toward them.

And now one swirling glass globe heading straight for one of those missiles.

Ah.

There's another *whump*, and another, and another, and one more, and after each one another sphere appears on the screen. All five of them are out there now, and each one targets a different missile, locking on and heading right for it.

I'm not quite sure what a glowing bowling ball can do to stop a lawn-dart missile, but I get the feeling I'm about to find out. And Heidi looks pretty confident—he's a clear sky-blue again, and I'm pretty sure he's humming to himself.

The first sphere closes on its missile, and Heidi says, "Okay, here we go." And we watch as the sphere and the missile zoom toward each other, the missile's tip looking set to puncture or shatter the globe's glass surface, but instead—

—it passes right through it.

The rest of the missile follows, the whole thing flowing into the sphere like it was made of water instead of glass. But then the missile's tip touches the sphere's other side from within—

—and it explodes.

The flash is bright enough to make me wince and to cause my nictating membranes to slide into place—hey, I'm not being gross, go look it up! They're like built-in goggles or sunglasses— and I see Tall's hand come up to shield his eyes, too. Guess he's missing those sunglasses right about now. We don't hear anything, of course, since sound doesn't travel through space— something I learned from watching 2001, thanks very much— but the important thing is, the ship doesn't rock back from the shockwave or anything. The other globes don't get tossed about, either. In fact, it looks like that explosion didn't go anywhere.

Somehow, the bowling ball contained the whole thing.

Now that sphere's glowing bright as a mini-star—it's not swirling or anything, and it's a steady yellowish white, but it's still more than any reading lamp I ever had—and it swoops about and heads back toward us.

"Uh, are you sure that's a good idea?" I ask. "What if it's radioactive now or something?"

"It'll be fine," Heidi promises, and he sounds completely relaxed. "My shells are made to hold energy, and they can take a lot more than those little things can dish out."

"I thought you said these were your cast-offs," Tall points out. "Doesn't that mean they have diminished capacity now?"

"Sure, but not for energy absorption." Heidi sighs. "They don't respond as well to commands, and they don't color-shift as easily—which you probably guessed could cause me all kinds of trouble." He chuckles. "One time I waited too long to swap spheres and I got locked out of the ship! There I was, hovering by the airlock, trying to go chartreuse, and all I was getting was rose and a little dull amber. Took me two hours afore I finally coaxed the right shade out of the darn thing!"

There's a mild *thunk* from the front, and Tall turns to look—allowing me to do the same—as that front panel slides open again and that first bowling ball sails back in. Up close it's even brighter, throwing lots of big shadows around the cabin and making the black velvet shimmer like a waterfall.

"Come here, my pretty," Heidi coos at it, and the globe obediently drifts over to him. "Now, what've you got inside, exactly?" They tap surfaces, and the slug-thing makes another appearance. I think it flicked a long, thin, forked tongue out to taste the other globe's contents, but I'm trying hard not to think about that. "Hm, interesting! That's a lot of energy for a simple missile!"

Something clicks in my head. "Hey, maybe it's Jorbinate!" I suggest. "That's what they mine down there, right? And it's used for fuel cells?"

If Tall could turn around and look at me right now, I bet he would. "Just when I think you're an idiot, you say the darnedest thing," he mutters, but nods. "That's probably exactly what it is. Makes sense they'd have the stuff laying around, why not use it?"

Heidi's alternating blue and green. "Ooh, yeah, that would do it," he agrees happily. "I don't think they use Jorbinate anymore—there were some problems with it being unstable under certain conditions, if I remember rightly—but as long as that didn't happen it was supposed to be some primo stuff."

"Unstable under certain conditions, but otherwise great?" I repeat, mostly to myself. "Isn't that like 'a single bite could kill you, but if it doesn't it tastes amazing'? There's a reason I've never tried fugu. That, and it's pretty much like buying a brand-new car just to have dinner—I'll stick with 'fish that doesn't kill you or bankrupt you' for a hundred, Alex."

"He talks funny, doesn't he?" Heidi asks Tall.

"You have no idea." Gee, thanks. Nice to know you've got my back, big guy.

To change the subject—and because it just occurs to me that it's been awfully quiet and drama-free for a few seconds, which is definitely out of the norm given recent events—I say, "Hey, weren't there five missiles out there?"

"There sure were." Heidi's gaze swivels around to the monitor—it's scary that I can tell that—and I look over there too, just in time to see the last globe swallow the last missile, contain its detonation, and go spotlight bright. "Looks like more dinner for Papa!" It's like getting shot at's the best things that's happened to him all week.

"Glad you could get something for your trouble," Tall tells him, and he doesn't even sound grudging about it, which really shouldn't surprise me. He's actually pretty good about wanting to see people get rewarded for their work. He's super-conscientious about tipping delivery guys, too. So am I, actually, but that's because I've done that job and I know how much it sucks to truck a whole bunch of food up a fifth-floor walk-up in the pouring rain, only to have the guy stiff you or, worse, give you like five cents or something. Those're the people you really hope order again, because then they're probably getting some kind of surprise along with their food. "Can we pinpoint where those missiles came from?" He cracks his knuckles ominously. And no, that's not a given—I've seen him crack his knuckles humorously, angrily, resignedly, and even ironically a few times. It's a talent. "I think it's time I had a little chat with whoever sent them."

Chapter Twenty-five
Earthworms are easy

Heidi has no problem tracking the missiles—also known as "lunch," for him—back to their launch point. He brings his ship right over that spot, and offers to beam Tall down to the surface.

"I'm gonna stay up here, if'n it's all the same to you," he says as he parks the ship over Joribau—even from here the planet looks like just a big, dull rock. "I'd hate to get in your way, and this way I can have the ship ready to go when you've got what you needed. 'Sides"—he pats one of the blinding spheres nestled beside him—"I want to get better acquainted with my new supplies." The way he says that is totally smarmy, and I have this sudden, horrible image of him cozying up to the sphere in question, a wine glass in one hand and a cigarette in the other, telling her how pretty she is and not to worry and what a big, scary universe it is out there and how he'll protect her from all those bad people, she just has to stay close to him and keep him happy. Wow, I think I just creeped myself out.

"That's fine," Tall replies, and I have no idea if he got the same mental image I did—probably not, he's told me before I've got a knack for conjuring the most twisted images possible, and for once I haven't shared—but if so you can't tell at all from his voice. It's full-on brusque—he's definitely in get-in-and-get-it-done mode.

"Here." Heidi whistles, and a little thing pops out of the console. It looks like a button or a sticker, small and round and mostly flat, but the surface is the same iridescent swirl as his shell. I try not to think about that too closely. Ugh. "It's a short-range communicator—good enough for here to surface, and a little below, but if'n you're going deep down you'll need to climb again afore it can reach me. Just tap it and talk and if you're still in range I'll hear you and beam you back up." He strobes blue and green and a little orange. "Good luck!"

"Thanks." Tall slaps the sticker on his shirt cuff, where his jacket'll hide it from view, and nods. Then Heidi flickers and suddenly everything turns blue and grey and white before vanishing into a haze. That fades back out a second later, and we're definitely not on his ship anymore.

I was right, I think, looking around—Joribau's a dump. There's nothing but rock here, all around. Rock, rock, and more rock. And it's all brown, or orangey-brown, or reddish brown, or reddish-orangey brown. I feel like I've finally found where all those unwanted Burnt Sienna and Burnt Umber crayons go to die. Joy.

There's lots of nooks and crannies and valley and peaks, at least. This place'd be ten times worse if it was that much brown *and* perfectly flat. Instead I feel like I'm back in Arizona, on my way to the Grand Canyon and already admiring all the mesas and plateaus and weirdly carved rocks. Only the sky here's not a nice, cheery blue. It's not anything, really. There's just space and the stars out beyond. Which is weird.

"Where's the sky?" I ask Tall. "And if there isn't one, how're you breathing?"

"Same way you would be if you were here," he replies absently as he scans the area. "Those nanites."

Oh, right. I forgot that, when we first met up, Mary injected us both with nanites. They let our bodies convert elemental particles into oxygen so we can breathe anywhere, even in outer space. Turns out there's lots of space dust and stuff out there for the micro-machines to latch onto. It's the Space Dust Diet! And doesn't that sound all kinds of unappealing.

"Okay, where's this guy we need?" This limited color palette's starting to get to me already. I need more variety in my life. That's also why I have eight different types of mustard in the fridge—you just never know whether you're gonna be in a plain-yellow or spiced-brown or flower-infused mauve sort of mood. Of course I can't see that last one anymore, but I can still taste it. Figuring out when to order a new jar's a bitch, though.

There's no sign of anyone but us here—nobody coming over to say hi, nobody running at us with guns blazing, not even anyone yelling at us to cut out all the racket—and Tall hits the same realization I do, because he says "He must be underground—it's a mine, after all," a half-second after I think it. Hey, maybe I'm somehow pushing my thoughts at him through the camera mic? I try thinking "I want to dance the watusi right now!" at him as hard as I can, but when he turns and starts walking toward one cluster of rocks and a dark opening in their midst there's no hint of dance to his steps. Would it kill him to do one little twirl? For me?

But no, he's walking as solidly and soldierly as usual as he heads into what proves to be a cave or a cavern—I can never remember the difference, and I learned years back that my original guess of "it's a cave with an urn in it!" wasn't right—or maybe just the mouth to a tunnel. There's no light, of course, but Tall, always prepared, pulls a tiny flashlight out of his pocket and we're good to go.

"So, who do you think is down here?" I ask him as he tromps along. The flashlight's only providing enough light to see a few paces in front of him, really, which is good for not stubbing your toe or falling into a pit but not so great for figuring out what's around the next bend or just how far this rough corridor—because it's starting to look more like that than a simple cave—goes.

"No idea," he answers, going for as few words as possible, as always. "But I aim to find out."

'Aim to find out'? What's next, 'you're darned tootin'? I think Heidi's starting to rub off on him. Which might not be a bad thing—Tall'd probably benefit from a more colorful vocabulary. Though I'm pretty sure they'd fine him or something if he used phrases like that at work.

He walks on for a bit, with me trying to stay quiet so we can both listen for any noises up ahead, and it's definitely a tunnel now—the walls are mostly straight up and down, the floor is reasonably level, and there're thick beams supporting the ceiling. Small globes perch in the corners of those beams, and for a second I think Heidi's sent his drones down to check on us, or maybe we've found his old storage locker, but as we get close to one I see it's just a floodlight, the kind you'd mount on a garage door. Or in a long, dark tunnel.

"I don't suppose we can switch the lights on?" I ask quietly. Not that I'm afraid of the dark or anything, and I'm not even there, really, but this whole "can't see ahead of you" thing is really bugging me.

"Maybe," Tall admits after a second, "but then whoever's here would know we're coming."

Oh, right. That'd be bad. I resign myself to staring at Tall's feet and the ground right ahead of them.

More trudging. The tunnel twists a little here and there, and I think it's going down—I remember what Heidi said about that, and hope we aren't going to need to be picked up in a hurry. Not much we can do about it, though. It's not like Tall's gonna stop until he finds who he's looking for.

Finally, after more than two hours—for once it not only feels like hours, it's actually been hours, according to my watch—the floor levels out a bit. And maybe it's just wishful thinking but the area up ahead doesn't look quite as dark. Like there's a light somewhere a little farther out—the proverbial light at the end of the tunnel.

I just hope it's not a train.

Tall must see it too, because he switches off his flashlight, tucks it back away—and draws one of his pistols instead. "Don't make a sound," he warns under his breath, and he creeps forward, gun up and held in both hands.

And for once, I do what he says. Just to prove I can. And

because I've already had Heidi be able to hear me. If whoever's down here can too, I don't want to be the one that gives away where Tall is.

Yeah yeah, I'm a soft touch when it comes to my friends. As long as they don't want to borrow money. Or my car. Or my girlfriend. Or split a beer—somehow, you're always the one that gets stuck with nothing but backwash. But I'd give a friend the shirt off my back, if he really wanted it—though usually they're just as happy to have a clean one out of the drawer.

I do draw the line at my boxers, though.

Anyway, Tall edges ahead, and now there's definitely a light there. Enough so I can see there's a bend in the tunnel, and the light's coming from around the corner. Tall pauses right before it, back against the wall, gun at chest level, breathing a little heavy, and I know he's prepping himself for the classic heroic dash-around-the-corner moment. Better him than me. I'm more of an ellipses fan, really.

Sure enough, he bursts into action, leaping around the corner and leveling his gun immediately at—

—a Jacuzzi.

Okay, not what I expected.

Nor is the guy soaking in it, who looks up in surprise, gulps, and slumps down so he disappears under the water.

Yes, it's a Jacuzzi. Or at least a knockoff brand, but it's the classic big round standing tub, with wood paneling around the sides and what really looks like a fiberglass shell within, filled almost to the brim with steaming-hot water.

Though, admittedly, most of the people you see in those

things?

Don't look like earthworms.

I mean, really look like them—the glimpse I had of this guy before he submerged showed a bald, pink head, completely cylindrical and then tapering at the top, with rings around it like it's segmented. When Tall marches over to the tub and hauls him back up, I see I was right. Yep, he looks like an earthworm. With eyes, admittedly, imbedded deep in the folds, though it looks like the mouth's still a circular ring up top. Arms, too, long and almost tentacular—which creates some really interesting results if you type it in and use AutoCorrect, you should try it sometime but probably not while texting your old biology teacher—but no legs, just the body continuing down. He's like a snake-man, but earthworm instead. Weird.

Though I suppose it makes a certain amount of sense for somebody who lives in an underground mine. I wonder if he can tunnel his way through solid rock?

Not that Tall's taking a chance on that. He's got the guy out of the tub and up against a wall before I can say "Holy bathing earthworm, Batman!", with one hand firmly around the guy's . . . neck?

"Talk," he snaps, and Mr. Wriggly just cringes. And drips.

Then the whining starts.

"Please," he gasps, and it takes me a second to realize he's talking out of that enlarged blowhole, too. "Please don't hurt me! I didn't do anything wrong!"

"This mine was decommissioned years ago," Tall points out harshly, "and you just shot at our ship!"

"Oh." Wormy deflates a little. "Well, except for that."

"And you've been supplying mind-control powder to take over Earth," I supply, and I'm both relieved and a little hurt when he doesn't react. Guess he doesn't have Heidi's . . . whatever lets him hear me directly. "Pump him for info, big guy," I urge Tall instead.

"Don't worry, I've got this," he mutters back, then shakes Earthworm Man. "Who do you work for?"

Cringe, cringe. Whine, whine: "Please, I just do what I'm told!"

"And what were you told?" Tall tries. Ooh, good one! Especially since Bio Experiment One actually answers—guess he wasn't told not to:

"I prep the powder, ship it, and scare off anybody who gets too close." I've got to admit, I've had jobs that were a lot less well-defined. I wonder what kind of benefits he gets?

"And who told you do that?" Tall asks next.

"I—can't say," Long and Bendy whimpers.

Tall shakes him a bit. "You can, and you will," he snarls. "It's just a question of what happens to you between now and then."

I don't think I've ever seen an earthworm turn pale before. Which makes sense, since it's not like I study them a lot. Usually I only see them on fishing hooks, and if they quake and quail right before they're pierced, I've never noticed. This guy, though, it's hard to miss. Not that I blame him, entirely. Tall's really good at the intimidation thing.

But why am I hearing bubbling?

I look around, but of course my field of vision's limited by the way Tall's facing. "Hey, Tall, look around for a sec, would you?" I ask. He does, and I scan the area. Ah, it's just the Jacuzzi—I guess El Wormo Supremo had the temperature set to scalding, and now it's boiling over a bit. I prefer mine a little less like a crockpot, personally, but to each his own. "Okay, thanks—back to the interrogation."

He nods and zones back in on his captive, who's now even paler and wriggling just like the aforementioned worms on hooks. "No, please," he's saying, but he doesn't seem to be looking at Tall anymore. Instead I think he's gazing over the big guy's shoulder. "You've got to let me go! It's not safe!"

"What's not safe?" Tall demands. "Is somebody coming to save you? I'd like to see them try!"

"No," The Wormster replies, still looking past Tall. "We're all going to die unless you let me go right now!"

Something in his voice tells me the guy's not kidding. "Let him go, man," I tell Tall quietly. He doesn't budge. "Seriously, let him go. If it's nothing, you can just thrash him again." That works, and he drops the dude on the ground, where he only lays for a second before bursting past us—right toward the Jacuzzi.

And then he starts to panic.

"No, oh no!" He's wailing and carrying on like it's the end of the world. Maybe his soap's melted away or something? "We're all doomed!"

"What do you mean?" Tall asks. No answer, so he grabs The Worm's arm and yanks him around. "Talk!"

"It's the humidity," Mr. Worm moans. "Jorbinate can't take high humidity. It gets unstable. If that happens—"

"—the whole place could blow," I finish for him.

Tall gets the picture, and his grip on the guy tightens. "Then why in the nine hells do you have a Jacuzzi in here?" he asks in a deadly soft voice.

Worm-boy goes completely still. Blinks. Then whispers, "It's my skin. I've got eczema. I need to soak or I itch like crazy."

"And for that you've killed us?" I wonder aloud. "What, you've never heard of lotion?"

Tall's still got Sir Worm by the arm, only now he's hauling him back the way we came. "Come on," he says. "We're getting out of here. How long before it blows?"

The earthworm's trembling in his grip but trying to keep up, and I actually feel for the guy. Eczema's no joke, really. "An hour, maybe two," he gasps. "Could be a little more."

And we're about two hours below the surface. Swell.

Tall picks up his pace.

There's not a lot of talking on the way back. Though, after a few minutes of stumbling, I do ask whether our unplanned companion knows how to turn on the lights—Tall relays that, the guy nods and stops long enough to open a panel built into one of the beams, types in a code and pushes a button, and now we can see. That helps, and Tall breaks into a controlled jog, pretty much dragging Señor Worm behind him.

About an hour in, I tell him to start calling up to Heidi.

He tries at ten-minute intervals after that. It takes another three tries before he gets a response.

"Yeah, I hear you, keep your shirt on!" Oh great, we must have interrupted his mid-day meal. "You need me to pull you out?"

"Me and one other," Tall agrees. "He's right next to me, a foot to my right." He's let go of the guy, I notice, which is probably for the best—I'm getting flashbacks to *The Fly*, and I don't really want to see Tall and the earthworm-dude merged together. Especially since there's no telling where my camera would end up if that happened. Uck.

There's that flash of blue and gray and white again, and then we're back on Heidi's ship.

"Get us out of here!" Tall snaps, dropping onto one of the chairs. The earthworm just kinda curls up in the corner. At least he's dry now, and he's right, his skin does look really flaky and irritated.

"What's going on?" Heidi asks, but he's already warming the ship up.

"The whole planet's going to explode, that's what's going on!" I shout. "Like, any second now!"

Heidi freezes, and he flashes pure white. "The whole planet? All the Jorbinate?"

"It's unstable at high humidity," Tall explains. Heidi hasn't budged. "What?"

Our bowling-ball buddy answers slowly. "That much Jorbinate," he says finally, "all that energy, the chain reaction . . . we'd never be able to get far enough away in time. Sorry, buckos." He's gone yellow, a pale dandelion yellow that runs down in sheets through him. I can't help but think he's crying.

"Now, hang on," I tell him, as much to stop that display as anything else, "there's got to be a way out of this. We've gotten out of impossible scrapes before, right?"

But Heidi's still flashing. "We're just not fast enough," he says again. "Nothing is. That blast'll vaporize everything within a light-year."

Oh, crap. "Uh . . . how close is that other planet over there?" I ask.

"You mean Meribau?" Heidi does this bobble thing I'm guessing is a shrug. "Maybe a hundred million miles."

Great. So not only are we—well, Tall and Heidi and the Worm That Whines Like a Man—about to die, but so is an entire planet?

No, I decide. Not on my watch. Which doesn't make much sense, really, because if all of them could fit on the face of my vintage PacMan watch—it really plays!—I wouldn't have to worry about where to put them. But whatever, you know what I mean. I can't let this happen.

But how do we stop it?

We can't stop the planet from blowing up. And we can't get far enough away in time. So what's the alternative?

We've gotta find a way to contain the blast.

"Heidi," I shout. "Your shells. How many've you got stashed away?"

"Uh . . ." he flickers pink again for a second. "A couple dozen, maybe. Why."

"I don't suppose you can link them together somehow?"

He gets it right away—I'm really starting to like this guy—and his color goes from yellow to pale blue. "Yeah, I can! I can merge 'em into bigger containers if I want—I could even make 'em all into one big one!"

Tall's been following along, which isn't surprising—stupid he ain't. "You think it'd hold the full blast?"

"It's worth a try!" Heidi whistles, compartments open all around us, and suddenly we're inundated with his discards. Man, when he said a couple dozen he was definitely downplaying it! There's gotta be at least fifty here! He starts gathering 'em, and mushing 'em together, and breathing a little life into 'em—literally—and soon we're looking at one humongous one. It's so big it's crowding us up against the black velvet walls, smushing down on the consoles and the displays.

There's only one problem.

How the hell is that thing gonna fit outside?

But when I ask that out loud, Heidi just laughs. "No problem," he says. He flickers, and suddenly it's gone and we can breathe again. And looking at the monitor, I see why—

—he teleported it outside.

Right next to the planet.

We all watch as the sphere floats toward Joribau, looking like the universe's biggest soap bubble. Toward it, and then around it, swallowing it whole.

And just in time, because the trailing edge's only just jiggled up against the planet's surface when the whole thing goes off like a firecracker.

Whoomp!

Even with my eyelids in place, it's blinding. And enough force leaks out to make the whole ship rock, causing Tall to lose his balance and fall back onto the seat he'd just vacated, and

Worm-itude to topple over like a puppet with cut strings. Heidi wobbles but stays afloat.

The screens all go white and then black, some kind of program cutting in to shield viewers from the intensity, most likely, but as they fade back into view now we can see what looks like a small, fierce sun—

—only it's trapped within a big, shiny glass globe.

It's like the first-ever sunglobe.

I wonder if there's a market for that?

"I can't believe that worked!" Heidi's looping around in circles like a kid with his first remote-control plane—I would've gotten the hang of it eventually, too, if not for those electrical wires. And that weathervane. And then the water tower. Anyway, suffice to say he's clearly thrilled. So am I, and I'm not even really there!

I can tell Tall's pleased, too. "Nice one, DuckBob," he congratulates me. "And thanks."

"My pleasure, amigo," I assure him. A quiver off to one side catches my eye, and I remember why he's there in the first place. "Say, your new friend might be appreciative, too—and grateful enough to maybe answer a few questions."

"Good point." Tall steps over and crouches beside Live Bait. "Okay, now that we've saved your life," he starts, "how about you answer my question finally? Who do you work for?"

He quivers for a second, but finally nods. "Sure, sure. His name's Monsinal Sha'ar. But I don't know where you can find him. I just get a signal when he wants me to ship out more of the Sublimate, that's all." He sighs. "Guess that's all over and done now."

"How long've you been doing this job, anyway?" I ask, and Tall relays the question a second later.

That gets another sigh in response. "Thirty-three of your years, give or take," he replies. "Though most of that was just the waiting."

Wait, what?

"What do you mean?" Tall asks, and the guy responds right away. Obviously he's finally realized that cooperating is in his best interest here. The fact that his former home and workplace are practically burning his retinas probably doesn't hurt.

"I used to work the mines," he says, leaning back against the wall as he talks. "Just one of many. Monsinal was there, too, until he took me aside one day to suggest something better than just digging all day for somebody else. He'd figured out, partially by accident, what happened when you turned Jorbinate into a gas—what got left behind was Jorbinate Sublimate, a powder that altered the brain's nano-receptors, making people do whatever you said. He taught me the process, then took off, taking the first batch with him. A week or so later he got in touch and told me he needed more, and where to send it. So I did." He shrugs. "They eventually shut the mine down, but I stayed behind—once everybody else was gone it was easy for me to produce more Sublimate and send it off whenever he needed it. That went on for a few years, then suddenly he disappeared. No more messages, and no more money. I'd set some money aside, though, and I don't really need much, so I just waited."

"Then what happened?" Tall asked. I was on the edge of my

seat. Not quite literally, though—I've toppled off chairs enough times to know better by now. Comes from being so top-heavy, with the bill and all.

"I got a message a few months back," the Man-Worm replies. "Another order, after all this time! So I sent it. I've been getting them steadily ever since." He sighed again. "Not anymore, though."

I'm glad there won't be any more zombie powder, but there's still a bunch of it back on Earth—and plenty of zombie-making cookies already loose in the wild.

Tall's been thinking, apparently. "Where were you sending the shipments?" he asks. He doesn't sound angry anymore, or at least not at the worm. I think the guy's sob story got to him a little, too. Imagine sitting there all those years, just waiting. No wonder he needed a good soak!

"Earth," is the answer, of course. "A place called Westchester, in New York."

Tall nods. "What does this Monsinal Sha'ar look like?"

"Tall," the Worminator tells him. "Your height, but skinnier. Big poofy black hair slicked back, long sideburns. Dark skin, blue with whorls on it."

I can practically see the guy he's talking about. Wait a second—I *have* seen him!

"Tall," I shout. "The guy in the MiB cell, the one you peeked in on! The John Travolta look-alike! That's him!"

Tall nods, and sighs. "Yeah."

"What's wrong? Why aren't you doing a Happy Snoopy Dance," I demand. "We found him!" The way Wormy's staring and shrinking back, it's obvious Tall's not looking at him any-more, and he's trying to figure out what kind of voices this big stern guy in black is hearing and what exactly they're telling him to do. I can't bring myself to feel bad about that.

"We did," Tall agrees. "There's just two problems." He rises to his feet again. "First, he's in a holding cell, which means I've got to break *into* headquarters this time."

Oh. Right. "What's the second problem?"

He shakes his head. "If I remember right, that guy's been there the past thirty years." Which would explain the long silence—I'm guessing the MiBs don't exactly allow conjugal vis-its or long-distance calls for their prisoners. Especially not the kind of long distance we'd be talking.

I can guess what that means. "Somebody else ordered those last few shipments. This Moonshine guy isn't the one we're after."

Great. This whole situation's been twistier than a late-night dance party, and it's just gotten worse.

Chapter Twenty-six
In the out door

"**Okay, explain to** me again why you're still planning to break into your own workplace—most people try desperately to break out, you know—and talk to this guy?" I ask as Heidi turns the ship around and points it back toward Earth.

Our spherical friend is sulking a little, evident by the decidedly unlovely shade of brown he's currently displaying— I didn't even know you could glow brown, but he's managing it—because Tall wouldn't let him take the Joribau-sun back with him. "It belongs to the people of Meribau," Tall had explained. "They just lost the second planet in their system, which is going to play havoc with their orbit, their tides, all sorts of things. It's only fair to give them the miniature star as payment. They can use that energy to stabilize things again."

"Yeah, and who's gonna pay me for those globes?" Heidi had muttered. "Those things ain't cheap, y'know." But he didn't argue further, and I think most of it was for show anyway. I do hope he stops sulking soon, though—the brown is really starting to get to me.

But back to the topic at hand. "We know Moonshine Whatever-whatever isn't the one behind all this," I remind Tall.

"Somebody else obviously found out about his little operation and horned in on it. That's who we need to be going after."

"I know that," Tall says, using that belabored tone parents often take when being forced to explain things for the third or fourth or twelfth time to their kid. He uses this tone with me a lot. "But we have no idea who that is or where they are. Monsinal Sha'ar might. Whoever it is, they obviously got that information from him, so he's still our best lead."

Oh, right. Yeah, that actually does make sense. I hate it when that happens.

"Okay," I try again, "but you can't just walk in there. You escaped, remember? If you go back they'll just toss you back in that same little cell, and this time they'll throw away the key."

He cracks his knuckles—still ominous, but with a little more anger and a hint of malicious glee this time. It's like the ragout of knuckle-popping, a little something for everyone. "They're welcome to try." Yeah, I would not want to be a MiB right now. Or ever, really. Especially after seeing that office space. I'm still having nightmares. Tall has said that they've got really good health insurance, though. And they get in free to all the museums.

It's obvious I'm not going to talk him out of this—once Tall's got an idea in his head, that's pretty much it. One time he really wanted to watch some cheesy football movie, and while normally I'm totally up for that at the time I was more in the mood for a big action flick. Tall literally sat down, folded his arms over his chest, and glared without speaking until I gave in.

Okay, yes, that was only five minutes. I just couldn't take it anymore—the silent treatment has always worked on me, ever since that time my brother went without talking to me for a week. Admittedly, he had laryngitis at the time, but I had no idea what that was so I was both scared and impressed. Point being, Tall tends to lock onto things. He's kinda like a pit bull that way. Also, in the way he sometimes chases after cars, and how he likes to bark at people. If only he liked milk bones, I'd be set for birthday presents for years.

"So what's the plan?" I ask finally. If you can't beat 'em, join 'em—especially from the comfort of your own home.

"The plan?" I can actually hear him frowning. "We head back to the Core, call Mary, have her get the Grays to beam me back to MiB headquarters, go to the holding cells, speak with Monsinal Sha'ar, find out what he knows, and leave. Simple as that."

"Oh-kay." Hey, it's obvious even to me by now—nothing around here is ever simple. And nothing ever goes according to plan.

But Tall's pleased with himself for coming up with something so clean-cut and by-the-numbers, so I'm not going to say anything. Or sleep much.

It only takes a few hours for Heidi to ferry us back to the Galactic Core bus stop. "You sure you wouldn't rather stick around?" he asks as he drops us off in the parking lot across from Red's. "I wouldn't mind the company, and you guys've proven you're handy to have around." He winks. "And it's not like DuckBob's an extra mouth to feed."

"Thanks." Tall actually sounds a little disappointed himself, and I suddenly remember his earlier gripes about how his job seemed like mostly paperwork these days. "That's actually tempting. But I have to take care of this."

Heidi nods. "Well, you know how to get hold of me if you change your mind, or if you just need a lift again." He's strobing green, yellow, pink, and blue, which I'm guessing means he's sorry to see us go but pleased to have helped and proud he made a difference. Or he could just have gas.

"Thanks, Heidi," I tell him. "You're all right." Especially for a glowing bowling ball o' doom, but I don't say that part. I really am getting better at this whole tact thing!

"You too, pal," he replied. "Keep an eye on the big lug, okay?"

"You got it." Hey, I pretty much do have an eye on him, literally, so that's not a hard promise to make.

We part ways, and Tall heads into Red's for a quick bite, which makes me insanely jealous again. I've got to talk to Ned about finding some way for me to travel, or at least go out for lunch! Two hours later—and yes, that pretty much is a quick bite at Red's—Tall's just stepping back out into the parking lot when his cell phone rings.

"Yeah?" The MiBs have definitely trained him well, he doesn't give his name or anything, just demands to know what the caller wants. Me, I usually answer with "DuckBob at your service" when I'm in a good mood, "American Avian Society" when I don't want to talk, and "Yeah, I'll have a large pepperoni and an order of garlic knots" when I just want to mess with people. "Got it. Thanks." He hangs up, straightens his tie, brushes a few final crumbs from his jacket—and disappears in a burst of light.

When I can see around him again, he's standing in the big Toys R Us on Times Square. Why am I not surprised the Grays have been to that toy store? They probably love riding that big Ferris wheel in the center—I can imagine them going around and around all day long.

We're maybe twenty blocks from MiB headquarters here, which is pretty much dead on-target considering how far we came. Plus Tall asked them not to drop him right at the building. Hell, if it were me I'd have asked if they could put me in the building, but I guess you'd never know who you might materialize in front of. Or where in the building, exactly—showing up smack-dab in the middle of the women's bathroom would be embarrassing, even though Jones is the only woman there and so the odds against her being in the bathroom at that exact time are really pretty good. Which actually makes me wonder why there's a women's bathroom there in the first place. Did they really anticipate letting women join again when they remodeled? Was the building originally something else and they left most of it alone, including the women's bathroom? Is it a front somehow, like you go in there and turn the knob on the third sink or flush the fourth toilet to open a secret passage somewhere?

Or am I just reading too much into things again?

"So how's this going to work?" I ask as Tall exits the toy store—and without buying anything, which only proves he's got more willpower than I do—and begins marching toward his office. "You just gonna walk in, order anyone you see to spontaneously nap or something, and make your way down to the cells? You got lucky last time," I point out. "Only three guys, and all of them cookie zombies. I wouldn't count on that kind of luck again."

"I'm not," Tall promises, but he doesn't elaborate. I hate that—it's like when someone says something like "I read the funniest thing today," and then stops there, waiting for you to say "Oh, really?" or "How fascinating!" or even "Wicked cool!" before continuing. Look, if you've got something you want to say, go ahead and say it. Don't expect me to feed you those lines, because I'm more likely to get stubborn and refuse to say anything at all on general principle. Like now. Let Tall keep his little plan to himself. I just hope it doesn't blow up in his face. On general principle.

We're only three blocks from the building when Tall suddenly slows and swerves toward the curb—and the row of pay phones there. I'm amazed. I didn't even think there was such a thing as a pay phone anymore. Hell, I'm surprised people even still have landlines! It's so much easier to just get a cell and be done with it, and they can go pretty much anywhere. Of course, I might just think that because Ned did something to my cell and now I get signal out here, which is hella impressive. It's not like there's a radio tower for at least a few hundred light-years. Then again, I am hooked into what's basically the largest, most powerful emitter array in the universe, so if you can't find a signal from here the whole shebang's probably frozen over or something.

Anyway, there are these three pay phones, each in its own

little nook. It's very quaint. One of the phones, not surprisingly, has gone walkabout—there's a cord hanging there, two frayed wires sticking out of the end, and that's it. One of them is still there but looks like the last person to use it may have been a giant slug—it's coated in something thick and lumpy and green-ish with white streaks. I really hope it was a giant slug, actually, because this is New York and we are famous for our pigeons. The third one, though, looks a bit grimy but otherwise okay.

Why is that, anyway? Have you ever noticed how, when there are three things, there's always one that's okay but the other two are seriously dodgy, and usually in completely different ways? Did the story of Goldilocks somehow tap into some great cos-mic truth, that in every trinity there's one that too much of one thing, one that's too much of another, and one that's dead cen-ter and just right? And now I'm picturing the Hindu trinity for some reason, with Shiva saying "I'm too cold" and Brahma say-ing "I'm too hot" and Vishnu smiling smugly and saying "I am just right." Good to know those Eastern Religion classes I took in college weren't a total loss.

Tall scoops up that third receiver, drops some coins into the phone, and dials a number. I hear ringing. Then it picks up, and a voice says, "Metro Investment Brokerage, how may I direct your call?" Which I have to admit is clever, because who wants to talk to investment brokers? I'm guessing most wrong num-bers never make it past the second word.

"I'm a day trader—get me the Actuarials Archive," Tall replies, and there's a click. Then a different voice says, "Report."

"Potential infestation of Comcobi slaver-wasps," Tall says

crisply. "Hive sighted at Strawberry Field, just below the foot-bridge. Full maturity in less than an hour."

"Copy," is all the other man replies. Then the line goes dead. Tall hangs up, turns, and watches the building.

"What the hell was that?" I ask him. "And what is a Comcobi slaver-wasp?"

"It's like a cross between a wasp and a pro wrestler," Tall answers, though I can tell he's focusing most of his attention on the MiB building ahead of us. "Big, mean, ugly, winged, poison stinger. They paralyze you and cart you off to sell as a slave, a pet, a host, whatever. Hives are shot out and fall to Earth, then sit and gestate until they're ready to hatch. Each one contains a few hundred slaver-wasps. They can strip an entire town lifeless in an hour."

"Uh, right." I gulp. "Next time, remind me not to ask." I get it, though. "So you figure they're gonna send out the big guns to deal with this hive, leaving nobody but the mailroom clerk to get in your way?"

"That's about the size of it." I can hear the smirk in his voice. I'm just glad, for once, I don't have to see it, too.

"And what if it's the real deal?" I ask, because the notion of being carried off by something that looks like a pirate ship but captained by giant wasp-men in vests and boots and eye patches is more than a little bit terrifying. "I mean, I know you made this one up, but what if there's a real menace while they're out looking for this one?"

"They're still monitoring for disturbances and alerts," he assures me, "so if there's another threat they'll deploy people for that as well. This'll only keep them busy for an hour at best, but unless something equally dangerous hits it'll be their top priority right now. And there hasn't been a slaver-wasp hive here since 2009." The way he says that makes it clear he knows that for dead certain, and I decide I really don't want to know any more about how or why. I just hope he's right.

But sure enough, suddenly there's a flood of dark-suit-wearing men charging out of the building and toward cars, trucks, minivans, and for some of them just racing past on foot. Wow, apparently Comcobi slaver-wasps are as big a deal as Tall said. I'll have to remember that the next time I need to get rid of somebody.

Also, I'm going to want about thirty cans of insect repellent. And a few dozen of those fog-bomb things, too.

"So how many do you think just cleared out?" I ask Tall as he starts walking toward the building again. He's not rushing, definitely doesn't want anybody to pay him any attention, especially his co-workers. Because of course the black suit and the glower aren't dead giveaways. Fortunately, the last few stragglers are so busy chasing the rest of the team they don't even glance in our direction, and Tall waits until the last one has disappeared down the block before just up and walking to the entrance, pulling the big front door open, and stepping inside.

There's nobody in the lobby but us—well, Tall—and once those doors shut behind us it's eerily quiet as well. Quiet as the grave, which isn't exactly a comparison I'm keen to make.

Tall doesn't waste any time reminiscing. He makes a beeline for the elevator bank—and then marches past it, to a small door set in the lobby wall.

"Wait, what're you— ah." Because Tall has swiped an ID card of some sort, a panel next to the door has winked green, and then he's pulled the door open to reveal a narrow set of industrial metal stairs winding down, down, down.

"You're not seriously planning to walk down, are you?" I ask Tall. "Isn't it something like eleven stories below ground? Would you even still be able to breathe after climbing down that far?"

"I am, it is, and yes, I'll be fine," Tall answers. "Don't worry about it—I'm in peak physical health." He chuckles as he steps into the stairwell, pulling the door shut behind him. "Besides, down is a lot easier than up."

Which doesn't really bode well for any escape plans afterward. Why couldn't they have put their holding cells on the second floor, or even the third? Good natural light, decent noise, lots of restaurants and stores all around. I don't think that small consideration is really too much to ask.

Chapter Twenty-seven
Picking up excitation

Four minutes later, Tall's barely breathing hard. I, on the other hand, can't seem to catch my breath.

Ever watch one of those Imax 3-D features? The ones where you're riding a roller coaster or plummeting over a waterfall or scaling a mountain? The ones where you feel like you're really there, it's so crisp and clear and big and all-encompassing you can practically feel the water's spray on your face, taste the thin high-altitude air, hear the screams of the people all around you?

Now imagine that the latest feature is someone barreling down flight after flight of narrow metal stairs, nothing but rough whitewashed cinderblock walls around with harsh fluorescent bulbs overhead and sturdy metal fire doors at each landing. "Barreling" doesn't really begin to cover it, though. "Controlled falling" might be closer. Or "flying downhill really really REALLY fast," if you wanna be nice.

I'm pretty sure Tall's feet have only touched the ground for a step or two on each flight. He basically leans out and down, grasps the railings with both hands halfway down that set of steps, and then leaps out and swings wide, letting go at the top of his arc so he can plummet down, down—and land with his feet solidly on the landing below the last step. Then he swivels to the next flight and repeats the process.

Except he's taking maybe half a second on each swivel. And about ten seconds on each flight of stairs. It's all going by in one sickening, nonstop blur. I feel like I've been strapped to a metronome that was set to seven-eighths time and then plugged into an accelerator or fed ground coffee straight from the can. Lean, swing, land, swivel, lean swing, land, swivel—my whole body is vibrating in sympathy, and I swear my arms are starting to ache from gripping my chair so tight by sheer reflex.

"You. Are. Insane!" I finally manage to gasp as Tall lands one last time, right next to the door labeled "B11." "You could have killed yourself doing that!"

"It was the fastest way down," he answers, straightening and brushing off his jacket and adjusting his tie. "We're on a tight schedule." Seriously, he's not breathing any harder or faster than if he'd just walked quickly across the room. I'm starting to wonder if he had most of his real organs traded out for cheap alien knockoffs when I wasn't looking.

But I give up arguing as he pulls open the door and steps into the lobby of B11, the same doctor's waiting room I saw last time. There's nobody else here, no MiBs standing guard. So far so good. Tall crosses to the inner door, swipes his card again—I guess they never bothered to deactivate the thing when he took off, which seems strange but I'm not gonna look a gift ID in the mouth—and enters the hall beyond.

The guy we want is in the third cell on the right.

"Monsinal Sha'ar?" Tall asks as he enters, though the way

he spits out the name it's less a question than an accusation. It's amazing how he can make anything sound like that—I've heard him order dinner before and the delivery guys are always really apologetic and swear the restaurant will shape up and behave next time.

"Yes?" The Martian Manero doesn't look too fazed, but I guess he's had plenty of practice dealing with MiBs.

"I need to ask you some questions." Tall closes the door behind him, grabs the one chair—Sha'ar's sitting on his bed and has a deck of cards laid out in front of him, solitaire-style—spins it around, and drops onto it.

"After all this time?" Sha'ar smiles and spreads his hands wide. Except for the weird skin he could be right out of a Solid Gold flashback video or a Bee Gees movie. With the skin he looks like a giant chameleon that landed on somebody's favorite tie and got mighty confused. "I assure you, I have not done anything new." Okay, at least the guy's got a sense of humor. After so many years stuck in here I guess it's that or lose it completely.

I'm also wondering how they handle laundry in this joint, because his white suit looks pristine, as does his shirt. For that matter, his hair is perfect and his shoes are shined to a high gloss. I don't see any spare clothes, though, so do they press everything while he's still wearing it, or what? Is there a com- plimentary robe with "Imprisoned Alien" stenciled across the back or something?

"This is about what you did back then," Tall explains, and he's gruff but not up to chewing rocks. After all, this guy's been locked away in here since before Tall was born. Kinda hard to hold a grudge at that point. "You used Jorbinate Sublimate, didn't you?"

Sha'ar sighs and lifts a card, idly flipping it between his fingers as he talks. "Yes, I did. I'm impressed, Agent—at the time, no one knew what it was called or where it came from. I gather you've got some new sources."

I can almost hear the skin of Tall's cheeks creasing as he smiles. "Fah-te says hi." That's Worm-with-hands's name, Fah-te, which to me sounds like "Fatty" but whose fault is that? I'm just glad I'm not the one who has to repeat it with a straight face. Then again, Tall is grinning, so maybe he wasn't immune, either.

"Ah." Sha'ar turns and leans back against the wall, his head tilted up, eyes closing for a second. "You know, I have not heard from or really thought of him in at least two decades. Is that cruel of me? He was a loyal employee, not quite a partner and not quite a friend but certainly someone I felt I could trust with our business and with our secrets. I hope you did not hurt him?" Sha'ar's voice is soft and whispery, and makes me think of old books where the paper's so worn it's soft like cloth and just as supple. Somehow I have a hard time picturing this guy as an evil mastermind—he sounds more like he should be reading kids stories in the library after school. Admittedly, from behind a screen or something.

"He's fine," Tall replies, and surprises me by adding, "and he didn't give you up easily. But I saved his life so he felt he owed me."

Sha'ar nods. "Of course. He is very loyal, and very

conscientious about his debts." He smiles and twirls that card again. "Well, since you clearly know how I came by the Sublimate, what else can I tell you?"

Tall leans forward and I see his hands tighten on the chair top. "What was the plan?"

"Oh, that?" He actually laughs, this refugee from the glam years. "The same as most, I suppose—to take over the world. Rule it, or at least have it pay homage—I was less interested in the day-to-day responsibilities than in the massive wealth and power I would have accrued."

"And how did you plan to do this, exactly?" Once again, dog with a bone.

The alien dips his head. "I included the Sublimate in a drink I created, and spread it widely to affect as many people as possible. Once they'd tasted it they craved more, so it was easy to keep them under control. Then, when I had enough, I was going to have them storm the capital and take over. The United Nations would have been next, and then each country individually, with the effect spreading until the entire world answered to me." The way he says it, so calmly, sends shivers up my spine.

"What was the drink?" I demand into the mic, and Tall repeats the question a second later.

That prompts a second laugh. "It was a new soda," Sha'ar answers once he's recovered. "I called it Sunlight."

I.

Am.

So.

Stupid.

Of course! It all fits! Sunlight came out in the late seventies to early eighties and caught on like crazy. It's still around now, and still popular, even though I'm assuming it doesn't have the Sublimate in it any more, just the usual sugar and caffeine and flavoring, but I remember everybody still being absolutely nuts about it by the time I came along.

"What happened?" Tall asks next, and Sha'ar sighs.

"I got careless," he admits. "I tried to expand my operation too quickly, tried to control people too overtly, and someone noticed. The next thing I knew, my company was being sold to another, my factory was shut down and all my supplies impounded, and I had two agents showing up at my door to escort me here." He waves an arm around the tiny cell. "And I have been here ever since."

"Someone's started your operation back up," Tall informs him sharply, like it's this guy's fault somehow. "Somebody who knew about the Sublimate. Who did you tell?"

The guy actually looks startled, though it could be an act. "No one!" He leans forward slightly. "I never told a soul how I had done it, or where I had gotten the powder. They asked, of course, the agents who brought me in, but I refused to answer. I have not heard its name outside my own innermost thoughts until now."

I'm thinking about that. This poor schlub's been sitting here rotting for the past thirty to forty years. So why is it only now that somebody got hold of more Jorbinate Sublimate? If whoever it was had already known what he was using and where it was from, why not go get more back then? Why wait all these years?

Unless they didn't know, and only just found out. But how?

"What happened to the stuff that got confiscated?" I ask Tall. "Did they destroy it or lock it away somewhere?"

"Probably destroyed," he answers under his breath, and it doesn't look like Sha'ar caught the exchange. "They couldn't have been sure it didn't give off poison fumes or something, so they wouldn't have risked keeping it around."

Great. If it had been here we'd just have to figure out where it went next and who got hold of it. Without that, though—how the hell would they even know what they were looking for?

Tall's obviously been thinking along the same lines, because his next question is, "How many agents stormed your operation, in all?"

"Just those two," Sha'ar answers. He gathers the cards without looking down at them, tidies up the stack, then shuffles it. Then again. He's good, Vegas casino-good, fast and skilled and with just the right amount of flourish. "I think there were local officers to cordon off the building," he continues, "but your fellow agents didn't let them come in contact with any sensitive material."

Great, yet another case for a MiB being involved in all this. Even if was several decades ago.

But wait . . . I grab my mic. "Tall," I say quickly, "find out who they were. The two agents." They were the ones on the scene, after all. If anybody had access to the Sublimate—and the means to smuggle even a little sample out—it'd be them.

"What were their names?" he asks. "The two agents?"

But Sha'ar shakes his head. "It has been over thirty years," he reminds. Funny thing is, he doesn't even seem mad about that. I guess he's had time to get used to the idea. "I cannot remember."

Tall tries a different tack. "What did they look like?" Smart—there can't have been that many MiBs back then, he should be able to find a picture that matches the description. Assuming he can get access to the pictures.

I glance at my watch. He entered the building fifteen minutes ago. And told me the slaver-wasp decoy might keep the other MiBs busy for an hour at most.

But it's hard to rush a memory. Especially after so long. Sha'ar's got his eyes closed, his brow furrowed, and sweat starts popping out along his forehead. It's like he's trying to pull that memory to the surface through sheer will, one step at a time.

But after another minute he opens his eyes, and his disappointed expression isn't reassuring. "I can no longer remember the second agent," he tells us quietly. "I am sorry. But the first one, him I remember. I do not know that I have ever met another human being that thin, so much so that I initially wondered if he might be one of the Lamgedar, who are in fact two-dimensional." Heh, sounds like a lot of the women I used to date.

"What else?" Tall asks, but there's a sigh hidden behind his words. Like he can already guess where this is going.

"Hm." Sha'ar rubs at his chin. "Yes, well, let's see—thin I already said, sharp features, hair similar to mine but not as tall"—he pats his own hair, which could probably brush the ceiling if we let it loose—"and a well-cut suit."

Tall shakes his head. "And you're sure you can't tell me anything else about who might have gotten hold of that powder, or at least found out its name and where it's from and how to contact Fah-te?"

"I promise you, I have not said a word to anyone," Sha'ar states again. He looks around and smiles. "After all, who would I tell?"

Tall rises to his feet. "Thank you for your time." He turns to the door, uses his key card to open it, and twists to pass through the narrow doorway.

"Any time," Sha'ar answers, and in his eyes I can see how lonely he must have been over all these years alone. Then we're out in the hall again, with no noise but Tall's breathing and the clomp of his feet as he stalks toward the lobby.

"You know who that is, don't you?" I ask when he's still a door or two away. "Tell me you do, because I sure have an idea in my head."

"Smith," Tall mutters, reaching for the doorknob. "It's Agent Smith."

"Yeah, that's what I thought, too." But why wait so long, then? Maybe he had to because—

The door swings open—and I find myself staring down the barrel of a gun. "Don't move, Agent Thomas," a voice declares, "or I will be forced to shoot." It's a deep voice, husky—and not in a good way.

Agent Jones.

Because this day couldn't really get much worse.

Chapter Twenty-eight
It's all so clearly understated

"Agent Jones." Tall sounds perfectly calm as he confronts her across her weapon.

Me, I'm freaking out.

"Shoot her!" I shout into the mic. "Or take her gun away! Yeah, do that first so she can't shoot you, then—shoot her! Knock her out! Put her in a sleeper hold. Make her look away for a second and turn invisible, then dart past when she runs on by! I don't know, do something!"

Yeah, okay, I can get a little excitable at times. But here we are, we've got a new lead on what's going on—though it's one I almost can't believe—we're deep inside MiB headquarters, the entire rest of the workforce could come boiling back in at any time, and suddenly here's Agent Jones to throw a monkey wrench into everything.

It's like it's her job. Or at least her favorite hobby.

"I take it you have recovered from whatever sent you on your rampage?" she asks. It's like she's reading off cue cards or something, she's that stiff—even Tall is looser and emotes more than this! Except that what she's asking, and how she's asking it—if you ignore the flat tone, and the large handgun, she does almost sound like she was genuinely concerned.

"I did," he agrees. Then he pauses for a second. "Agent Jones, I'm sure you've noticed the strange behavior of our fellow agents lately. Within the past week or two."

She cocks her head to the side like a bulldog being asked to shake. I really can't help it, every time I think of analogies with her it winds up being a bulldog. "I have nothing to compare their behavior to," she replies. "As you no doubt remember, I joined the agency only ten days previous." Man, it's like they're both using one of those text-to-speech programs, typing in these awkward bits of dialogue and having the computer spit out these strangely modulated sound bytes in return. I can practically hear the keys clacking.

Tall nods. "True, but even so you must have wondered why the other agents have been so . . . agreeable. So easily swayed."

Her hand cannon doesn't lower for a second, doesn't waver—she must have forearms of solid steel, I'd be pointing at the floor by now, or with my luck taking aim at my own big toe—but I can see she's considering this. "I have noticed that, for an agency charged with such aggressive protection procedures, everyone seems unusually willing to acquiesce to anything." Good lord, she's like a walking thesaurus! I am never playing her at Scrabble, especially since I bet she'd stick to the official rules just like Tall does. I still say sound effects should count for double.

"Someone has drugged the agency," Tall explains to her. "They used a chemical called Jorbinate Sublimate, which they mixed into the CampGirl cookies at the factory. Anyone who eats those cookies becomes severely receptive to verbal commands."

"Is that what led to your own strange behavior?"

"It is." He grinds those two words so tight they're practically powder. "I was told to cut loose and rampage through the streets. So I did."

"How did the others stop you, then?" Still that gun. It's like it isn't even there, the way the two of them are—stiffly—conversing. Like it was newspaper on the table in front of them. Only then, human nature being what it is, at least one of them would've tugged it around and started flipping through it by now, looking for either the comics or the sports scores.

"The only way we know of to snap someone out of the trance the chemical induces," Tall replies, "is to command them to snap out of it." This has been a public service announcement of the Tall and Terminally Unfazed Brigade, I add quietly, but I don't say it out loud. Tall wouldn't have laughed, anyway.

She frowns. At least, I think she does—the line between her brows deepens a notch, but she was already kind of glowering, so it's hard to tell. It's more like she ratchets the frown up to Defcon Two, I guess. "And you expect me to believe all this?"

And that, I have to admit, is a very good question. Damn it. How the hell does Tall expect her to believe any of this? It's completely ridiculous—an entire agency, and not just any old agency but the MiBs themselves, mind-controlled through boxes of CampGirl cookies? Talk about nuts! And what kind of proof do we have? The other MiBs are all still gone—I check my watch, half an hour to go—and Tall can't touch the things anymore, so unless Jones wants to try downing some of those cookies herself, we've got no way to show her what they do to people. And there's no way she's falling for that one.

"It's a lot to swallow," Tall tells her slowly. "But it happens to be true. The detainee in 12-A, Monsinal Sha'ar, was the first to discover how to create Jorbinate Sublimate, and to realize its properties. He's why I came back, to find out who learned about the chemical from him."

Jones nods. "And?" I'm starting to think she's actually got invisible wires holding that gun up.

"The only people who knew about it were the agents who apprehended him." Tall sighs. "One of them was Agent Smith. I don't know who his partner was at the time."

Jones barks at him, and it takes me a second to realize she's laughing. Either that or she's just mistaken him for a passing car. "So, what? You want to go ask Agent Smith if he has been drugging the rest of the agency? I don't think that will go over very well."

"Naw, Smith'll get a good laugh over it," I mutter. "He's so easy-going, I'm sure it'll be fine." Yeah, right.

Tall doesn't bother to repeat my crack, or even to acknowledge it. "Perhaps not," he says instead. "But it's the only move I have right now. We need to identify the person behind all this and stop them from pursuing their plans further. Until we do that, the entire agency's been compromised. We can't trust anyone."

What's this "we," white man? I want to ask him. But Jones actually beats me to it.

"You say 'we,'" she tells him, "as if you and I are somehow working together on this. We are not. I am an agent in good standing. You are an agent currently on administrative suspension, and recently escaped from custody. I am not helping you—I am re-capturing you." The gun finally moves after all this time, as she waggles it to remind him it's there. Like any of us have forgotten!

"Think about it," Tall urges her. "You can apprehend me, yes, but who knows what will happen then? The other agents will still be under mind-control, and whoever did that to them will still be out there. Imagine what someone could do with the agency at their fingertips. We can't let that happen!"

"I will look into the matter once you are back in your cell," Jones promises after a second. "If matters are as you say, I will devise a plan. I cannot trust you to assist me, however."

This time it's Tall who laughs, his usual rough-edged, gravely chuckle. "Assist you? Agent Jones, I am the primary on this case. I have been on it since the beginning, and I possess all the relevant information. There isn't any time to bring you up to speed on it, either. You would have to assist me, not the other way around." Great, we're standing here with a gun pointed at us and he's busy arguing over pecking order.

"Tall, she's got a gun trained on you," I remind him quickly. "Just agree to whatever she says and go along with it until you can turn the tables on her, okay?"

I'm totally unsurprised that he doesn't go for it. "You've seen me both under the cookies' influence and not," he tells Jones now. "Tell me you didn't notice a difference!"

"I did," she agrees. "There were times you were docile and accepted any statement or request as an order that could not be gainsayed. Then there were other times when you bulled ahead like a runaway train, not accepting direction from anyone." A tiny little smile flickers across her lips as she mentions that second style, which takes me aback. Did Agent Jones just talk about how stubborn and bullheaded Tall is—in a wistful, admiring sort of way? As cranky, overbearing, arrogant secret agents go, is Tall a hunk?

"Then you can see for yourself that I am not currently under that influence," he tells her, apparently completely missing her brief fangirl moment. I wonder if he'd even have any idea how to respond anyway. Tall doesn't strike me as the type that's too suave with the ladies. "Thus you know I am acting of my own free will."

"And what's to stop you from eating cookies again at some later point and reverting to docility?" Jones asks him. At this point I'm wondering if her gun is just a replica painted to look good and then filled with helium so it not only stays up but supports her arm as well. Oy.

I don't have to see Tall to know he's grimacing. "I had a crash course in immersive aversion therapy," he manages to spit out. "I couldn't eat another cookie if I wanted to." And given how many boxes he went through right from the start, I don't think he'd want another CampGirl cookie if he could at all avoid it, anyway. Though maybe I'm just being gleefully malicious here, seeing as how I'm actually rubbing my hands together right now and cackling, "All the more for me, mwa-ha-ha!" Under my breath, of course.

Amazingly enough, Jones actually seems to be considering his suggestion seriously. "Explain to me again why I cannot simply lock you up and proceed myself," she asks, but it doesn't have the same force as her earlier statements. It sounds rhetorical to me. And yes, I know what that means. Hell, I make rhetorical statements all the time! It comes from never expecting anyone to reply to me. Which is probably why I sometimes startle if people do respond—I'm just not used to it. Ignore, yes. Sneer, sure. Throw money, occasionally. Throw food, often—hey, you'd be amazed how many free lunches you can cobble together that way, especially on the subway! But actually answer? Yeah, not so much.

"I have already explained," Tall replies, and he's using that "speaking to the slow kid" voice again. I love it when he breaks that out and it isn't aimed at me. "I have been following this case since it broke. I am possessed of all the pertinent information. I am now immune to the lure of the CampGirl cookies, despite the addictive nature of their new additive. And I am a senior agent, whereas you are still a rookie."

"A senior agent currently on probation and possibly still labeled a fugitive," Jones corrects, but after a second and a blink she holsters her pistol. Finally! To be honest, I'm not even sure how she manages it—I can't imagine her arm has any flexibility after being held ramrod-straight like that for so long. But somehow she does it, though she may have cheated and used mirrors, because one second I'm staring down the barrel of that thing—admittedly, from several million light-years away, but it looks like it's right in my face—and the next it's nowhere in sight and she's rebuttoning her jacket. I bet she's a whiz at the ol' shell game.

"Very well, what is our next move?" she asks Tall like she hadn't been threatening to shoot him a second ago. I wonder what it would take to unnerve her, or any of the MiBs? An act of God? An extinction-level event? Everyone being quiet and calm on the subway? I know that last one would freak me out!

"We need to ask Agent Smith some questions about his old case," Tall replies. He turns without another glance at her and starts toward the stairwell door. "There's no time to lose." No "hey, thanks for not shooting me, Agent Jones!" No, "Hey, welcome aboard the 'Stop-the-crazy-cookie-zombies' train!" Nope. Nada. But then, Tall's never been a people person. He'd have done great in HR.

"Why don't we just check his work history?" Jones asks, falling into step beside him. Which is disorienting for me, since it means all I can see of her now is the barest edge of her shadow at the lip of my peripheral vision—but her voice is coming through loud and clear. A little too loud, actually. She really needs to take some lessons in adjusting her volume. I think she's got "inside voice" confused with "baseball stadium voice."

"Because we don't have time," Tall replies. "I'm still considered a fugitive, as you pointed out, and the rest of the agency will be returning within the next twenty minutes. I cannot afford to be here when they do."

"I can put in the file request and meet up with you," Jones offers. "That would be the most efficient use of our time."

He only pauses a second before nodding. "Fine. Do that. Meet me at the Malibu Diner."

And he steps into the stairwell, takes a deep breath, and grabs the stair railings about halfway up with both hands.

Oh, boy.

Chapter Twenty-nine
Doing the avoidance dance

"**What did you** find out?" That's the first thing Tall says when Agent Jones catches up to him at the Malibu Diner. Tall's sitting in a booth near the back—not the very back row, which I know he'd prefer due to the whole "back to the wall" thing, because there's a big group of people back there being very geeky and very loud and frankly looking like they're having a lot more fun than we are—facing the front, and he's got a burger and a plate of fries in front of him, which he's been picking at since they showed up a few minutes ago. I don't think lingering over the food is helping it any, though. He'd have been better off just putting it out of its—and his—misery right away, because now in addition to be poorly cooked it's semi-cool and partially congealed. Yum.

She slides into the booth opposite him, catches the waiter's eye, nods, and taps Tall's coffee mug with a forefinger. They must've had training in that, because Tall was able to get the waiter's attention right away, too, and that never happens. Especially not in an old-school New York diner like the Malibu. The waiters here have clearly taken special "customer-evasion technique" courses—they can walk in your direction, drop food off at another table in front of you, take orders from a third table, scan your general vicinity, and turn away, all without once ever making eye contact or acknowledging your upraised hand. It's kind of amazing, really, and certainly impressive— when you're not the one trying to get your check and get out, or trying to complain that your medium-rare cheeseburger with Cheddar and fries done extra-crispy showed up well done with American cheese and fries only half a step up from raw. At the best of times it turns into a strange food-based dance, customer and waiter moving toward yet away from each other and spinning in circles around one another, demanding attention but never granting it if they can help it. At its worst it's all-out war, leading to more and more aggressive maneuvers until one side finally snaps. I've gone so far as to wave menus over my head, clang flatware against water glasses, make up loud songs about the terrible service, and other shenanigans. One time my buddies and I got so fed up waiting for the waiter to take our order, we called in a delivery order instead—and told them "the table in the back right corner," when they asked for our address.

Of course they got the order wrong.

Anyway, Jones waits until she's got her coffee and has taken a sip before replying. "I put in the request," she answers. "Four to twelve hours before we hear back. I checked Smith's personnel file, as well, but it doesn't list his home address." She grimaces— I think. "The rest of the agents have returned. A slaver-wasp hive? Really?"

"It worked," Tall points out, jabbing the burger again with his fork. It still just lies there, looking horribly unappetizing.

"I'm guessing you tested several of them for the cookies' influence, and for freeing them from it?"

"I did." She reaches out to steal a fry, thinks better of it once she touches one, but is left holding the flabby, pale blonde piece of potato and finally brings it to her mouth, chews methodically, and swallows. "Your claim appears to be correct. Everyone else in the agency seems to be under the cookies' command. Telling them to snap out of it, however, cancels its influence."

"Yeah, until the next time they eat more cookies," I point out, though I'm talking as much to myself as to anyone else. "We've already seen how addictive they can be."

Tall doesn't reply to me, or repeat what I said to her. I think he figures she already knows that much. Hey, just because it's obvious doesn't mean I won't say it anyway! "Are you still willing to assist me?" he asks her instead.

She pauses a second before nodding.

"Then we need to find out where Agent Smith lives, and confront him in his home." Tall frowns—I can tell from the starstruck look that crosses Jones's face. Yuck. "The question is, how're we going to do that when it isn't in the database?"

That gives me an idea, though. "Hang on," I say, swiveling around in my chair and kicking my computer to wake it up. Hey, it works for siblings, roommates, campers, and the occasional bedmate, why not computers? At least I draw the line at punching, head-butting, sitting on, peeing on, and upending. There's a reason I never liked mornings. "Do you know Agent Smith's full name?"

"No," Tall answers for them both. "He's always just been

Agent Smith." I see Jones raise an eyebrow—he said that under his breath but she heard it anyway.

"All right, all right—how old would you say he is?" I ask. Not having a full name makes it harder but not impossible.

"How old is he?" Tall pauses to consider that for a moment. "He captured Monsinal Sha'ar in the early seventies, so he was definitely a full agent by then. That means he was at least twenty-one, which would make him sixty or older now."

Sixty? Really? Wow, I'd have pegged Smith as forties, probably. I hope I look that good when I'm his age! Hell, I wish I looked that good—body, not head—now!

Anyway, I add that to the list I'm already inputting: government affiliation (even if he's got some sort of cover job I figure he's got security clearances out the whazoo), early to mid-sixties, average height, seriously narrow build, glossy black hair worn short and slicked back, gray eyes, New York city area and environs, male, white, last name "Smith." Then I tell my system to go fetch.

I've said it before, there are some very definite advantages to living in the Matrix Center. One of which is a computer that's basically plugged into the entire galactic database. Ten minutes later—as I'm watching Tall polish off the last of his New York-style cheesecake, which actually looks pretty good, and seeing Jones demolish a chocolate éclair, my search engine turns up a hit.

"Hey, I've got something!" I tell Tall, scanning the screen as the results show up. "Yep, I've got two Smiths that fit the bill. One, Henry Patrick Smith, lives in Manhattan, down in the

Village. The other, Edmund Franklin Smith"—I read the details and grin. "The other leaves in Nutley, New Jersey, a short train and bus ride away."

Tall shares this data with Jones. "It would have to be Nutley," he states after that. "The Village would be too noisy and chaotic after a full day as a MiB. He'd want somewhere quiet and peaceful to relax in, somewhere he could recharge a bit." He glances up, catches the waiter's eye immediately—how the hell does he do that?—and makes the universal sign for "Check, please!" Either that or he's asking for a small bird to show up and start pecking at his nose. I'm guessing it's the former. "Let's go."

Jones doesn't argue, she just shoves what's left of that éclair into her mouth and slides out to stand by the booth. "Right." She leads the way out, and doesn't stop or appreciably slow down until she's standing under the striped awning out front.

Tall has stopped off long enough to pay the cashier on the way out. I don't see Agent Jones offer him any money for her coffee and éclair, and Tall doesn't ask her or hesitate at all before putting all of it on his card. Wouldn't that make this almost a sort of semi-date, then? I shudder.

The minute he's outside as well, Jones turns on him. "You've been holding out on me," she accuses. Her stern expression would work a lot better if not for that dab of chocolate beside her mouth. "You've got someone else helping you."

"I do," Tall admits. "But not anyone from the agency. It's—"

"No, don't tell her!" I shout into the mic. "Don't say my name! Don't—"

"—DuckBob," he finishes without even pausing to

acknowledge me. Which is funny, considering he's acknowledging me.

I didn't think Jones's face could get much more wrinkled, but now it goes all prune-like. "That duck-headed clown from the Matrix? He's helping you?"

"Hey!" I squawk. "This duck-headed clown saved the galaxy, thank you very much!" With a little help, admittedly, but still, some respect would be nice!

Much to my surprise, Tall stands up for me. "DuckBob may not look like much," he admits, which makes me bristle a bit except that he continues, "but I have continually been surprised by his astuteness and his ability to hit upon innovative solutions. It was he who first deduced that the cookies were the source of the problem, and it is only with his help that I was able to discover as much as I already have about them."

Jones considers that, idly rubbing at that bit of chocolate. "Well, I suppose he wouldn't have been made Guardian of the Matrix if he was completely useless," she conceded finally, which is about as faint praise as I can imagine. "Fine. And he's the one who just fed you Smith's address?"

"He is. DuckBob has access to almost every database in existence," Tall explained, taking her elbow and guiding her away from the diner and toward the corner, where a subway entrance awaited. "He cross-referenced what details we had for Smith and came up with the address." He's right about the databases—I can get information about almost anything or anyone. Which sure surprised the hell out of Bobby McIntire, you betcha, especially when his confidential test results showed up on his Facebook page. That's what you get for making me eat dirt in second grade, Bobby. And don't worry, I'm sure some antibiotics will clean that right up. As far as the divorce, well, I guess posting those videos might have been overkill but you shouldn't have kept them in the cloud, now, should you?

"Well, I hope he got it right," Jones grumbles as they descend the steps. "I'd hate to go all the way out to Nutley for nothing."

"Yeah, well, I'd love to send you out there for nothing, and leave you there," I grumble back. "Good thing Tall's with you, so it's not worth the trouble." It's surprisingly easy to mouth off to people when they can't hear you. I'm particularly good at doing that to people on TV, though I have to be careful about that now—my TV out here can be highly interactive, and more than once I've said something to some character on a series or some contestant on a show, only to have them turn and glare at me and snap something in reply. Yeah, the Matrix, where the line between reality and reality TV is so blurry you can lose it in the water ring from your drink.

Chapter Thirty
When a house calls, answer

The ride out to Nutley is . . . unbelievably boring. I thought it was bad enough traveling with Tall, who can be silent for hours on end and can sit so still you'd think someone had unplugged his power pack, but at least when we were traipsing around the galaxy together I could mess with him, get a rise of him, have some laughs. The thing is, he's learned to tune me out now—it helps that I'm not there, just a voice in his ear or in the bones of his jaw or whatever. And Jones is just as motionless and taciturn as he is. Maybe moreso. Actually, I suspect they're actually having a "who can be more like a badly dressed statue?" contest but I can't be sure because they never actually said as much. Still, about the only time they move over the next hour and a half is when they transfer from the subway to the bus, and once they're on the bus they go right back to carved-from-granite mode. I've had more fun trying to race snails, and believe me, given the right motivation those little buggers can really crawl!

Of course, staring at them—or at Jones, since I can't actually see Tall unless he's in front of a reflective surface—isn't exactly riveting, so I only half pay attention. I check on the Matrix, just as an excuse to get up and walk around—there isn't actually much for me to do to it, other than stay hooked up, so really as long as it's still spinning and humming and all the lights are going, it's in good shape. And whenever it stops any of those I call Ned, anyway. I'm the Guardian, not the Repairman!

After I do that—and yes, it's working fine, that little flicker and that one wobble are supposed to be there. I think—then I goof off on the computer for a bit, answer emails, update my blog, etc.

Then I take a leak.

Oh, the exciting life of the Guardian of the Matrix. Whee. It's a good thing I'm easily amused or I'd be bored spitless.

Not that I can really spit much, anymore.

Anyway, finally Tall reaches up and tugs the cord—earning a little smirk from Jones, which I guess means she won—and they both stand up as the bus pulls over. "Wow, remind me never to take long road trips with the two of you," I remark as Tall pushes open the rear door and half steps, half leaps down to the side of the road. "Not unless I desperately need to catch up on my sleep."

He ignores that completely—see? It's like I'm not even there! Which I guess I'm not, exactly, but whatever, it's still rude!—and scans the area. So do I.

Uh, okay.

"Hey, isn't there supposed to be a city around here somewhere?" I ask. "Because all I see are . . . trees. And a road. And a few houses over yonder. Nobody told me Nutley was a county!" It's been a while since I've seen anyplace as empty as this. Not counting space, I mean. Which turned out to be a whole helluva lot more crowded than I'd ever expected. But this is—well, when I moved to New York, all those years ago, I swore I was never not going to live in a big city ever again. I figure I can make an exception for the Matrix, because of the whole "saving the galaxy and watching over it" thing. Plus the pay is good. But Nutley looks an awful lot like a small town, way too close for comfort, and even though I'm only here remotely I still feel my skin crawl. Which is an awful feeling, especially under all these feathers.

"We are on the outskirts of Nutley," Jones confirms. "But it is not a big city, no. It has a total population of approximately twenty-seven thousand." Well well, look who took some time to bone up on the facts! Must be trying to impress Tall. And twenty-seven thousand? Seriously? That's like half a neighborhood in the Big Apple!

"Listen, Smith lives at twelve-fourteen Orchard Lane," I tell Tall. "Let's just get this over with, okay? Being out here in the boonies is weirding me out, and your traveling companion isn't helping any."

"We need to locate Orchard Lane," Tall relays, leaving out the rest. Funny, I didn't think he had tact, either. Guess this whole experience is a learning experience for both of us. He pulls out his phone, clicks open a map of Nutley, inputs the address, and watches as it traces a route from his current location right to Smith's front door. Assuming it gets certain details—like which state we're in, for starters—right. I've had those apps send me all over creation. One time they tried to tell me the fastest way from Weehawken to Whippany was by way of Boise. Those first two are both in New Jersey, by the way. Boise, not so much. Tall doesn't seem too worried, though, as he gestures straight ahead. "This way."

Jones doesn't argue, and neither do I—hey, it's not like I'm the one who'd wind up lost, anyway! But his app must be government issue or something, because it doesn't try to steer him wrong once, and after about twenty minutes we're all staring at the front of 1214 Orchard Lane.

Smith's house is a nice little two-story job, all wood and shingles, with a pair of silver birches in the front yard on either side of a pleasant brick walk. There's a big porch, complete with an old-fashioned porch swing off to one side past the big bay windows, and the front door itself is all carved wood around an oblong of frosted glass. I feel like I've stepped back in time a few centuries, and should be sitting here sipping lemonade or maybe a mint julep and asking if the carriage is ready.

Tall doesn't waste any time admiring the architecture. He charges down the walkway and up the porch steps and pounds one oversized fist against the door. Jones is right behind him.

We wait.

Nothing happens.

"Maybe he's stuck in traffic?" I suggest after a minute. "Or he's taking a post-work nap?" I used to do those—still do, sometimes. And pre-work naps. And occasionally mid-work naps. Those were the ones my supervisors used to complain about but like I always told them, better I'm out for ten minutes than out of it for the entire rest of the day.

Tall pounds again.

Still nothing.

"We could leave a note," I offer, but just then I hear movement from inside. Tall must hear it too, because he stiffens and takes a step back, one hand going for his gun. Jones already has hers drawn—showing off again—and holds it up, both hands locked around its grip. Though after that stunt down in the cells I can't imagine she needs more than one hand to hold it steady— hell, she could probably manage with just her trigger finger and maybe her thumb, and let the other three fingers wrestle or paint each other's nails or something while they wait. Anyway, both of them are poised and ready when the door opens, and sure enough there's Agent Smith—

—only he's not dressed like an agent.

In fact, he's wearing . . . a white polo shirt with thin yellow banding around the collar and the sleeves. Below that he's got a pair of equally white shorts, and capping the other end of his almost inhumanly skinny legs are white socks and white tennis shoes. A white terrycloth headband holds his glossy black hair in place, and matching bands adorn each wrist.

Somewhere between work and now, Agent Smith has been possessed—by the spirit of Bjorn Borg.

It's horrible.

If he's at all surprised to see Tall and Jones there, one with a drawn gun and the other clearly ready to draw, Smith doesn't let on. "Agent Thomas, Agent Jones," he says instead, in that dry, whispery voice of his that makes you expect to see tumbleweeds drift by at any second. "Perhaps you should come in." And he steps back, pushing the door wide so they can slip past him.

Tall does so at once, without question or hesitation. That's him, though. He's all about swift, decisive action. Me, I'd probably have stood there until the cows came home, debating all my options and asking a whole lot of annoying questions and eventually finding out just what it took to make Smith snap and shoot me right there on his front porch.

From what little I can tell behind me, Jones isn't entirely thrilled with this turn of events, but she follows Tall in anyway, and doesn't let him get more than ten paces ahead as Smith maneuvers past them both and then leads the way into a cozy living room. The walls are done in tasteful wallpaper, the couches and matching armchairs are handsome but still look comfortable, the rug's a pleasant vine-and-leaf pattern done in pale greens and blues and purples, and the curtains are a filmy white with an embroidered design of snowflakes. I feel like I'm in Alice in Wonderland's Spring Collection.

"Have a seat," Smith instructs, and the way he says it makes it come across less as an invitation than as a command. Tall quickly takes one end of the couch, while Jones sinks into an armchair. Hell, I drop back into my desk chair, and I'm halfway across the Galaxy! "Now, what can I do for the two of you that required you to locate my home and breach my privacy?"

"Sorry, sir," Tall begins, and I can tell from his tone that he actually really does respect Smith. He sounds like a boy who's just disappointed his dad big-time—and yeah, I know that sound all too well. At least Tall hasn't blown anything up. Yet. "We wouldn't have bothered you but we need some information from you."

"And whatever this is couldn't wait until during work tomorrow?" Smith asks, just a hint of steel in his voice. Enough to make me shiver. "Besides, Agent Thomas, you are still on administrative leave." He frowns, and it's like a wolf showing all his teeth right before he tears into you. "I would be especially interested to know how you exited the facilities, in fact. I seem to recall speaking with you in the detainment level, and then—"

"—and then you woke up and I was gone," Tall finishes for him, which may be the bravest, riskiest, craziest thing I've ever seen him do. "Yes, sir. That's exactly why we're here, sir. You see, everyone in the agency has been compromised—everyone except Agent Jones and myself. Every other agent is now under the control of an outside force, and completely compliant."

"I see." It's clear from Smith's voice that he thinks this is all a big joke, and not a very funny one at that. He folds his arms over his chest—Jesus, he's so damn skinny for a second I think he's just gonna fold himself up like a used napkin and disappear completely from view! "All of us, you say? Including me?"

Tall sighs. "Stand up," he says by way of reply, and I can see Smith start to say something else, then look really damn startled when he pries his narrow butt off the couch and rises to his feet. "Hop on one foot," Tall continues. "Cluck like a chicken. Pretend you're a mime stuck in an invisible box." I always hated that one! "Tell me your mother's maiden name and your social security number."

Smith obeys all of those instructions, of course—turns out his mother's maiden name was Gist—and looks none to happy about any of it. "Now do you believe me?" Tall asks finally, and

Smith nods, slightly out of breath. Must have been the mime thing—those invisible cubes can be tricky!

"What—" Smith starts to ask, but then he stops, straightens, and his eyes narrow. "Monsinal Sha'ar."

"Precisely." Tall leans forward. "We need to know everything you can tell us about him, about his operation, about who else knew about him. Because someone has been using Jorbinate Sublimate." I can hear his jaw clenching—it's like a heavy rumble through my speakers—as he adds, "on us."

Smith nods. "There isn't much to tell," he says after a minute, sitting back down and closing his eyes for a second. "Monsinal Sha'ar had created a soda company and had begun producing orange soda, which he called Sunlight. But he added a little Jorbinate Sublimate to every bottle, and everyone who drank it became his slave. He got too eager, though, pushed too far too fast, and showed up on our radar as a result. We cut off his bank accounts, his electricity, his water and phones. Then we triggered the fire alarm at his factory, and once all the workers were clear we moved in and apprehended him." He gives a short, dry chuckle. "I'll give him this, he was polite and well-behaved, did exactly what we told him to do, never put up a fight. A model prisoner."

"He still is," Tall agreed. "After this is all over, we might want to see about commuting his remaining sentence. He's been alone in that cell for a very long time." I see his hands clench, and know he's forcing himself back on target. For now. "Who else knew about the chemicals?

But Smith is shaking his head. "No one. Myself, my

immediate superior Agent Trumble, Director Manaheim, and that's it. We were careful to keep local authorities on a need-to-know basis, as usual—they were told he'd been poisoning the sodas and nothing more."

"Where are Agent Trumble and Director Manaheim now?" It's the first time Jones has spoken in all this, and Smith raises an eyebrow as he glances over at her. That little facial expression is like a slap in the face, and I can see her pale a bit—which does not look good on her—but she holds her ground and after a second he smiles. Well, his lips twitch. I think that's about as good as it gets with him.

"Director Manaheim passed away in 1983," Smith answers, shaking his head. "Natural causes—he was already in his sixties by the time I started with the agency, and ours is hardly a low-stress work situation. Agent Trumble died a year later, shot accidentally by a panicked Velcanite at a routine traffic stop—the Velcanite had packed a Joruvian card-blaster in case of a mugging, and grabbed that up along with his galactic visa, shot Trumble right in the chest, he died instantly. He was a good man." He sighs. "So you see, neither of them could have been involved in this, and I assure you I was not." I believe him, too. First off, he's always struck me as the ramrod-straight, stick-up-his-butt type—no way he'd violate protocols and go off the reservation and all that other stuff. Second, he's clearly under the influence himself, and what kind of mastermind lets himself get doped with his own mind-control drug? Which just leaves one option:

"What about his partner?" I remind Tall, who nods and

repeats the question out loud.

Smith looks surprised. "My partner?" He purses his lips, and his eyes unfocus. "My partner. Yes, that's right, I did have a partner! It was . . . it was . . ." I don't know about them but I'm on the edge of my seat—yes, I'm being careful about it—but after a few seconds Smith shakes his head. "I don't remember the name. I'm sorry."

I'm pretty sure Tall looks as shocked as I feel. "You don't remember his name?" he says, and he certainly sounds stunned. "You? You remember every detail of every case you've ever worked, and every case you've overseen. You could probably tell me the color and pattern of the tie of the agent who first recruited you."

"Blue and silver, herringbone, Perry Ellis label, silk," Smith replies at once. "Very nice." His lips are still puckered in thought, if lips can think, and there's a noticeable new crease between his brows. "No, you're right, that is strange."

Tall sighs, but he doesn't sound as crushed as I feel. "It's not the first time I've seen this," he says, and I remember what he's talking about. The cookie factory! That guy Reg completely forgot he'd been the one to spike the cookies, until Tall ordered him to remember. Sure enough, the next thing he says is "remember your old partner, even if you were told to forget him."

Smith nods and opens his mouth, but shuts it again a second later. "No, I still can't remember. I'm sorry."

I can actually hear Tall's frown. It sort of twists his words sideways a little as he says, "That should have worked."

"Yeah, it should have," I agree. "But it didn't. So what now, chief?"

Tall shakes his head in response. "We need to find out who your old partner was," he tells Smith, and Jones nods agreement. "He's got to be the key to all this."

"Perhaps his work history will tell us," Jones offers. "The file request may have come through by the time I get back." But she doesn't sound too convinced, and it doesn't take a genius to figure out why. If Mr. Perfect Recall can't remember his own partner's name, why would some old report still have it? This guy's got to be more thorough than that.

"We'll think of something," Tall declares as he stands up. "Whoever's behind this, I'm not going to let him get away with it." Jones rises to her feet as well, and so does Smith. "Oh, one more thing, sir," Tall says as he starts to turn toward the door.

"Yes?"

"Snap out of it."

Smith's eyes clear, and the easy-going attitude he's been wearing since we got here vanishes, revealing the coiled-spring cobra-strike posture he's always had before. "And you waited until you were leaving to do that why, exactly?" he asks, each word like a little laser aimed at Tall's throat.

"Because I knew you wouldn't answer our questions otherwise," Tall admits, and I'm pretty sure he's giving his superior a nasty grin. "And I didn't have time to waste."

I'm surprised when Smith nods, just a tight little incline of the chin. "Understood. That will, of course, go in my report." I'm wondering if he's going to say anything about Tall's suspension—and how he and Jones are the only ones dealing with what's a clear and obvious threat to the entire agency, despite that restriction—when something beeps. Smith pulls a Bluetooth earpiece out of his pocket, inserts it in his ear, and taps it. "This is Smith." He listens for a second, nods. "Understood. Thank you." Then he sighs and glances over at Tall again. "You might want to contact your avian-adjusted friend and warn him to batten down the hatches."

"What? DuckBob? Why?" Tall says that the same time I blurt out "What? Me? Why?" It's like we're on the same wavelength! Which I guess makes sense, given the long-range frequency of this camera doohickey.

"Because our security sweep detected an unauthorized transmission from his location to our headquarters," Smith answers. "It bypassed all of our blockers and jammers, but the new systems were able to trace it back." He sighs. "And someone authorized a strike team to respond. With extreme prejudice."

"Extreme prejudice?" I try to swallow, but my throat's gone all dry and raspy. "Tell me that means they're just gonna say nasty things about my momma."

But Tall's already racing out onto the porch. "No," he answers as he moves. "It means you've got a dozen or more MiBs heading your way, weapons hot, with orders to kill anything that moves and then sanitize the entire area."

Gulp. And here I thought I was sitting safely on the sidelines. Who knew the sidelines were about to turn into Ground Zero?

Chapter Thirty-one
Get out of my head!

"Crap! What do I do? What do I do?" I'm up from my computer and pacing around the living room fast enough that my couch is edging back from me warily like it thinks I might suddenly pounce on it. Good to know—the couch can be scared into staying put. But I'm not really focused on that right now. I'm a little busy thinking about the strike team headed my way, all those MiBs just itching to shoot me or burn me or whatever they've got handy. And oddly enough, the thought that keeps popping into my head is "do I have anything for them to eat? Should I set out some chips and maybe some veggies and dip, or order some pizzas?" Thanks, Mom—you trained me so well even in a crisis I worry about entertaining.

Explains a lot about me, actually, doesn't it?

"Hang on, DuckBob!" Tall is shouting at me. A glance at the monitor shows him sprinting down some street in Nutley, and the dark flicker to one side says Jones is keeping pace. For now. "We're on our way! Mary!" He adds, and it takes me a second to realize that's not aimed at me. Hey, my lady and I are close but we are not interchangeable! "I need a pickup immediately, two of us, to the Matrix! DuckBob's in trouble!" If that doesn't get her attention, nothing will.

I glance around the room. "What should I be doing right now?" I ask. Do I have any weapons anywhere? Not really, no. I mean, I could try wielding my monitor like a giant shield, maybe, and freeze or at least severely frostbite anybody who gets too close. But that's not going to do me much good, not when they've got pistols or lasers or something else with more range than my armspan. I've got random foodstuffs, but even the dangerous ones usually require ingestion first and I doubt these guys are gonna want to stand still and open their mouths just 'cause I ask 'em to.

Though, come to think of it, they might. They're probably all cookie zombies, right? So they'll do anything anyone tells them to. Including me. Hm. I stop pacing and start grinning. This could wind up going easier than I thought.

Here's the really funny thing, the thing that probably happens in most war movies and thrillers but you don't actually see it. Normally, somebody says something like "Oh no, they know we're here!" or "Oh no, they're coming this way!" and then there's a few tense moments, and then just as they—and we—are starting to relax again, bam! Something or someone attacks. Right?

Except really, in most case it'd more like "Oh no, they know we're here!" or "Oh no, they're coming this way!" Followed by a whole lot of waiting. We're talking an hour or two, minimum. The heroes are all scared and nervous and wired—for the first few minutes. Then they start to settle down a little. They catch their breath. They remember they haven't eaten all day. They take a quick catnap. They bandage their wounds. And then they go back to watching, but they know there's probably still time, so why be on high alert?

Now take that and multiply it a time or three. The fastest Tall's ever made it out here—or back to Earth after here—is three or four hours. And that's when he's moving like a bat out of hell but still taking the bus and the car and all that, instead of asking the Grays for a quick teleport. So we're talking about three or four hours, minimum, from Earth to here. Which is probably gonna seem maddening to those poor MiBs with their SWAT gear and all that, stuck taking the train with all those weapons and all that body armor and so on. It'll be like that scene you see in every movie, the elite strike force all suited up and raring to go—only dragged out to the length of an entire mini-series. They'll probably crash from the adrenaline high and still have time to wake back up afterward.

Me?

I get a beer, make some lunch, eat, play on the computer—I mean, access the Matrix status reports—and talk to Mary. She offers to come over and help me fend off the attack, of course. And I tell her no, stay put, wherever she is. I actually don't know where she is at this point. Come to think of it, I don't even know if she has a place of her own, since it's not like I can ever go there—thanks to the Matrix, all of our dates are pretty much at my place automatically. It's possible she just hangs out on various Gray ships in between whatever missions they give her, or rents a hotel room in whatever city or planet she's in at the time. I should really ask her about that.

Anyway, I tell her not to worry about it. "Tall's on his way," I remind her, "just as soon as the Grays can beam him up." Apparently there's a queue. "And much as I'd love to have you here, and would appreciate the moral support, we'd both just be in his way." Plus, and this part I don't tell her, but if something does happen to me, somebody's gonna have to tell my mom.

Personally, I'd rather face the entire MiB agency than that. One of the best things about being stuck all the way out here in the center of the galaxy—I can't exactly go home on weekends.

It takes some doing, but I finally convince Mary that it's better if she stays where she is. And I promise to let her know once Tall gets here, and once everything's taken care of.

Then I take a nap. Because, really, what's the point in getting all worked up about it hours ahead of time? I figure I'll worry about it properly when they get here.

Which I know they have when I hear somebody kick in my front door.

"Hey!" I shout, clambering up from the couch—leaping off it is dangerous, as I discovered one time when I suddenly remembered I'd left the hot chocolate on in the kitchen and the couch, ever helpful, turned itself into something between a beanbag and a springboard. It's a good thing I looked up in time to smack bill-first into the ceiling, because otherwise I'd probably have cracked my skull. So this time I'm a little more cautious. And I'm careful not to get in sight of the front hallway as I yell, "stop shooting and drop your weapons!"

There's a satisfying clatter a second later. Yep, definitely cookie zombies.

"Everybody, drop your weapons!" I add even louder. And trust me, I can project—being heard was never a problem for me anyway and do you have any idea how much lung capacity a duck has, relatively speaking? Lots. I can hold my breath underwater for a good ten minutes or more. And I can shoot a sunflower seed across a regular cafeteria hard enough to leave a dent in the far wall. Try that at home! So yeah, when I raise my voice and project properly, I'm pretty sure all the MiBs preparing to attack me can hear.

Which doesn't mean I'm stupid enough to assume they were all listening, and are now all completely unarmed.

Nor do I assume that "unarmed" means "harmless." I've seen Tall take down a dozen invaders with nothing but hands, feet, forehead, and attitude. These guys may not be quite in his league, but they're head and shoulders above mine and there're twelve of them to one of me. Not my best odds.

So I need to even the playing field. "Go to sleep!" I holler. And there's the distinct sound, immediately after, of bodies falling over. Yes, I know it well—my Aunt Arlene was a narcoleptic, used to pass out if she laughed too much. We all competed to see who could make her drop off fastest. Cruel, I know, but at least she was always smiling. And between us and Uncle Joe we did our best to keep her away from any hard surfaces.

I wait another minute or two, listening as best I can. I don't hear anybody trying to sneak up on me, but that just means they're good at it. Still, I'm guessing at least half the strike team is down. Not bad for a guy whose best offense is usually his foot odor. Hey, what do you want, it's hard to keep things this big clean!

The question, though, is what'm I gonna do about the rest of the team? Maybe they've got earplugs in, or they're wearing headphones and jamming out to some "attack and destroy" action mix, or maybe this half is deaf and only uses sign language and smoke signals to communicate. Whatever it is, if they didn't disarm and then pass out already I've got to assume commands won't work on 'em. Which doesn't leave me a lot of options.

Though those options suddenly explode upward when I hear a faint jingling somewhere nearby—and the air in the middle of the living room starts to shimmer. I've seen this sort of thing before, so I'm not completely surprised when that area starts to glow, blue and then pink and then red and then back to blue, getting brighter and brighter all the time.

Then the glow fades, and there're two people standing there. Both of 'em are big and bulky, but one's taller and leaner. The other's got a face like a bulldog.

"Boy, am I glad to see you!" I tell Tall, clapping him on the shoulder and almost getting a punch in the face for my troubles. Which would've served him right, really—hitting me in my bill is a lot like slamming your fist into a concrete pylon, or so I've been told by a really pissed-off fellow commuter and a really intrigued EMT. I take a quick step back anyway, though. No sense antagonizing Tall when he's clearly raced here to rescue me.

"Are they here yet?" he asks, already dropping into that "ready for action" crouch of his, his pistol emerging from under his jacket.

"Yeah, they showed up a minute before you did," I tell him, nodding hello to Agent Jones—I can't hate her too much if she's here to save me—and getting a dismissive chin-jerk in reply. "I think I put half of 'em to sleep, though."

"What'd you do, tell them your fantasy football scores?" Tall grins, peering around the corner and down the hallway. And pulls back fast as someone shoots at him.

"Ha ha. I still don't see how it counts as fantasy football if I'm not allowed to use orcs and wizards and battle axes." That'd be a helluva lot more interesting—not to mention my team would probably stand a better chance. They couldn't do much worse. "But no, I ordered them to sleep."

Wow, it's been a while since I've seen Stare Number Six! But that's what I get now as Tall looks up at me, then nods. "Nice. Only took out half, though?"

"I think so, yeah. Not sure why." He shrugs and fires down the hall, which gets a small flurry in return. I hope they don't put too many holes in this place—I don't think Home Depot has sparkly purple crystal spackle. "So what do we do now?"

Tall glances over, not at me but at Jones, and nods. "Now we subdue the rest of the strike team," he answers, "and then deprogram them. Ready?" She nods—she's yet to say a word since she got here, maybe she figures that way it's less like she's going someplace she's not supposed to be or maybe she's just worried I've got a security system and I'd have voice records that she was here—and moves to the wall right behind him. Then she starts shooting toward the front door and Tall takes advantage of the distraction, rounds the corner, and takes off at a full run.

A second later I hear a dull thud, followed by a muffled grunt and another thump. That happens again, and a third time. "All clear here," Tall calls out then. It sounds like he might actually be breathing hard! Amazing!

"How many other entrance points are there?" Jones demands, glaring over at me like somehow this is all my fault. Hello, those cookies don't even affect me! And yeah, the MiBs are here to take me out, but only because I was trying to help Tall!

I'm trying to be nice, though, so I take a minute to consider her question. "From this room?" I ask. "Two—the one to the main Matrix chamber, there, and the one there to the kitchen and the bathroom and the bedroom."

"How many other ways into the building itself?" She's looking down the hallway again, her back to me, but I can hear her eye-rolling anyway.

"Oh." Yeah, I guess that might be important. At least I know the answer to that one without having to stop and think about it. "None."

She glares at me like my old Algebra teacher, Mrs. Hendricks, whenever she'd call on me. What? I'm not good at doing math under pressure! Especially when it involves letters—I like to keep my letters and my numbers separate, thank you very much! When they mix it just gets messy, in an abstract sort of way.

"None?" Jones repeats like she can't believe I'd dare even suggest that. Just like Mrs. Hendricks used to. "You're saying this is the only way in or out of this entire complex?"

"Yep."

She scrubs at her face with one hand. It doesn't help. "When Agent Thomas brought me here that first time," she rasps out, "I couldn't help but notice the arched portals gaping up above. What about those?"

"They're terraces." See, without numbers my answers are a lot clearer! And quicker!

"And is there some reason the strike team couldn't use those to gain entrance?" She tries grinding her teeth, but really I'm not impressed. Compared to Tall she's an amateur. I bet she can't even hit different octaves, let alone grind in dual harmony!

"Yeah, there's force fields on them," I tell her. Gently, because I feel bad for her lack of teeth-grinding prowess. "Air flows through, but that's about it. Even liquid gets stopped, in both directions." Which I learned all too well one time when I thought it'd be funny to lay in wait and lob water balloons at Tall as he showed up for one of his visits/spot inspections. Let's just say it's a good thing my feathers shed water so easily. And that I'd decided at the last minute not to go with grape Kool-Aid, as I'd originally planned.

I can see Jones visibly relax a little, which means she's now only as tense as your average day trader during a Wall Street blitz. "Ah. Well, good. So we just need to defend this one door and we're all set."

"Yep." It occurs to me that I haven't heard any shooting or fighting for at least a minute. I listen. "Uh, should you maybe go check on him?" I suggest. "I'd do it, but—" I hold up the cord tethering me to the Matrix.

"I'm sure Agent Thomas has matters well in hand," Jones says, and there's that hint of hero worship in her voice again, making it sort of high and breathy under the rough smoker's rasp. Not a good combo. "It's only six other agents."

"Uh, yeah, sure, okay." I scratch my head. "I mean, yes, Tall's a bad-ass, but what if—"

I don't have to finish that thought because the front door swings open and a long shadow stretches down the hall. "Exterior secured," Tall reports as he emerges in the doorway. He's got a pair of MiBs with him, one slung over each shoulder like they were hand towels. "Let's bring them all in, make sure they're secure, and then we'll get Ned to run that gizmo of his to deprogram them." Jones nods and brushes past him, presumably to go retrieve more downed agents though I suspect she also took the liberty of checking him for weapons on the way past—and I'm trying REALLY hard not to think about that one too much, thanks all the same—and Tall looks over at me. "You okay?"

"Fine." I sigh. "I mean, I feel a little violated, with them bursting in like that, and I'm annoyed, and now I've got all this onion dip that's probably gonna go to waste, but otherwise, yeah, I'm good." He gives me one of his looks—it might be Number Four but if so it's a kinder, gentler version than usual, maybe Four-A?—and shakes his head, then lumbers past to deposit the unconscious agents where Ned had set Brad up before.

After he's gone and I'm by myself again, I sink down onto my couch—which doesn't protest, for once—and rest my head in my hands. Though only for a minute, because this bill is heavy! I wasn't kidding about feeling a little violated. This place may be weird and wacky and Day-glo and the last known remnant of some ancient space beastie, but it's still my home, and those MiBs kicked down the door and started shooting it up. I'd be lying if I said I was happy about that.

But more than being scared or upset or even relieved—I'm pissed. Whoever's behind all this figured out I was involved and sent those agents here. After me. Well, mister, whoever you are and wherever you are, it's on!

Chapter Thirty-two
Answering in double-negatives

After the other MiBs have been restored to their proper minds—or whatever passes for such a thing when you're a top-secret government agent whose whole job is tracking, categorizing, and generally policing alien creatures the entire rest of the world don't even believe exist, much less run out on bar tabs and use up all the paper towels and hand soap in public restrooms—they're all appropriately embarrassed about breaking down my door and trying to kill me. They even offer to help repair the damage, though I don't take them up on that for a number of reasons. First off, even your standard MiB wouldn't know what to make of my humble abode, and how can they possibly patch it up if they don't even know what it is? Second, this whole place is still classified, and not a one of them has the clearance for it—I suspect half of the reason behind their offer to help is for an excuse to poke around.

Third, I've actually been wanting to put up a few coat hooks and maybe a small basketball hoop but I could never find a way to pierce the skull walls. Now I've got a half dozen or so holes, ready and waiting. I'll have to remember this and ask Tall to bring his sidearm the next time I need to install new shelves.

Anyway, Tall bundles the others off back to Earth—the slow, boring, interstellar bus way, presumably because they don't deserve the Grays' instant-teleport method—and Jones elects to go with them. She's made the trip once before, after all—which is one more time than any of these other yahoos, at least when they were in their right mind—and besides, she wants to check and see if that query she put in on Agent Smith has come back yet. I can't say I'm sorry to see her go, at least not with a straight face. She's not as terrible as she was the first time, admittedly, but that still doesn't mean we're gonna be late-night drinking buddies. Though a little alcohol—okay, a lot of alcohol—might do wonders for her personality. I've been told it vastly improves mine. And expands my vocabulary, which is a little disturbing—apparently I speak passable Welsh and nearly fluent Japanese when I'm drunk, which might just say something about how those languages evolved in the first place.

"So, what now?" I ask Tall as I hand him a beer—a regular Earth-variety one, I don't need any more excitement at the moment—and plop down on my couch with another. It's still behaving—I think all the commotion scared it.

"Now we wait for Agent Jones to see what she can find," he replies, taking a healthy swig from his bottle. "Hopefully, we'll get the name of Smith's old partner, and then we can set about tracking him down."

"You really think that'll work?" I ask him, and I'm not surprised when he frowns and shakes his head. "Yeah, me either. This guy's smart enough to erase people's memories after they meet him, and he even got to Smith somehow—he has to know enough to erase his old work history from your computers."

"It isn't quite that easy," Tall protests. He actually sounds a little hurt, like I've insulted his haircut or something. Hey, just because I don't want my head to look like a fresh-cut lawn or a gravel landing strip, don't let me stop you! "Our computers have the best security on the planet," he says, "or in the solar system. And we've brought in guys like Ned before to make sure it can stand up to alien interference, too. Plus it's all hard-shielded, so there's no way to break into it from off-site." Which I personally know to be true. Hey, what do you want? I've got oodles of spare time, a computer that can practically write a sonata while rebuilding a classic car engine and calculating the approach of a meteor swarm, a sensor array capable of tracking stray particles in solar systems on the other end of the spiral and determining each one's size, density, and frequency, and a penchant for sticking my bill where it doesn't belong. And I was curious what they had to say about me. But no luck. I couldn't get in, no matter what I tried.

"So this guy's been to your headquarters," I say. "Doesn't that mean you have him on tape? I know there're cameras everywhere."

"There are," Tall agrees, polishing off the last of his beer in two long swallows, "and we can check, but I'm guessing he was smart enough to hack into those and erase any footage." Which makes sense. Why be this careful in everything else and then get sloppy with something like that?

There is something that's bugging me, though. "Why couldn't Smith remember when you told him to? That worked before, on the cookie guy."

"I don't know." And I can tell from the way Tall says it that having to admit that is killing him. "There must've been something different about the two situations, but we have no way of knowing what."

We sit there in silence for a bit after that. Eventually I get bored—okay, as soon as my beer's done—and switch on the TV. Turns out one of the channels is having an all-day "If Our World Was Ending" marathon, so we sit and watch a few episodes of that. The "Supernova" episode is particularly good—I'm impressed how the focal character thinks to dry his laundry and cook his food using the convection heat beating down from the swollen sun, thus speeding up his pack-and-go time by at least a few hours. Waste not, want not!

The "Stolen by Space Pirates" episode is just past the credits when Tall's phone rings. "Yeah?" he answers, eyes still on the screen. It's like he's evasive on sheer reflex! He listens for a second, nods, sighs, says, "All right, thanks. I'll keep you posted," and hangs up. "That was Agent Jones," he tells me, which I kind of guessed. "She got Agent Smith's work history. His partner's name isn't listed."

"No real surprise there," I comment, leaning back and folding my hands over my belly. What, I think best when reclining! Especially while sleeping! "It is kind of weird, though."

He shakes his head at me. "How is that weird? You agreed earlier that he probably got to the files as well."

"Well, sure." I shrug. "I dunno, it's just—if you were trying to cover up who you were, how would you do it? If you didn't want people to track you through your old case files and blog posts and things."

"I don't blog," he corrects with that same tone you hear from super-elegant ladies who exclaim that they don't stoop to such-and-such behavior—usually right before sneaking off for exactly that. "But I would most likely create a false persona and use that to obscure my real identity."

"Exactly!" I try to wave my arms around but I forgot my fingers were laced together, and it winds up just looking like I'm doing some old breakdancing move. I'll have to remember that if I ever make it back for a college reunion. "But this guy, he doesn't insert 'Agent Stick-Up-Butt' or 'Grimjaw McShady' or anything like that. No, he just removes himself completely. It just seems like a weird choice to me."

Tall's thinking—I can tell because he's chewing on his lower lip, and because he didn't glare at me for the "stick-up-butt" thing, and after a moment he raises his cell phone again and dials somebody. "Thomas here," he says a second later—presumably the person on the other end just picked up. "Can you pull up that file again?" Ah, Agent Jones. She's a lot more pleasant like this, where I don't have to see or hear her myself. "Check the file history," he tells her next. "It should be under 'Status,' right after 'Check out,' 'check in,' and 'report.' Yes, right there. Now, what's the last entry before your check-out?" He listens intently. "Okay. Thanks."

"What's going on?" I ask.

"Agent Smith's file hasn't been recently altered," he tells me. "It was officially redacted—almost forty years ago!"

"Redacted? What the hell's that? Is it like 'reduced' but with a dramatic reading involved?"

Tall doesn't laugh—I don't know why I bother. I guess mainly because I laugh. Hey, I'm a funny guy! He does answer, though: "No, 'redacted' means to obscure or remove text." His frown deepens—I can practically see through that crease in his forehead, right into his skull! "Typically it's used to refer to government alteration of some official document."

"So you're saying the agency removed the name of Smith's partner, and it was years ago?" I scratch at my bill. "Man, I can see why he'd be pissed!" There's something tickling the back of my mind, and it's not the business end of the feathers gracing my neck. But what? Forty years ago, official censoring of agency records, all traces of this guy wiped clean . . . "Hey, would the agency erase memories, too?"

Tall nods. "Of course. I told you that's standard procedure when an agent decides to leave—or doesn't make the cut and gets sent back to a normal life." The sad little quirk to his lips tells me he's thinking the same thing I am, that a life like that, especially after everything we've seen and done, might not even be worth living. And even though I know he hasn't been entirely thrilled about his job since the whole saving the universe thing, there's no way he'd ever give up everything we've seen and done.

But I'm still going over his explanation. He said something similar once before, about going back to a normal life—and then it all clicks into place. Of course!

"Agent Mercer-Messer-Miezer!" Tall hits me with a Number Seven, and I hurry to explain. "The first WiB, remember? You told me she was there in the early seventies, and after they kicked her out they wiped her memory and set her up with a normal, boring life instead. She'd have to be, what, in her sixties or seventies today? Which is—"

"—about the right age to be a little old lady who bumps into Reg from the cookie factory and hypnotizes him into adding Jorbinate Sublimate to the cookies," Tall finishes for me. "Damn."

"And the timing's right for her to have been partnered with Smith," I add. "Then they wiped his memory of her, too, after she left."

"Which is why commanding him to remember wasn't going to work," Tall agrees. "When she uses the cookies to alter people's memories, she's really just hiding those memories away so nobody can find them—until I order them to go ahead and remember after all. But the agency's redaction methods are a lot more thorough. There really wasn't enough there for Agent Smith to grasp onto, or to even realize he'd been tampered with." He's nodding slowly. "I think you've just found our culprit, DuckBob." And I know I'm not imagining the respect in his voice. I wish I could bottle it and save it for later, like the next time I do or say something stupid. It probably wouldn't even go flat by then.

"Cool. So, now that we know who she is, how do we find her? I'm guessing she's not gonna make this easy for us."

Tall grins at me in reply. "Of course not. Where would be the fun in that?" He gestures toward my computer. "Come on, fire that thing up and let's get cracking."

I'm already off the couch—it goes into a sulk, but I refuse to let my own furniture guilt me into doing something—and a few seconds later I'm sliding into my desk chair and waking the system up. "What're we looking for?"

"We'll need her full name, first," he points out. He walks over to stand right behind me, both hands on the back of my chair, and frowns—I can see him reflected in the monitor. "Look for articles from the early seventies about young women recovering from a coma," he tells me. "That's always the agency's favorite cover story—it explains why the person hasn't been around, and covers over any odd behavior as they readjust."

I nod and type in the search request. A few minutes later, my computer dings—sometimes I think it mistakes itself for a Betty Crocker oven, which just tells me I need to try scooping brownie mix into the CD tray—and the results start to pop up on the screen. There's a good page or two of them, but a lot we can rule out immediately—like the ones talking about a twelve-year-old coma victim, or the ones where it's a forty-year-old housewife. That just leaves four possibilities, and I click on each one to read the full article and check out the accompanying picture. The first one looks to be tiny, a waif-like thing with big dark eyes and a dark pixie cut. The second one's got light hair of some color but she's not much better-looking than Agent Jones—plus she was in a coma for only a week, which doesn't match. But the third—

"That's her!" Tall grips my chair so hard I have to plant my feet to keep him from tipping us both over. Down, boy! "That's definitely her!"

I study the image. Okay, yeah, I can see it—she's tall, broad-shouldered, busty, with long blond hair and a strong but still graceful jaw and dark eyes. She could be Wonder Woman's blonde cousin.

"Olivia Ann Mercer, age twenty-five," I read, "thrilled hospital and family alike when this morning she suddenly woke from a two-year-long coma. Miss Mercer had graduated Sarah Williams College with a degree in Romance languages and had been traveling to Boston for a job interview when the bus she was in had a mechanical failure and flipped over. Miss Mercer was rushed to the nearest hospital, St. Luke's in Grandville, but somehow her identification got lost in the shuffle and she languished there for two years known only as Jane Doe, while her family believed her dead. It was only this morning, upon awakening, that she was able to let the hospital staff know her name and who to contact. Doctors say that Miss Mercer is showing signs of a remarkable recovery, and they hope to be able to release her to her family soon."

"Sounds about right," Tall says, and I can tell from the dreamy tone that he's still gazing at her picture. Yeah, okay, she's a hottie, but focus, please!

"Two years, though?" I ask him. "I thought you said she was only a WiB for a month?"

He nods, making my chair shake. "She was, but she had to undergo training first. They wiped out all memory of that as well. At least, that's how it's supposed to work—I did hear once that the early memory wipes weren't always perfect, and sometimes random images or names could crop back up."

"Yeah, well, sounds like she kept a lot more than that." I reread the article. "At least we know her name now." I type that in and hit "search." "Let's see what we get." What we get turns out to be page upon page of information—seems there're a lot of Olivias and Anns and Mercers. Who knew? But I group the whole name and this time the results are sparser. The first one, though, knocks me for a loop:

"Olivia Ann Mercer, age sixty-five, passed away on Tuesday from a fatal heart attack. She is survived by her sister Doris Lehaine, her brother Rick Mercer, and her grandchildren Melody, Anne, Daniel, and Jack. Services are for family only, but donations in her memory can be made to the Red Cross and to United Way." I check the date. "According to this, she died six months ago."

"Just before everything started," Tall says. "Hmph. You've got access to DMV files, right?"

I laugh. "Please! I spent a whole day one time giving fake tickets and DUIs to people I hated in high school."

He gives me a big "I'll ignore that—for now" sigh. "Look for any women, age sixty to seventy, who applied for a driver's license within the month or two before her death," he orders.

"Got it." Makes sense—she'd want to have another identity ready before she faked her death—and I'm assuming that's what's going on, because I can handle aliens of all stripes just fine but if it turns out we're dealing with real, genuine, bona fide, honest-to-God ghosts, I quit.

But sure enough, I get a few hits. "Here's a Mavis Delilah Rhodes, age sixty-eight," I read off, "and a Nancy Caroline Fry, age sixty-one, and a Waverly Irene Brooks, age sixty-four."

"That last one," Tall says, leaning in. "Pull up her application. It should have her photo."

It does, and sure enough it's a shot of an older but still striking woman with almost platinum-blond hair—natural, from the look of it—and a stern expression. "How'd you know?" I ask Tall.

He grins at me. "Waverly Irene Brooks. WiB."

"Ah." Great, our crazy revenge-minded take-over-the-world lady has a sense of humor. Delightful.

"Her DMV record lists her address as Westchester, New York." I pull the address up on the screen, then call up a map and zero in on it. Then I check around a little more. "No sign that she's left." I go to a different site. "Yep, the post office is still delivering her mail to that address, no forwarding requested." It makes sense that she'd set up there, too. We know that's where Monsinal Sha'ar and Fah-te had set up their drop point for the Jorbinate Sublimate, and she'd want to stay close to that. And still be able to bop into Manhattan to keep tabs on the MiBs, and maybe take in a show.

"Excellent!" Tall squeezes my chair one last time—what'd it ever do to him?—and turns toward the front door. He's already got his phone out, and is typing in a text to someone as he walks away.

"Wait, where're you going?" I actually have a pretty good idea, which he confirms when he glances back and gives me what I can only call a wolfish grin, since it looks all lean and hungry and even a bit furry. He really needs to shave soon. "I don't think confronting her by yourself is really smart—at least call Agent Jones for backup!"

But Tall shakes his head even as he pulls the front door open. "This one is all mine," he insists. I hear a faint humming somewhere, and the air around him starts getting brighter and brighter. Uh oh. There's a color shift or two, and a big flash, and when it all clears away Tall is gone.

I just hope he knows what he's doing.

As for Olivia Ann Mercer, I hope she's ready. Because she may not even know what hit her.

Chapter Thirty-three
Why, Granny, what big semi-legal automatic weapons you have!

I pull up my Tall-cam just in time to see him hop into a car—another MiB pulls up in it, one of their standard "ooh, look at me I'm so subtle!' black sedans—and walks away, leaving the keys in the ignition—and take off for Westchester. I guess all's forgiven now that the whole agency's experienced the joy and wonder of being a cookie zombie. Or maybe Enterprise was just out of dark sedans.

I can see Tall's face in the rearview mirror as he drives up through Manhattan, and he looks furious, his jaw clenched and his brow so low he practically needs a forklift just to raise it high enough to peer out from under. His hands grip the steering wheel so tight I'm surprised it doesn't twist up like a pretzel. Of course, Manhattan traffic always makes me feel the same way—I'm convinced most New York drivers actually got their licenses from cereal boxes and their training from action movies—but this is clearly more than that. And while I'm a big fan of watching Tall tear through things—and people—like they're paper dolls, I'm not sure that's the best play here.

"Listen, Tall, let's think this through," I urge into the mike.

"I'm serious. You don't want to just go charging in there half-cocked. This lady's one tough customer, and she's probably already expecting you. What're you gonna do, knock on the front door?"

"That's exactly what I'm going to do," he mutters through his teeth. "Only I'll be using this car as the knocker."

Okay, that can't be good.

"What if you've got the wrong house?" I point out. "What if she's in a bunker out back? What if she's kidnapped some innocent little kid and has him tied up in the foyer to prevent just such a response? Are you really willing to risk little Timmy's life to satisfy your rage?"

That makes him pause—at least for a few seconds. "Yes," he finally answers. Great. Now he's gone full-on homicidal.

I call Mary instead. "Can't you get the Grays to zap him back here?" I ask her. "Then we could come up with a real plan instead of this 'look at me charging in like a knight at a joust, only it turns out I'm up against a Panzer tank' bullshit."

"They will not relocate him, or anyone else, without the subject's express permission," she tells me. "It is part of the accords they formed with the agency, allowing them to continue operating on Earth and in its vicinity." Presumably because people weren't too happy about the whole 'abducted and probed and then tossed back like a tagged wildebeest" experience.

"So what can I do?" I ask her. I'd be tearing at my hair but feathers are a lot shorter and harder to grasp. Good thing, because a bald duck-headed man would be a REALLY look for me.

"Stay close to him," Mary urges. "Make sure he knows you are there to support him, and give him the benefit of your insight and your observation." See, this is why I love her. She sees the good in me, when most people just see all the other stuff. Which, admittedly, is usually a lot louder.

'Got it," I promise. "Thanks." I wish she was here, but she's doing some kind of scouting mission—when I called I thought I caught a glimpse of what looked like wispy clouds, only made of lava. Not sure I really want to ask her for the details when she does get back.

Anyway, I focus on Tall, though I let him drive the rest of the way in silence, and soon the apartment buildings and sub-way tracks have swapped out for large houses with even larger lawns and wide, quiet streets with the occasional luxury car. So this is how the other half lives. Though, actually, I don't know which half that'd be. Could be the ducks, because we do pass a few small ponds and I'm betting they only ever get tossed high-end organic bread.

The address I found for Waverly Irene Brooks turns out to be big, sprawling house broken almost haphazardly into small segments that exist at various heights and angles to one another. It's like somebody took a regular ranch house, got it stinking drunk, and then let it stagger around until it smashed up against a cliff or something and broke apart a bit but still managed to hold onto its components, however loosely. Great, it's the Drunk House.

Tall pulls up the nice big circular drive and stops right in front of the house. At least something I said earlier must have gotten through, since he doesn't just stomp up to the door and kick it in. Instead—he rings the doorbell.

I half expect big nasty deathtraps to go off all around, or a sabertooth tiger to leap down from the porch awning and swallow Tall whole, or at least an electrified net to envelop him and taze him into unconsciousness. Instead there's the sound of footsteps from within, then the click of a lock, and then the door opens.

And there, at long last, is Olivia Ann Mercer.

Her pictures don't really do her justice. She's tall, six feet I'd guess, and still built like a brick outhouse, even at her age— broad shoulders, impressive bust, tight waist. Her hair's a sil-very white and pulled up in a tight bun and she's got a few lines around her eyes and mouth and across her forehead, but oth-erwise she looks exactly like the stunning young woman who flustered an entire top-secret agency into almost killing itself trying to impress her. And I can totally see why.

"Ah. Yes. I wondered when you would find me." Her dark eyes flick over Tall, no doubt tallying the location of every weapon he's carrying, and they stay hard and cold even though her lips curl up in a smile as she steps back, opening the door wide. "Won't you come in, Agent Thomas?"

"Thank you, Miss Mercer," Tall replies, refusing to let her see that knowing his name flusters him though I suspect it does at least a little bit—hell, it has me quaking, and I'm a million light-years away!—and steps in. It's a nice foyer, rough stone slabs for the floor and a wide open space behind where the floor drops away to stairs and then a lower level while the ceiling goes up above a few others stairs to an open walkway running overhead. It's like what would happen if Escher had taken up with Frank Lloyd Wright—and then the pair of them had decided to sell out and start making McMansions in suburbia.

"Can I take your coat?" Miss Mercer asks, striding past Tall and stopping just at the top of the stairs heading down. "Your sunglasses? Your sidearm?"

"No, thank you." Tall matches her fake politeness. He is at least part bureaucrat, after all. Probably on his cousin's side. "I doubt I'll be staying long."

"Come, we'll talk in the family room." And she leads the way down the stairs, along a short hallway, and into an enormous room. Seriously, this room is almost as long as the Matrix Chamber, though not as wide. And the ceiling in here has got to be at least twenty feet up—again, no match for the Chamber, but still seriously impressive all the same. "Being a WiB for a month ten years ago must pay a helluva lot better than I thought," I mutter. "Or she's wicked good at the day trading."

"Can I get you anything?" she asks, settling into a comfortable-looking armchair and gesturing him toward the matching one or the couch, both set up opposite it and across a coffee table made from an entire slab of redwood. I know because I had one like it, back in college. Awesome table, really distinctive, got lots of admiring looks—right up until people barked their shins on it. Those untreated edges are sharp! "Coffee?" Mercer continues. "Tea? A few cookies, perhaps?" I can't quite read the look in her eyes when she says that. Maybe if I knew Braille.

"No thanks," Tall answers, choosing the other armchair.

Maybe he's thinking of my couch and assuming hers will be equally difficult to escape, though hers has yet to move or even quiver or change color. Amateur. "I'm on a strict no-cookie diet these days."

"I thought you might be." She actually laughs like this is funny, though I don't see how. Must be MiB humor. "I'd love to know how you managed that, actually. The addictive element is extremely strong." There's a teacup on the table in front of her, saucer and everything, but she doesn't reach for it. Maybe she's saving it for later.

Tall doesn't even bother answering. Me, I would've said something patently ridiculous, like "I just thought of my old gym teacher in a skin-tight bathing suit every time I heard the word 'cookie' and that killed any inclination to ever go near them again." Actually, now that I think about it, yuck! Suddenly I don't want any cookies, either! But Tall's done playing games. "What exactly do you want, Miss Mercer?"

She spreads her hands—I can't help noticing they're big, strong, but graceful, with long, tapered fingers and short but well-tended nails done in a bronze polish. What? So I'm observant—and may have spent a few months, at my most desperate, working at a nail salon. So what? I never did pedis, though—even I have my limits. "What do I want?" she replies. "Revenge, for starters. The world, after that. There really isn't much in between, is there?" Her smile is slow, sultry, and vicious. It's like a shark decided to get dolled up for an elegant night on the town.

"Revenge?" Tall sounds genuinely confused. "For what? You were offered a spot in the agency. It didn't work out. You knew when you accepted the offer what would happen if you left. You were compensated for your time, and reinserted into your life with as little alteration as possible."

"As little alteration as possible?" She's up out of her chair so fast Tall actually starts, and I'm pretty sure I see him reach for his pistol. "You took two years of my life! And tried to convince me that nothing had happened, that I'd been in a stupid car accident and then been comatose all that time! You don't think that's a problem? You don't think knowing what really happened, knowing I'd been a part of something I could never talk about, never find again, and never convince anyone else even existed, you don't think that took its toll on me? You don't think that scarred me for life? You don't think I deserve something for all that?"

"Geez, repeat yourself much," I mutter. "How many times can one person say 'you don't think' in a single rant, anyway? What was she, a debating champ?" I repeat myself a lot too, of course, but usually it's just things like "Hey, now!" or "Really?" or "Worcestershire sauce!" That last one drives Tall nuts, mainly because I'll insert it after every third or fourth word for a while, just to watch him twitch. And because I really like Worcestershire sauce.

Tall keeps his cool, and doesn't draw down on her either, though he does rise to his feet as well. Probably so she doesn't tower over him—ha, see, that's not so fun, is it? "That shouldn't have happened," he tells her. "The agency had only recently developed the process, and there were still a few flaws. It's seamless now—you won't remember anything."

I'm sure he thought that would be helpful somehow, all but telling her flat out that "we're going to wipe your memory again, but don't worry, this time we'll do it right!" I could've told him, though—as far as comforting statements goes? That one, not so much.

Clearly Miss Mercer feels the same way, because she swells up like a squeezed water balloon. "So you think you can just walk in here and tell me you're going to wipe my memory a second time, make me forget everything that's happened, and that'll be okay? You think I'll say thank you or something? Not a chance, buster!" Buster? Yeah, that's about the first time I've really believed her age—who says "buster" anymore? What's next, "gee, willikers!"? "Boy, howdy!"? "Darn tootin'!"?

"I didn't mean to upset you," Tall says, and I'm pretty sure he's being sincere. For one thing, he's speaking clearly, without any grinding. "But obviously having these memories has caused problems for you, and we can fix that."

"Can you?" She takes a step closer, and now she's in his face. "Can you really? Can you give me back the last forty years of my life!?!" She screams that last bit, so close I can count her molars—she has eleven of them, which makes me wonder where the last one went. Is it packed away in a drawer somewhere, just in case she needs a spare? Did she get one wisdom tooth taken out but decide she needed to keep the rest or else she'd be unwise the rest of her life? Did the MiBs take it out and replace it with a poison tooth, and then take that one back when they booted her, in which case I've got to be real careful about being around Tall when he bites down on something hard?—and her eyes look all wild and wide, like my old cat right before he went into his "look at me, I'm a whirling dervish of death, aren't I cute?" routine. Uh-oh.

"Tall, look out, man," I warn, but even as I say that, a smirk forms on Miss Mercer's face. At least I don't have to look at those molars anymore.

"I don't think so, Agent Thomas," she says, stepping back a pace, and now her voice is cool and calm. Too calm. "In fact, I don't think I'll be letting you do anything." She sits back down and picks up her teacup. "Are you sure you wouldn't like anything to drink?"

"No, thank you." He sits down as well. Too damn polite, sometimes. If I were him, I'd stay on my feet, both so I could loom over her—Tall's world-class at looming, too, I've asked him more than once if he studied that in college—and so I could back away quickly. But instead there he is, sitting down like this is still some demented social call. "Look, I'm sure we can work things out here. There's no reason for anyone to get upset."

She smiles, but it's not a good smile. "No, I suppose not." Then she leans forward slightly. "Actually, can I tell you something?"

Tall leans in as well. "Of course."

"Don't listen to her, man!" I shout. "Think of Admiral Ackbar! What would he say?" But he doesn't listen. He's too captivated by her, which I guess makes sense—he's pretty much had a crush on her since he first found about her, and now here she is in the flesh, and still looking pretty damn good for all her years, and he's basically stunned. Plus I already knew he had a thing for Valkyries, tall, busty, broad-shouldered blondes, and Olivia Ann Mercer is practically the model for that type.

So I can't do anything but groan when she tosses the contents of her cup full in his face. I'd laugh at how silly that gesture was, but I've already guessed that she doesn't do anything silly. And the way she smiles right after, slow and lazy like a cat about to pounce, doesn't help any.

"There, now," she says, setting her cup back down and straightening in her seat. "Don't you feel better?"

"I suppose so," Tall answers, and it's a good thing I'm by myself because I'm pretty sure the curses I loose could blister paint and cause deafness, tremors, and partial paralysis. As it is, my couch quivers and tries to curl into a ball in the corner. That doesn't even slow me down, though, because I recognize the slightly slurred tone in Tall's voice all too well:

He's gone cookie zombie again.

"I did worry that you might have made yourself immune to the Jorbinate Sublimate itself," Mercer confides as she rises to her feet again, but more slowly this time. After all, there's clearly no hurry anymore. "But I'd hoped it was just the cookies themselves you'd managed to find a way around. I'm glad to see I was right. Stand up." My perspective shifts as he complies. "Good. Now, come with me. I haven't decided exactly what to do with you yet, so for now I'll put you in the spare bedroom. For safekeeping."

I'm forced to watch as Tall follows docilely as a broken dog. Great. Now what're we gonna do? I can't snap him out of it, and I don't know if I can reach Ned or Mary in time. Who else can help, though?

Then I realize who. And I have to grit my teeth. But I need to do this, and not just for Tall. For everyone. So I force myself to go over to my computer and hack into Tall's phone records, then pick up my phone and dial.

"Who is this?" The raspy voice demands as soon as it picks up. This is definitely in the training manuals.

"It's DuckBob," I answer. "Listen, Agent Jones. Tall—I mean, Agent Thomas—needs your help."

Chapter Thirty-four
When bad pranks pay off

It doesn't take much to convince Jones that Tall's in trouble. About nine words, in fact: "So we found Mercer, and Tall went after her—"

"He what?" Okay, she may not be much at the whole gnashing-of-teeth thing but when it comes to frothing over the phone, this gal's world-class. I think my chin actually gets damp, even. "He went after her alone?" Then apparently her words catch up with her brain by way of her ears, and she stops. I know exactly what that's like, since I say things without thinking all the time, and then hear them and about half the time go "huh?" The best are the ones where I then realize, "Hey, that was actually pretty clever of me!" I may be an idiot, but my attitude has flashes of pure genius.

Jones is clearly having a moment like this, at least of the "wait, I said what?" variety. "Who is Mercer," she asks after a second, and I feel so bad for her, I just want to tell her, "It's okay, honey, keep practicing, someday you'll sound like you're shooting your words out at me machine-gun style instead of dribbling them on the floor at your own feet because you're chewing marbles at the same time." This probably isn't the time, though, so I just keep quiet and listen as she adds, "and what do you mean, 'she'?"

"Olivia Ann Mercer was a MiB," I explain, happy to actually know what I'm talking about for once. "Or maybe a WiB, I'm still not clear on that. She was the first female agent, back in the early seventies—and she was Smith's partner when they busted Monsinal Sha'ar. But it didn't work out, so she got drummed out and her memory was wiped, as were all records of her."

"Which is why Agent Smith couldn't remember she even existed." Yeah, Jones isn't stupid. I make a mental note of that in case we're ever playing poker together.

"Exactly. But apparently it didn't take with her, so she still remembered all of it. And, well, it's kinda driven her a little cuckoo." On the whole I think that's a pretty good rundown, especially a quickie version.

"So Agent Thomas went to confront her? What happened? Is he all right?" That definitely sounds like more than friendly and professional interest, but I let it slide for now. Instead I peek at my Tall-cam. He's in a bedroom, definitely a spare room by the way all the furnishings are a little on the generic side, with no photos or personal items. It's the same room Mercer led him to, and then she told him, "Stay here and keep quiet."

"He's in her spare room," I answer. "She dosed him again, though not with cookies at least, and so he's just sitting there quietly, waiting for orders."

"Tell him to snap out of it!" she urges, and of course if I could've I would have, but I already know better.

"Won't work," I reply. "You've gotta be there in person, over the mike doesn't cut it. Somebody's gotta get in there with him, wake him up, and get the hell back out."

"Fine." I can hear Jones moving about on her end. "I'm on my way. I should be there within the hour. You think about our next move, in the meantime." Then she's gone.

"Our next move"? Oy. But I do have the time to study this from all angles, and I'm hoping something springs to mind. Something beyond "sic an angry WiB on a revenge-crazed ex-WiB," which seems to be the current plan.

An hour later, Jones calls me back. "I'm pulling up in front of Mercer's house. Nice place."

"You should see the inside," I mutter. Jones hears me, though, and smiles. I can tell because her next words are stretched oddly: "That's the plan."

Then she's out of the car.

"Wait, what're you gonna do?" I ask. "Tall got zombified because he waltzed right in. If you do the same, you'll just be another zombie, too. And it's not like I have a lot of MiBs in my Favorites, so if you get stuck here, you're on your own."

That makes Jones stop, one big, beefy hand resting on the top of the car, the other clasping the upper edge of the still-open driver's side door. Yes, I can hear this sort of thing over the phone—it's amazing what good hearing I have, considering I don't have any actual external ears. And yes, I hate it when people call me while they're in the bathroom. Boundaries, people—boundaries.

"We need to find another way in," she admits after a minute. "And some way to steer clear of Miss Mercer herself. Any ideas?"

I'm flattered that she's even asking my opinion—and I wish I had something better to report—but after a few seconds' thought I have to sigh. "I didn't see any other exits," I tell her, "though in some spots it was hard to make out anything. I think you may be stuck with the front-door approach. And try to find some way not to breathe, either. She could have it in spray form, too."

Jones grunts. "Don't breathe. Right. This should be easy. What about contact? Will enough seep into my skin to affect me?"

It's a good question, and I honestly don't know. "You should keep from exposing yourself anyway, just in case," I tell her, which is actually true on a lot of levels. Ugh. "In fact, wrap a burka around yourself, and keep your head low."

Then I have what might be my best idea ever. "No, never mind the burka," I assure her. "Listen, how secure is your phone?"

"Very."

"Excellent! Here's what you do . . ."

Which is why, twenty minutes later, I'm still on the line with Jones when a large vehicle of some sort comes racing up the block, sirens blaring, and screeches to a halt right next to her car. There's the thud of door opening and closing, and the thump of feet hitting the ground, then the bustle of a bunch of people hustling about.

"You the one who called?" Someone asks, and his voice is heavily muffled.

"Me? No," Jones answers, lying through her teeth. Turns out she's better at that than grumbling through them or grinding them, so that's good, at least. "I got called in, too. I'm with the government." She doesn't bother to say which branch, and somehow they don't ask her. I guess they've got bigger things to worry about.

"All right, we'll secure the location—you stay back here behind the perimeter," Mr. Muffler orders. "Everybody ready?" There's a whole bunch of replies, all similarly swaddled. "Right, let's do this by the book!" And then there's footfalls again, followed by a loud crash.

So yes, it turns out that it really is good to know how to call in and report a possible biohazard situation. And no, you shouldn't do something like this to just anyone, not even an obnoxious co-worker who hogs all the chocolate donuts. Though Donny did deserve it—it's just not right leaving everyone else with only sprinkles, plain, and coconut. I don't care if he was a big deal in the seventies. Besides, the hazmat team didn't mess him up too badly, and I hear most of his hair did eventually grow back, so it's all good. And right now, remembering how to do that and being able to relay that to Jones turned out to be perfect.

Because of course they're all wearing full hazmat suits. With oxygen tanks. No outside contact at all. No way for Mercer to zombify them. Check and mate, sweetheart!

I'm still congratulating myself when I hear a whole lot of rustling. "Yo, what's going on?" I ask.

"I'm suiting up," Jones replies, and there's a clatter that I'm guessing is her setting the phone down on something for a minute.

"Suiting up? You're going in there?"

"Of course," she answers, and now she's all muffled too. "I've still got to get to Agent Thomas."

Ah, right. "Bring a spare," I point out, and the rustling that follows tells me she knows I'm not talking bowling. Then she hangs up on me.

Well, that's fine. I switch back to my Tall-cam. He's still in that same spare bedroom, sitting on the bed, just waiting there. I can hear the hazmat team moving around through his mic, but when the door opens a few minutes later it's not them I see—

It's Mercer.

Ah, hell.

Chapter Thirty-five
But where's the Jell-O?

"It seems someone thought to call in the cavalry," she says as she approaches him, and again I'm struck by what remarkably good shape she's in. If I didn't know any better, I'd swear she was in her thirties and just had prematurely silver hair. I'd say I hoped I look that good when I'm her age, but I already know I will—turns out ducks age handsomely, so I'll probably get some silvering around the eyes but otherwise there won't be much change. Go, me! Regardless, Mercer glides across the room with a casual grace that reminds me she's still very dangerous. And that Tall's a sitting duck—which is a bit of role-reversal, for sure.

"And they're well equipped to avoid my usual safeguards," she continues as she stops beside him. "Any idea who sent them?"

"Most likely DuckBob," Tall answers—damn that zombie-juice! That stuff's worse than truth serum, which Tall assures me can be beaten, or at least worked around. Wish I'd known that back in the day—I wouldn't have been so scared when the Feds threatened me with it over that one incident. "If it's a bizarre but strangely effective plan, it's usually his." Awww!

"Well, fortunately for me I also plan effectively," Mercer

snaps, and hands Tall something. Something big and dark and heavy and distinctively gun-shaped. Crap. "We're leaving now," she tells him. "You need to protect me from these people. Don't let any of them get near me."

"Yes, ma'am." The sudden rise in viewpoint tells me he's standing, and I hear as well as see him cock the gun. Great. I'd call Jones to warn her, but she wouldn't hear the phone ring through her suit. And it's probably too late, anyway. There's nothing I can do but watch as Tall leads the way to the door, cracks it open—and shoots a large, bulky, orange-suited figure lumbering down the hall. *Zot!* Then he's through the doorway and moving quickly, taking out the Hazmat team like this is a video game and he's one of those kids who spends all his time in his parents' basement practicing kill shots and one-liners but terrified of speaking to people in real life. Which makes me wonder about Tall's childhood, for sure.

Even as a cookie zombie he's horribly efficient, and in less than a minute there isn't another soul moving besides him— and Mercer, who's right behind him. I can see her shadow on the wall. "Excellent work, Agent Thomas," she assures him as they make they way toward the front door. "But don't let your guard down—there could be more of them."

Truer words were never spoken, because no sooner does she say that then a bolt of blue energy sizzles through the air from around the corner—and nails Tall full in the chest. Wham! He goes stiff as an ironing board, his own pistol falling from his hands, and topples like a felled tree. Which plays havoc with my perspective, let me tell you.

"You must be Olivia Ann Mercer," Jones says as she steps into view, pistol leveled at Mercer—at least I think it is, since I'm viewing all of this sideways. I practically have to stand on my head to make sense of it. Which is easier than you might think—the bill provides an extra contact point at each end, so it's more like a tripod. I've gotten really good at yoga as a result.

"I am," Mercer replies, and she starts to crouch down, but freezes as a second energy bolt fires just past her. "And you are?"

"Uh uh," Jones warns. "And I'm Agent Jones." She moves in a step or two.

"Ah. The new me, I presume?" Mercer straightens. "I must say, no offense but the agency's standards seem to be slipping."

"We can't all be former beauty queens," Jones snaps back, and from the angry rasp I'm guessing Mercer's little dig got to her. Which is of course exactly what Mercer wants. "Don't let her rattle you!" I shout, but it's no use. The only one who can hear me through this thing is Tall, and he's busy being a popsicle. All I can do is sit and watch as the two women sidle closer, sizing each other up. The current WiB and the former one. It's a striking difference, certainly—they're both tall and broad-shouldered but Jones looks like a linebacker or a heavyweight boxer stuffed into a suit, while Mercer really does handle herself like a beauty queen, regal and dignified and lovely.

Right up until the moment she looses a roundhouse kick and knocks the pistol from Jones's hands. Oh, right, this former beauty queen was a WiB as well—and apparently her work history isn't the only thing she remembers from her time with them.

She follows the kick with a backhand that could probably dislocate a jaw—but Jones blocks with a heavy forearm, then throws a punch that snaps Mercer's head back instead.

"Naw," Jones retorts as she pounds a fist into Mercer's stomach, doubling her over, "I'd say their standards are still pretty high."

She goes to bring her elbow down on Mercer's neck, finishing the job, but the Hazmat suit slows her down just enough for Mercer to twist to the side, evading the blow. She grabs Jones's wrist instead, yanking down hard and dragging her off-balance, then sweeps the agent's feet out from under her, sending her sprawling. But Jones does a fan-kick, making Mercer stagger back and pinwheeling her back to her feet as well. Damn, these two can fight! I think Tall could maybe take them, but most other opponents would get a serious beat-down, male or female, and here they are duking it out in front of me! It reminds me of some matches I saw in high school, when we used to sneak over to this one place that had female mud-wrestling and—even better—Jell-O wrestling. I'd get up and grab some popcorn but I don't want to miss a second of it.

They trade a couple more blows, and it looks to me like they're pretty evenly matched—Jones is a little stronger, and a lot younger, but that Hazmat suit's hampering her a bit, while Mercer's not quite as spry but she's still a tough old bird and she's picked up a lot of tricks over the years. Like grabbing Jones's helmet and yanking it sideways, making it impossible for her to see the blows Mercer then lands on her. Fortunately the suit is also taking some of that impact, and Jones responds by simply shoving hard in front of her—she doesn't have to see to connect at that range, and the powerful push sends Mercer flying. By the time she's back on her feet Jones has her mask twisted back around, and is advancing on her slowly and steadily.

"Give it up," she warns. "You can't win."

"Not if I play fair, perhaps," Mercer admits, levering herself up with one arm. "But I gave that up years ago." And she raises her other hand—which is holding Tall's gun.

Once again—crap.

There isn't time for Jones to go for her own pistol, wherever it landed, nor anywhere to dive for cover. So she does the next best thing—she sweeps one arm down and out and around, like she's bowling.

And scoops up the end table beside her, hurling it right at Mercer.

"Aah!" I guess she wasn't expecting to be attacked by her own living room furniture—besides me, who is, really?—because Mercer instinctively throws both hands up to shield herself. The table slams into her anyway, knocking her back to the floor, and her pistol goes flying.

By the time she's recovered enough to shove the wood shards off her and look around, dazed, Jones is standing over her, a pistol in each hand.

"Game over," she declares. "You lose."

Then she shoots Mercer. Twice. Just to be sure, I'm going to assume.

Once Mercer's frozen, Jones pulls off her helmet and crouches down beside Tall. "Agent Thomas, can you hear me?"

she asks.

"Yes," he answers, though it's a bit slurred. Good to know the paralysis from their guns doesn't last all that long.

"Good. Snap out of it," she instructs. She watches him closely, so much so that I can see his reflection in her eyes, which is a little weird, but I swear I can see it when his face shifts.

"Agent Jones?" he asks. "I take it you've apprehended Miss Mercer?"

"I have," she answers. "Once you're recovered we can bring her back to headquarters. You can call it in on the way." Which, I take it, is her way of letting him know that this is still his collar. Which is surprisingly cool of her. Maybe I misjudged Agent Jones a little bit. Hey, bulldogs can be very friendly, once you get past the scowl and the barking. And the biting and snarling. And the bad breath.

"Thank you." Tall nods, and sits up. Slowly. "DuckBob, you there?"

"Oh, you betcha," I answer. "Never left, amigo. Who do you think called Jones in?"

"Thanks." Tall leans forward, then he shakes his head. "Who would have thought there'd be this much trouble over a few cookies?"

"I know, right?" I sink back into my chair—I was sort of up and hopping from foot to foot during the big fight. I do that during movies sometimes, too. Fortunately, those theaters that have the little soundproofed booths in the middle for parents with babies so they can still watch the movie without their kids disrupting it for everybody else? Turns out they're surprisingly cool about letting other people hang out in there, too. Well, me, anyway. It doesn't hurt that most babies think my looks are utterly fascinating. I'm like the perfect baby distraction. As long as they don't try to gnaw on me.

Anyway, I relax a bit while Jones helps Tall to his feet. Then they bind Mercer's wrists—and gag her for good measure—and hoist her up as well.

"Who called the Hazmat team?" Tall asks as they step around the groggy crew and head outside. They'll probably chalk it all up to "incidental contact with an incapacitating agent" or some such. And in a way, they'll be right. Tall can certainly incapacitate people!

"I did," Jones admits, "but it was DuckBob's idea." See, she's even giving me credit for something! People can change! "Must be a holdover from his clearly misspent youth," she adds, "and doubtless only one of many questionable and even illegal things he's done over the years."

Well, hey—even the nicest bulldog's still gotta growl at you from time to time. Right?

Chapter Thirty-Six
Saved by a one-hit wonder

"**So, will it** hold this time?" I ask Tall as we sit on deck chairs out in the Matrix Chamber. I've got my feet in the wading pool, of course. Tall is actively ignoring that fact—and wincing every time I splash him.

"It should," He answers, taking a pull from his beer. Tulaskan Glacial Ale, guaranteed to chill your insides or your money back. I've got the heat cranked in here to simulate a sunny, summer day, so a super-cold beer feels good right now. Admittedly, I'm not a hundred percent sure what I found was really the thermostat—it may be some kind of microwave-based security system, slowly cooking us from the inside out—but it's warmer in here, so I'm not gonna complain. Or say anything to Ned. He gets a little irritated when I mess with systems I don't fully understand. Like TiVo.

"The process is a lot more effective these days," Tall continues. "Miss Mercer won't remember anything about her days in the agency, or any of her recent activities."

"How's that gonna work, though?" I ask sipping my own beer. My fingers are going a little numb, so I set it down on the ground beside me afterward. "I mean, sure, you can erase those two years, but she's been carrying those memories ever since, and it's obvious she's been scheming on ways to pay you all back this whole time. How can anything wipe out a single thread of thought that stretches over forty years and probably influenced most of her activities throughout?"

"I don't know, honestly," Tall admits. "I just know that the tech guys say it should work. The agency will be keeping a close eye on her, though, just in case."

That still weirds me out, him talking about the agency like it's a separate entity—and the fact that now it is. "I can't believe you quit," I tell him again. That's got to be at least the twentieth time, but it's true. I think I'm in shock. "You love being a MiB! It's your whole life!"

"Well, maybe it shouldn't be!" he snaps back. Then he sighs and stares out across the pool. "Look at me. I'm thirty-four years old, I'm not married, I'm not in a relationship, I barely have any hobbies, and my closest friend is a former alien abductee who now manages an interstellar security system and can't leave his workspace." Aw, I'm his closest friend? Really? I don't know whether to feel flattered or horribly depressed. "You're right," he goes on, "It was my whole life. But there's got to be more to life than just working all the time. And I think it's high time I found some of that."

I reach for my beer, find it without knocking it over, and raise it to my bill so I can sip from the straw—trust me, it's better this way, things get messy otherwise. "Hey, I'm the first to admit that work shouldn't be the only thing you do," I tell him. "You want to get out and party more, make some more friends, join some clubs, take up woodworking, hit the dating scene, I'm all for it. But what happens if you find out it's not for you? Some people really are all work, man."

He shrugs. "Maybe so. In which case, I'll go back. Or move on to some other job. But I need to know for sure."

"You think they'll take you back?" The agency never struck me as big on second chances.

He actually grins at me. "I'd like to see them try to stop me." Yeah, I can just picture Tall striding back into MiB headquarters, plonking down at his old desk, and saying, "I'm back—like it or not!" and glaring at anyone who tries to object until they just give up and go on with work like he never left. Heh.

"I still don't see how you kept your memories," I say. And he laughs again. Grinning, laughing—I'm starting to wonder if this is like Cookie-zombie Tall, version 2.0.

"That's all you, my friend," he tells me, holding up his bottle. So naturally I clink it with mine. Hey, some habits are hard to break. "I pointed out that, if they wiped me, they'd have to bring someone else up to speed on you and the Matrix, which was a security risk. Or they could make me a Confidential Contact, let me keep my security clearance, and allow me to continue acting as your go-between. Even if I'm not your official agency liaison." He takes another sip, and shivers for a second. "And they went for it."

I lean back in my chair and stretch, locking my arms behind my head. Which, unfortunately, means I clunk myself in the head with my beer, since I forgot I was still holding it. "Yeah, it's pretty cool not having a MiB watchdog on me anymore. I feel like I've been let off the leash. Even though you're still reporting back, it's not the same somehow."

We sit in silence for a few minutes, broken only by the sounds of our drinking and my occasional splashing. "How's the cookie thing going?" I ask finally.

"Good," Tall answers. "Agent Jones is spearheading the cleanup. They've isolated almost all of the boxes from the affected batches, and they've deprogrammed everyone already affected." He grimaces for a second. "Damn, that's annoying."

I grin. "Stuck in your head again?"

"Yes!"

"Hey, what can I say?" I drain the last of my beer. "I'm a musical genius!"

After taking Mercer in, the MiBs were still a little stumped on what to do about all the potential cookie-zombies. They couldn't exactly go door-to-door and tell each person, "hey, snap out of it!"

So I figured out a way to do it for them.

Rosy was only too happy to help, which made things a lot easier. She brought my proposal to the CampGirls Central Committee, championed it for me, and I'm sure the MiBs brought some pressure to bear as well. Which is why, a few days later, the CampGirls unveiled their official Cookie Song: "Snap Out of It!"

Yes, I came up with that. And wrote it. Well, okay, I used a synthesizer program, which behaved about as normally as anything else around here—I think really my computer has to get a lot of the credit. But I did the lyrics!

The song's been a huge hit, and not just among the CampGirls and their families. It's topping all the charts, which has been great for the organization but even better as a way to make sure everyone's heard it and is singing it. Because, of course, it's a total earworm. People everywhere are walking around telling each other, "snap out of it!"

What? It works!

And it annoys Tall to no end. Bonus!

"So what're you gonna do now?" I ask him, mainly because he's starting to fix me with Stare Number Two again and I need to distract him from that song ASAP. "Got any ideas for another job?"

Apparently that was the right thing to say, because just like that his scowl transforms into a smile. "Already taken care of." He finishes his beer and sets the empty bottle down. "I'm going into business. With Heidi."

"Seriously? You're gonna be an interstellar trucker with an animate bowling ball filled with steam, goo, and a miniature sandworm?"

He actually shrugs at me. I'm not sure I've ever seen Tall shrug before. "Why not? We get along well, it pays well, and I'll get to travel. A lot. Maybe I won't stay with it forever, but for now it sounds like fun."

Fun. Hm. The idea of Tall having fun doesn't really fit with my concept of reality—but it looks like I may have to alter that a little. And maybe that's not a bad thing.

"Good for you," I tell him. "Go live a little."

"I will," he says, rising to his feet. "Right after I jog around this room a few dozen times." He reaches down and a hand the size of a Volkswagen latches onto my arm and yanks me out of my chair. "And you're jogging with me."

"What? No! You can't!" I protest as he drags me away from the chairs and starts circling the chamber. "I'm not wearing the right shoes! I just drank—I have to wait an hour! I have a doctor's note saying no heavy exercise, or having to watch old *Bonanza* reruns!"

Help!

About the Author

Aaron Rosenberg has not been altered by aliens, as far as he's aware. He is, however, very silly, and he and DuckBob share similar taste in shirts. When Aaron isn't busy taste-testing fried chicken and barbeque or watching movies or sleeping, he's writing. So far he's written roleplaying games (including the award-winning *Gamemastering Secrets*, plus work for *Warhammer*, *Dungeons & Dragons*, *Deadlands*, *Vampire: The Masquerade*, and many others), children's books (among them the middle-grade series Pete and Penny's Pizza Puzzles, and books for *iCarly*, *Ben10*, *Chaotic*, and *Transformers Animated*), educational books (including books about cryptology, the Bermuda Triangle, and various biographies), and of course novels (like his two WarCraft novels, his Warhammer trilogy the Daemon Gates, the Stargate: Atlantis novel *Hunt & Run*, and the Eureka novels *Substitution Method* and *Road Less Traveled*). He is also the author of the Dread Remora space-opera series and one of the creators of the O.C.L.T. paranormal thriller series. If he did meet Grays, he'd probably ask them to increase his typing speed. Aaron lives in New York City with his family, and makes sure to always have a MetroCard and a finger puppet handy. You can read more about his life and his books at gryphonrose.com or follow him on Twitter @gryphonrose.

Missed out on DuckBob's first adventure?
No problem!
Here's the first chapter of

Chapter One
DuckBob, meet the Universe.
Universe, meet DuckBob.

Ever have one of those days where nothing ever seems to go quite right? Where you miss the train by seconds each time, fumble your change at the snack machine, click away from the porn site too slow to fool your supervisor, kick yourself in the head when you're trying to tie your shoe, take a swig of your beer only to realize it's a canister of baking soda instead?

That's pretty much every day for me.

The name's DuckBob. DuckBob Spinowitz. No, that's not a nickname or a pet name or any of that other funny stuff. It's my name. I had it legally changed. Figured it was easier to join 'em than try to stop 'em, and when you beat 'em to the punch, it stops being funny. A little. Sometimes. Why "DuckBob"? Well, okay, here's the thing—

—I've got the head of a duck.

I know, right now you're thinking, "oh, he's got a flat nose" or "he's got a weak chin and a high forehead" or "he must have feathery blond hair." No. That's not it at all.

I.

Have.

The head of.

A duck.

Really. My head? It's that of a mallard—a Wood Duck, to be precise. Complete with black-tipped red-and-white bill, white below the bill and down the front of the neck, a touch of yellow rising up from the bill and leading to a white streaks above red eyes, and emerald green feathers covering the rest, with a few white streaks mixed in.

A duck.

Only, y'know, man-sized.

I've also got webbed feet. And feathers instead of hair. All over. Soft downy feathers, looks just like fine hair until you feel it. Speckled brown down the chest and on the feet, tan across the arms and hands, emerald green on the back (yes, all the way down!), and white on the belly, groin, and legs.

It's pretty slick-looking, actually. If I were a crazed xenobiologist with leanings toward ornithology, I'd say I was an impressive specimen. I even won a few awards at bird shows, before I was disqualified—seems the entry and the owner can't be the same person. Purists.

Plus there was that whole "disrobing in public" thing. But hey, is it my fault they wouldn't take my word for it about the feathers, y'know, Down Below?

On the plus side, I can walk in the rain and not get wet. And swimming? Fuggedaboutit.

No, I wasn't born this way. And no, I don't want to talk about it. Just another example of the colossal bad luck that routinely plagues my life. Because that's what it was—bad luck. I mean, was it my fault I was hiking through a restricted area in the Catskills in the dead of night, waving a lighter in one hand and a neon-orange fishing pole in the other? While naked?

Long story. There was a girl involved. At least I certainly hope so, because otherwise I've got no excuse.

Beyond that—let's just say that, all those stories about alien abductions and crazy experiments? They don't know the half of it. Those little gray buggers are downright cruel.

So you're probably thinking, "Okay, this guy's half man, half duck. That's weird. I'll bet he's a superhero, with a face like that—DuckBob the Aquatic Avenger. Or a mad scientist. Or a professional deep-sea diver. Or at least a sunglasses model."

Nope. Sorry. I'm just your ordinary average guy, and when I'm dressed I look completely normal, 'cept for the whole duck-head thing. I'm no superhero. I work at—aw hell, does it even matter what the name is, really? It's an office job, okay? I'm a pencil pusher, and not even a glorified one. I shuffle papers and push buttons in a little cubicle all day. Then I leave.

Whee.

Some life, huh? Well, it beats the alternatives. At least that's what I like to tell myself. Hey, whatever it takes to get through the day. For me that usually includes watching a few minutes from old Donald Duck cartoons at some point. It's about the only way I can convince myself things could be worse. Look like this, not be able to talk straight, and be forced to walk around with my butt and my business hanging out all the time? Yeah, that would pretty much be the last straw.

Anyway, I'm used to being the butt of some cosmic joke. That being said, I was still surprised when I walked into work one Tuesday and two guys suddenly showed up alongside me and grabbed me by the arms. Big guys, too—they lifted me right off my feet, and I'm not small myself. Plus the bill weighs a lot—I've got amazing neck muscles.

"Hey, what's the big idea?" I demanded as they turned and carried me back out the door. "I've gotta punch in!"

"Mr. Spinowitz?" One of them asked. He had a face like a microwaved potato—squishy and overflowing—and a voice like a hoarse bulldog. He was wearing a suit, a dark one, and I was pretty sure I heard fabric tear each time he shifted.

"Yeah. Who the hell are you guys?"

"We need to speak with you about an urgent matter of national security," the other guy said. He was taller than his buddy, athletic where Mr. Potato Head was just squat. (I'm big-boned and slightly rotund, by the way. It's the slacker lifestyle that does it.) Matching suit, though. I thought that was sweet. Like jewelry but washable.

"National security? I was just curious what sort of brownie recipes it had," I said quickly. "I didn't try any of the other stuff, and even if I did Missus Gries down the hall had it coming! I'm sure the twitching will stop soon!"

The shorter guy raised an eyebrow but shook his head. "That's not why we're here."

"What, then?" I thought for a second, then gasped. "Oh, come on! I know the porn was from Yugoslavia but I only traded an old Steve McQueen movie for it! It's not like I was selling state secrets! It's not even a clean copy!"

By this time we'd reached the curb, and a big black sedan idling there. Mr. Potato Head opened the passenger door and slid in, then Mr. Tall shoved me in after him. I've never understood the whole "dark sedan with government plates" thing, actually. Why that kind of car? Why not those crazy monster SUVs, so the agents can drive over anyone who gets in their way? And nobody'd escape custody—it's not like you can get out of one of those without a ladder and some pitons. Or go for sports cars, classy and great in a car chase. Or the old kidnapper classic, the white Econoline van— cheap, ubiquitous, and now with faster sliding doors! Or maybe something to counteract their whole "we're not really on your side after all" image. I bet government agencies wouldn't seem half as scary if they all drove brightly colored compact cars or minivans with "My Kid's an Honors Student" bumper stickers.

Instead, there I was in the back of a dark sedan. The windows were tinted—I could have made faces at my co-workers and they'd never have known. Not that I can do many faces anymore— duckbills are not very versatile. I'm great at Charades, though. As long as it involves water fowl.

"Where're we going?" I asked as the car pulled away—there must have been a third guy driving but I couldn't see him. "Who are you? What do you want from me? Say, what's that?" That last one I asked while pointing at the Empire State Building, just to get a reaction. I did. They looked at me like I was a moron. I know that look all too well.

With a head like mine, it's hard getting people to take you seriously.

"Our superiors want to speak with you," the taller guy answered.

"They never heard of the phone?"

He glared at me. "It's a matter of national security."

"Yeah, you said that already. Couldn't they have used a nationally secure phone?"

That got snorts from both of them, and I think from the driver as well. "No such thing," Mr. Potato Head said. "You have any idea how easy it is to tap into a cell phone conversation?"

"No. Could you show me? I'd love to know what my boss says about me." Though actually I think I have a pretty good idea. "Quack, quack" is surprisingly easy to lip read.

They didn't answer, and we spent the rest of the ride in silence. I hate silence. It gives me time to think.

Finally we pulled into a building down near the south piers. A warehouse, it looked like, on a narrow street full of warehouses. I didn't see a sign or a street number or anything. Which I guess was the point.

"Out," Mr. Tall demanded once we'd stopped and the garage door clanked shut again. He got out first and Mr. Potato Head shoved me from behind to make me move, then clambered out after me. Maybe his door was broken. I looked around as I got out but it just looked like a warehouse. There was a guy standing there watching us, though. Average height, skinny as a razor blade, with features to match and glossy black hair that looked painted on. Same suit as my escorts but his looked better on him.

"Mr. Spinowitz? I'm Mr. Smith," he said, offering his hand. "Thank you for joining us."

"I didn't really have a choice," I pointed out, but I shook hands with him anyway. Hell, I was in a nondescript warehouse somewhere in Manhattan with at least four guys, all of them probably armed. Being rude didn't sound like a good idea.

"I apologize for our insistence," Smith explained. "But this is an urgent matter and we couldn't risk you refusing our invitation."

"Okay, so I'm here." I glanced around again. Nothing to see but rusty walls and stairs and railings, concrete floor, the car we'd pulled up in, and us. "What's this all about?"

Smith started to say something, stopped, and started again. "We have a situation, and we think you may be uniquely qualified to handle it for us," he said finally.

"Qualified? Me? You haven't read my performance reviews. What makes me so qualified?"

Smith pointed at my head. "That."

"Oh."

"Yes. You see, we've been approached by extraterrestrials. We have no idea what they want, and none of our attempts to communicate have worked. But you've encountered them before—we hoped that might have granted you some rapport with them."

I stared at him, at the guys behind me, and then back at him again. "Let me get this straight—you've got some aliens you want to talk to, and you want me to do the talking because I got abducted and given a duck head so you figure I can relate to them better? Are you mental?" Okay, I might have forgot about the whole not-pissing-off-the-men-with-guns thing.

"You may be correct," Smith admitted. He actually didn't look pissed-off at all, which was unusual for anyone I talk to. "But we have little to lose at this point, and it seemed an avenue worth exploring. Would you be willing to make the attempt? For the good of your country?" Man, this guy was good! Those callers from the Fraternal Order of Police had nothing on him!

I took time to think about it, though. I didn't want to just jump into anything. "Yeah, okay, sure."

"Excellent!" He actually rubbed his hands together. I thought they only did that in cheesy movies. "Come along, it's right this way." I followed him to the back of the warehouse, which had several doors. The floor above continued back past this point so I was looking at the doors to several rooms rather than a whole set of back doors. Which makes sense because why would anyone need more than one back door, especially all in a row? Why not just have one great big giant door? Smith gestured toward the door to the left. "After you."

"Oh, the alien's in there?" He nodded. "And you want me to talk to it?" Another nod. "Alone?" Nod number three—one more and I walked. "But you just said 'after you'—doesn't that mean you're going in with me?"

Smith smiled then, which looked like something you'd see on a buzzard that suddenly found itself at a breakfast buffet. "I lied." He indicated the door again, and rested one hand on his side. Right below the bulge I suspected was his gun—either that or he had a hideous growth under his left arm. Either way I figured I'd better do what he wanted.

"Okay, okay, I'm going." I turned the knob and pulled the

door halfway open. At least it looked dark on the other side, no blinding lights and sets of examining tables and rows of glistening tools. Not that I think about such things. Much. Ever.

"Right." I took a deep breath. "Here goes." And I stepped inside.

And promptly screamed as the door slammed shut behind me. Then the lights came on, showing me four plain metal chairs and a small folding table—and the little figure sitting in one of the chairs facing the table.

Short, skinny, gray skin, huge head, huge eyes, no hair. An alien. Just like the ones who . . . anyway, an alien.

Though I wondered where he'd gotten the Halloween-themed footy pajamas. Those didn't seem like standard issue. At least the black-bat pattern went with his skin tone and his eyes.

I was trying hard not to panic. I figured I could always do that later, in a pinch. I'm good at spontaneous panic. Also, shooting spitballs. I've got wicked velocity.

Right now, though, I figured the best thing was just to get this over with. Face my fear. All that.

"Uh, hi." I like to think my voice didn't shake much at all. I walked over to the table and leaned over it so we were roughly face-to-face. "I'm Bob. DuckBob. Um, have we met?"